# GHOSTS OF TIME

# GHOSTS
# OF TIME

✦ ✦ ✦

# STEVE WHITE

GHOSTS OF TIME

A Baen Book

Baen Publishing Enterprises
P.O. Box 1403
Riverdale, NY 10471
www.baen.com

ISBN: 978-1-4767-3657-0

Cover art by Don Maitz

First Baen printing, July 2014

Distributed by Simon & Schuster
1230 Avenue of the Americas
New York, NY 10020

Library of Congress Cataloging-in-Publication Data

White, Steve, 1946-
 Ghosts of time / Steve White.
     pages cm -- (Jason Thanou Time Travel series ; 4)
Summary: "Special Operations office Jason Thanou of the Temporal Regulatory
Authority must once again plunge into Earth's blood-drenched past to combat the
plots of the transhumanist underground to subvert the past. This time they are
attempting to use the chaos of the American Civil War to escape the Observer Effect:
the immutable law that recorded history cannot be changed. The Fall of Richmond
looms and in the Shenandoah Valley insurgency brews. The time travelers must join
the raiders to prevent a transhumanist trap from dooming the mission from the start.
Meanwhile, the leader of a secret slave underground possesses an incredible secret that
may change Jason's fate--and that of the future itself--forever"-- Provided by publisher.
 ISBN 978-1-4767-3657-0 (paperback)
1. Time travel--Fiction. 2. Gods, Greek--Fiction. 3. Bronze age--Greek--Fiction. 4.
Fantasy fiction. I. Title.
 PS3573.H474777G46 2014
 813'.54--dc23
                          2014009912

Printed in the United States of America

10 9 8 7 6 5 4 3 2 1

# GHOSTS OF TIME

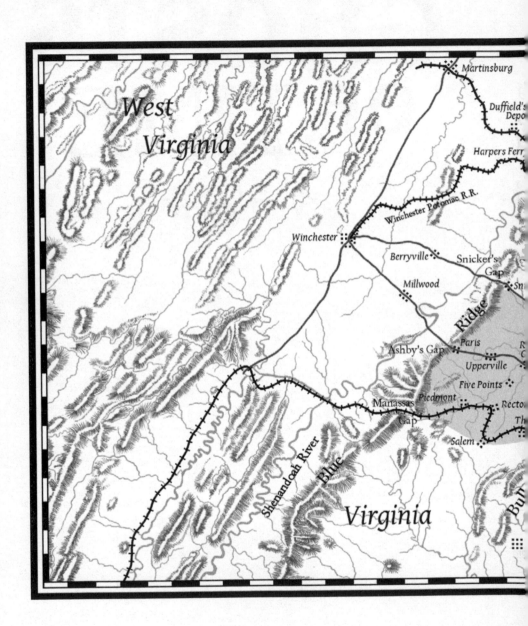

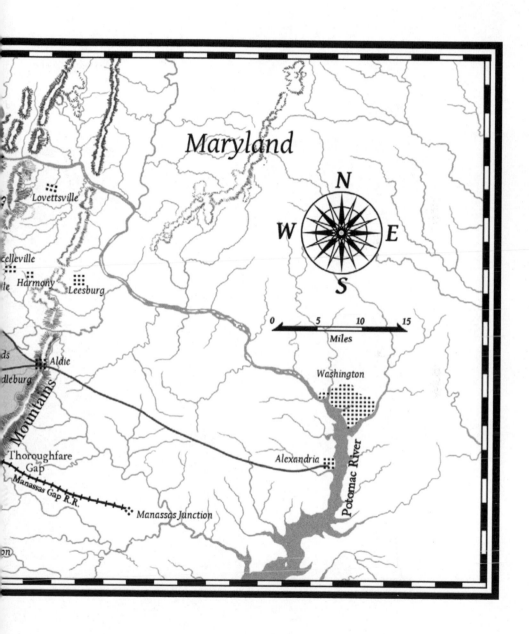

# CHAPTER ONE

It might almost have been the Caribbean.

Not really, of course. The Caribbean was far away indeed, across the unthinkable gulf of forty-eight and a half light years, no mean journey even in these days of the negative mass drive. And the afternoon sunlight that sparkled eye-wateringly on these tropical waters was that of Psi 5 Aurigae, a G0v star slightly more massive than Sol and perhaps half a billion years younger. And the vegetation that clothed these islands was not the wild, rank jungle that Jason Thanou remembered. This world of Hesperia, colonized only three generations ago, was still incompletely terraformed. Even in areas like this where biotech and nanotech had transformed the original naked rock and sand into soil, the scientifically selected, carefully nurtured terrestrial flora still stood in regimented rows. Only later, with the passage of time and the introduction of additional species, would it rebel, diversifying and efflorescing into something like what Jason had struggled through on Hispaniola.

And yet in spite of everything, as Jason flew his aircar westward over the Verdant Sea and gazed to his right at the mountainous islands that marked the boundary of the Cerulean Ocean to the north, he could almost imagine that those islands were the Greater Antilles, and that those peaks rearing above the orderly forest were the Blue Mountains of Jamaica, in whose shadow Port Royal had flourished in all its gaudy and unabashed sinfulness.

Port Royal had vanished almost seven centuries before, in 1692. But Jason had seen it with his own eyes, for he was head of the Special Operations Section of the Temporal Service, enforcement arm of the Temporal Regulatory Authority which held exclusive jurisdiction over all time travel. Only a couple of months before, in terms of his own consciousness, he had sailed those seas beside that preposterously engaging scoundrel Henry Morgan . . . and a certain she-pirate who was very difficult to forget.

He shook his head. Hesperia, his homeworld to which he had returned on a much-overdue leave, would never be mistaken for Earth, even though the two planets were near-twins in all physical parameters, and not just because of the newness of this world's imported ecology. Earth's aura of age went deeper than biology, into psychic realms that could not be measured or detected but which all but the most insensitive outworlders could feel in their souls as they walked through history-littered landscapes suffused with the memory of thousands of years of human experience in all its fervor and urgency.

Presently Jason flew over the continental shelf, and the shallow water below took on the greenness that gave the sea its name, courtesy of masses of the seaweed-like aquatic vegetation that was one of the highest expressions of Hesperia's mostly microbial indigenous life. Ahead lay the continent of Darcy's Land. A long beach backed by sandy bluffs extended as far as the eye could see to the south, but a few miles to the north the bluffs rose into a range of low hills extending down to cliff-faces at the sea. Lines of white surf rolled up and down the sand as the tide came in. (Hesperia's moon, believed to be a captured asteroid, was smaller than Earth's but orbited more closely, hurtling around the planet so swiftly that its motion was clearly visible at night. So the tides were at least equal in strength to the mother planet's, and more irregular. Sand erosion was a problem.) Low-built, light-tinted villas lined the crest of the bluffs, and it was toward one of these that Jason steered his aircar. It settled to the ground with a hum of grav repulsion and a swirl of dust from its ground-pressure effect.

The canopy clamshelled open and Jason stepped out into the hot sunlight. As always on visits home from Earth, he couldn't avoid the feeling that Hesperia's 0.97 G gravitation somehow seemed lighter than that, as though Earth's burden of history somehow added to the planet's mass. He yawned, having still not completely readjusted to his homeworld's rotation period of 27.3 standard hours. Then he smiled and waved as a handsome woman wearing a loose flowing gown emerged from the villa and walked along a palm-shaded walkway toward the landing stage, smiling in return at her son.

Helena Jankovic-Thanou was eighty-one standard years old (a little over seventy-nine in Hesperia's slightly longer years), but that was a less advanced age in this era than it had once been. She still walked with a sprightly step, and her hair was a dark iron-gray. Her straight features, light-olive skin and dark-brown eyes were those of her son, but when she gave Jason a quick kiss on the cheek she didn't have to reach up to do it. At five feet eleven, he was below average height for human males from Earth and other approximately one-gee planets in this day and age. It was a useful attribute for one whose work required him to pass inconspicuously in earlier, less well-nourished epochs. He inherited his relative shortness and solid muscularity from his father, who had been noticeably shorter than the willowy Helena, and positively stocky. When Paul Thanou had died in a storm at sea, his widow had bought this small villa in the tropics.

"How is Daphne doing, dear?" she inquired.

"Fine. She sends her love." Jason had been visiting his older sister in one of the archipelagoes in the eastern reaches of the Verdant Sea, where she followed in their father's footsteps by working on one of the terraforming projects. Their mother had always been more comfortable with that than with her son's somewhat unorthodox career choices. It hadn't been so bad when he had joined the Hesperian Colonial Rangers, a paramilitary constabulary whose functions included suppression of the lawless elements that had sprung up on the frontiers of the terraformed regions as a kind of toxic sociological byproduct. But when he had accepted an (admittedly extremely well-paying) offer from the Temporal Regulatory Authority . . . !

"Good. Oh, by the way," Helena added as an afterthought, "there's a gentleman here to see you."

"Oh?" Jason was puzzled, having already touched bases with all his old friends and acquaintances.

"Yes. He just came down here from the Port Marshak spaceport. He's waiting in the study."

All at once, Jason's danger-tendrils tingled. Despite many attempts over the centuries to exploit quantum entanglement, there was still no such thing as instantaneous "interstellar radio." Messages had to be carried by shipborne courier. It was one of the reasons for the effective political independence the colonies all enjoyed, however vociferous their protestations of loyalty to Mother Earth. At the same time, when Earth found it necessary to go to the expense of sending such a courier. . . .

"Tell me, Mother: does this gentleman by any chance have the kind of features—plump cheeks, receding chin, slightly buck teeth—that vaguely suggest a rabbit?"

"Well, er, I wouldn't exactly have put it that way, dear. But now that you mention it . . ."

"Uh *huh!*" nodded Jason with the dourness of confirmed pessimism. He stalked to the villa and proceeded down an airy gallery where the afternoon sunlight was filtered through hanging ferns, to a vaulted room. The visitor rose to his feet from a recliner.

Irving Nesbit didn't really resemble a rabbit nearly as much as he once had. He had accompanied Jason's party to the seventeenth-century Caribbean, and to Jason's amazement had come out of that crucible of horrors and hardships with some of the physical and mental softness melted away. "Commander Thanou!" he beamed. "It is a pleasure to see you again."

"And it's something of a *surprise* to see you, Irving," said Jason, accepting Nesbit's extended hand. "After . . . what happened following your retrieval, I was worried that the Authority wouldn't be requiring your services for jobs like this. Or for anything else."

Nesbit looked rueful. His presence on the Caribbean expedition—to the despair of Jason, who had always regarded him as enough to give spineless bureaucrats a bad name—had been the work of Alastair Kung, a powerful member of the Authority's governing council who regarded the often unorthodox Special Operations Section as a necessary evil of whose necessity he was not totally convinced. In effect, Kung had sought to use his lap dog as a watchdog, keeping Jason on the straight and narrow path of the Authority's sacrosanct operational guidelines. Instead, on their return Nesbit had excelled himself and floored everyone by vehemently defending Jason's flagrant irregularities—surely at the price of his career, Jason had been certain.

"It's true that I was in bad odor with Councilor Kung for a while,"

Nesbit acknowledged. "But in the end even he was forced to admit that you had no choice but to take the actions you did, and indeed that your boldness may well have averted disaster."

Jason nodded. He knew what Nesbit meant, and that "disaster" might well be too weak a word.

On an earlier expedition to Bronze Age Greece, Jason had discovered the Teloi aliens who had once been worshipped as gods by the human race that they themselves had created by genetic manipulation of *homo erectus*. He and his companions had seriously weakened them, and by the time he had gone back to 490 B.C. to investigate their possible survival they had been a shadow of their former selves. But on that expedition he had uncovered something in its own way even more appalling. He had discovered that the Authority's carefully regulated time travelers were not the only interlopers in the human past.

A little over a century before, Earth (with the help of its returning extrasolar colonists) had freed itself from the Transhuman Dispensation and its twisted dream of distorting the natural human genotype into a grotesque hierarchy of gods and monsters. It had taken a torrent of blood to wash the motherworld clean of the Transhumanist abominations, but at least the job had been done . . . or so it had been generally believed. But, as Jason had discovered, surviving Transhumanist remnants had gone deep underground, licking their wounds and recovering their strength . . . and stealing Weintraub's work that had led to the invention of the Fujiwara-Weintraub Temporal Displacer. But they had avoided some flaw in Fujiwara's mathematics, as a result of which *their* temporal displacer was far more efficient and compact than the Authority's town-sized installation, and could be concealed. And they were using it to subvert the past. They could not change recorded history—the poorly understood "Observer Effect" saw to that. But they were filling the past's "blank spaces" with a secret history of conspiracies, genetically-engineered plagues, sociologically-engineered cults and delayed-action nanotechnological viruses that would all culminate in a Transhumanist triumph on *The Day*—a date somewhere in Jason's future which the Authority devoutly wished to learn.

It was to combat the Transhuman underground that the Special Operations Section had been formed, and granted a degree of latitude which gave Kung and his conservative ilk attacks of the vapors. And it was for this purpose that Jason had led an expedition—with Nesbit in tow—back to the seventeenth century, when the Teloi on Earth were all long dead and consigned to the realms of myth. But the Transhumanists were only too active—and the Teloi had returned, in a new and virulent form. An interstellar war had left their race extinct save for a hard core of military fanatics, the *Tuova'Zhonglu*, who for thousands of years had skulked about the galaxy, stewing in their own megalomania and grimly determined to reassert their dominance when the time was right. And the Transhumanists had tricked them into an alliance which had nearly culminated in the acquisition by the Transhumanists of Teloi military technology. To forestall that nightmare possibility, Jason had gone into space with his companions—including Captain Morgan, who had no business being there three centuries before Yuri Gagarin. That, in turn, had forced Jason to go back to the same time period as his own slightly younger self and restore the rightness of history by wiping the impermissible parts of Morgan's memory. For Kung, that had been the final straw. It was only Nesbit's unexpected support that had made it possible, and Jason had been properly grateful.

Now, however. . . .

"Well, Irving, I'm glad you're back in favor. Although come to think of it, sending you here may have been intended as a form of punishment, given the way Kung feels about the outworlds." *And their inhabitants*, Jason mentally added. *Especially me.*

Nesbit looked slightly ill at ease. "Actually, it was Director Rutherford who sent me."

"I had a feeling it might be coming to that," Jason sighed. Kyle Rutherford was the Authority's operations director, possessed of wide powers but subject to the council's oversight. Over the years, he and Jason had had their ups and downs. Some of the downs had resulted from Rutherford's occasionally cavalier attitude toward leaves of absence. "So, Irving," Jason continued in what Nesbit by now recognized as a deceptively mild tone of voice, "do I gather that you're back in your old job as Rutherford's bearer of ill tidings?"

"Well . . . er. . . ."

"What deliberately inconspicuous 'special circumstances' or 'emergency contingency' clause is it this time, Irving?" Jason's voice grew even milder. "I know from experience that you can quote me Part, Article, Paragraph and Subparagraph."

"Director Rutherford thought that, in this instance, perhaps you would want to voluntarily cut your leave short."

"Did he indeed?"

"Yes. You see, the matter at hand concerns your next-to-last mission."

"What?" Jason blinked with surprise. "You mean the one to April, 1865?" Jason had only just brought a Special Ops team back from the final cataclysm of the Confederate States of America, where he had foiled a Transhumanist plot while Richmond burned, and departed for Hesperia on leave when Nesbit had been sent to summon him back to Earth for the seventeenth-century Caribbean expedition.

"The same. I'm not privy to the details—'need to know' and all that sort of thing—but it seems that evidence had come to light suggesting that at some point in our own near future the Transhumanists will launch an expedition back to a point in time earlier in 1865 than their previous expedition, in an effort to undo your work."

Jason stared. "Irving, do you realize what this means? This was one of their nano-tech time bombs, deigned to disable technologically advanced equipment! On The Day it would have sent much of North America back to the nineteenth century—only worse, because people in the nineteenth century knew how to cope with such conditions."

"This is precisely why the Authority views the matter with such seriousness. You must be on hand in that time period, in the latter phases of the American Civil War, to counter this new attempt to put their nefarious plan into effect."

"Why me in particular?"

"It is obviously a job for the Special Operations Section. And Director Rutherford feels that you, as leader of the previous expedition, will be in the best position to deal with this threat. After all, you have already received orientation in the period, including language and—"

"All well and good. But has it occurred to anyone that—depending on the exact dates to which I'm temporally displaced—this might result in me being present in the same area and time-frame as myself? That's only happened once in the history of the Authority, and you of all people ought to remember what a flap *that* caused."

"I certainly do." Nesbit suddenly took on a look of crafty calculation. "Councilor Kung will no doubt be absolutely livid."

Jason's face lit up. "Yes, he will, won't he?"

"In fact," Nesbit continued with careful expressionlessness, "he might even have a stroke."

"That *could* be a danger, couldn't it?" Jason brightened still further. "Especially considering how overweight he is."

"I would be deeply concerned for his health," said Nesbit solemnly.

"As should we all," Jason intoned with equal solemnity.

"He would be a great loss."

"I couldn't agree more." Jason was smiling broadly now. He walked over to a side table which held a cut-glass decanter filled with Hesperian rum from the easternmost islands of the Verdant Sea, where sugarcane had successfully taken root. It wasn't competitive with the mellow products of Earth's present-day West Indies, but it was a considerably smoother article than the ferocious kill-devil the two of them had somehow survived drinking in their days among the buccaneers of the Spanish Main. He opened the decanter and poured two glasses.

"I believe the sun is over the yardarm, Irving. Now, tell me more about this mission."

# CHAPTER TWO

When Jason and Nesbit landed at Earth's Pontic Spaceport on the steppes north of the Black Sea, Rutherford happened to be at his Athens office rather than the Authority's displacer facility and operations center in Australia's Great Sandy Desert.

So they separated, and as Nesbit departed for the far side of the world by suborbital transport, Jason took a short aircar hop to the southwest. Presently he passed over the Aegean, into haunted regions where the memory of human experience reached back beyond history into myth. Jason, who had witnessed the origins of both, gazed downward and brooded over the things he had seen and done.

His mood intensified as Athens came into view. The last time he had seen it, it had been an early fifth century B.C. huddle of perhaps seven and a half thousand people clustered around the Acropolis—an unprepossessing womb within which the future had gestated. That future would have been aborted had the Athenians not triumphed at the Battle of Marathon. Jason himself had fought in that battle. How much difference his individual contribution had made was impossible to guess. But there was no such uncertainty about what he had done in 1628 B.C., arranging for the older generation of Teloi to be trapped forever in their artificial "pocket dimension" along with most of the advanced technology that had enabled them to masquerade as gods.

Jason wasn't the only one who had ever brooded over the

philosophical implications. Indeed, such questions were never far from the Authority's thoughts, although no one had ever come up with satisfactory answers. It stood to reason that time travelers must surely change the past whenever they took any actions, however small. But it was an established fact that observed, recorded history could not be changed. The activities of time travelers always seemed to have outcomes that resulted in the world from which the time travelers had come. Something always prevented any act that might do otherwise. No one could cause the Persians to win at Marathon, or kill one of his own ancestors. There were no paradoxes.

This was the famous "Observer Effect" that afforded the Authority a degree of comfort. Evidently, anything a time traveler caused to happen in the past had *always* happened. Most people, not wishing to think about that which didn't bear thinking about, comforted themselves with the catch-phrase "reality protects itself." But some continued to be troubled by the uncomfortable realization that there had to be a gaping hole in the logic. And the matter had become still more troubling—urgently so—with the discovery that the Transhumanists were also at work in the past.

Jason shook his head to clear it of concerns that could become mind-eating obsessions if dwelt on. He concentrated on transmitting his destination to Athens traffic control as he entered its purview. He brought the aircar into the orderly streams of aerial traffic that flowed around the Acropolis, serene within the faint shimmer of its protective temporal stasis bubble. He looked down and smiled, for he knew the secrets a collapsed tunnel under that hill held, and he remembered the unnatural being whose grave it was—a gene-engineered replica of the Greek god Pan, created by the Transhumanists and their Teloi allies for their own twisted purposes. Then he brought his mind back to the present and lowered the aircar onto the landing stage atop a building just beyond the Philopappos Hill. Not a very tall one—Athenian building regulations saw to that—and Rutherford's office was on its top floor. Jason had called ahead, and there were no delays as he was ushered in.

As always, the first thing Jason noticed when entering the office was the wide virtual window which offered a view of the Acropolis from a considerably higher level than that which the office in fact occupied. Only then did he turn to the left of the door, where

Rutherford sat behind his desk against a backdrop of display cases filled with objects snatched from the past. He already had two visitors, one of whom Jason instantly recognized.

"Alexandre!" Jason exclaimed, extending his hand to the short, dark, wiry, Corsican who had saved his life on more than one occasion.

"I sent for Superintendent Mondrago," Rutherford explained, giving his silvery Vandyke his patented self-congratulatory preening, "because I anticipated you would want him assigned to you, especially inasmuch as he was with you on your last jaunt into the American Civil War."

"You think of everything," said Jason sourly. "Anyway, Alexandre, congratulations on your overdue promotion."

"Thanks, Commander," said the ex-mercenary with a grin that made his face engagingly ugly instead of merely ugly. "But I still haven't quite gotten used to the brain implant . . . or to the title. 'Superintendent' doesn't seem to be a very good fit for what I do—even worse than when I was an 'Inspector.'"

"I know what you mean," Jason commiserated with a grin of his own. The Temporal Service had always taken a certain pride in its ability to function without formalized rank titles. That had changed with the advent of the Special Operations Section, which had needed a structured hierarchy for the same reasons as every other military or paramilitary organization. But the Authority had continued to shrink from admitting that the Section was, in fact, anything so horrid. So, to avoid any tincture of militaristic flavor, it had borrowed the system used by the Colonial Rangers, which in turn was a streamlined descendant of that of the London Metropolitan Police, which Sir Robert Peel had devised five and a half centuries earlier for exactly the same purpose. When the Section grew big enough to require another level of management at the top, higher than "Commander," they would have to make Jason a "Commissioner."

"And this," said Rutherford, indicating his other visitor, "is Dr. Carlos Dabney, a recognized authority on the history of the American Civil War."

"More properly, the War Between the States. Or the War of the Northern Aggression, as certain of my ancestors on the paternal side would have called it," said Dabney with a smile, standing up and shaking hands with Jason. He seemed fairly young to be a "recognized authority" on anything, but that was typical of the academics who passed the Authority's physical requirements to endure the hardships of Earth's earlier eras. He spoke Standard International English with a North American accent. His appearance was predominantly Caucasoid and entirely nondescript, but Jason felt there was something oddly familiar about him.

"Have we met before, Doctor?"

"Once, very briefly. I was a member of the expedition led by your Inspector Da Cunha, at the time you and your Special Operations team appeared at the fall of Richmond, North America."

"This is precisely why he is here, Jason," Rutherford interjected. "It works out very conveniently. He has already met the Authority's requirements, including acquisition of the local idiom, which will expedite matters."

"What? You mean he's going with us?"

"Precisely. I'm aware that it is highly unusual—unprecedented, in fact—for a non-Service member to go on more than one extratemporal expedition. But you are going to need an expert on the period. And no one could be better qualified. After all, he has already had some exposure by his participation in Da Cunha's expedition."

Jason was silent, for a cloud passed over his mind as it always did at the mention of Pauline Da Cunha. He turned to Rutherford, and their eyes met. The two of them had known each other long enough for words to sometimes be unnecessary. Jason's eyes asked, *Does he know?* Rutherford's eyes replied, *No.*

Jason turned back to the visibly puzzled Dabney, and his expression cleared. "Excuse me, Doctor. I know it's annoying to have people discuss you in the third person in your presence. But I need to know if you are aware of the dangers you may be getting into."

"I read and signed the Articles of Agreement before my previous temporal displacement, and have done so again now," said Dabney, sounding slightly miffed. "So I'm aware of the clauses releasing the Authority from liability for my safety."

"You don't understand. Those boilerplate provisions of the Articles refer to random danger and primitive conditions in backward, violent epochs. They were written with academic research expeditions in mind, like the one you originally signed on for. The Special Operations Section operates quite differently. We will be going back in time with a very specific objective: to abort a conspiracy of the Transhumanist underground. This may bring us into direct conflict with some utterly ruthless and brutal people—if, indeed, the word 'people' is applicable, as to which I admit a degree of skepticism. May I ask if you have ever had any form of military training or experience?"

"No," Dabney admitted, somewhat crestfallen. "But at the same time, I have always had a hobby of collecting antique firearms from the Civil War period—and firing modern made-to-specification replicas of them. In fact, I hold marksmanship trophies in that specialized field. I may not be quite as useless as you suppose, Commander Thanou."

"Well and good. But the Transhumanists are far less hesitant than we are about taking modern weapons and equipment into the past. In order to combat them, the Special Operations Section has been granted a limited exemption from the traditional prohibitions, allowing us certain very carefully disguised items." Out of the corner of his eye, Jason saw Rutherford wince at the reminder of something to which he had never fully adjusted. "What I'm saying is that, while I don't doubt that you'll be able to handle in-period weapons, you may be facing far more dangerous stuff than that, wielded by persons who are utterly indifferent to human life."

"Director Rutherford has explained all this to me, Commander. I assure you that I'm willing to accept the risks. Seeing the era first-hand was the fulfillment of a lifetime's dream. In exchange for a *second* opportunity, I'll face Transhumanists or anything else!"

Jason was momentarily silent. He had encountered this kind of selfless academic fanaticism before, and he didn't underrate it as a motivator. "I'm sure you mean what you say. But," he continued, turning to Rutherford, "Special Ops missions normally last only a few days or sometimes hours. They don't involve a lengthy stay in the past, so we don't have to endanger an historian." *And burden ourselves with the need to keep him alive,* he did not add.

"Actually, Jason," said Rutherford, looking slightly apologetic, "this isn't going to be one of your brief, tightly focused Special Operations raids. It's going to have to be more along the lines of your last expedition, the one to the seventeenth-century Caribbean."

Jason went expressionless. "A fixed-duration expedition, in other words, using the standard TRDs."

Rutherford's nod was still more apologetic.

The Fujiwara-Weintraub Temporal Displacer required a gargantuan installation, and a power surge that only an antimatter reactor could supply, to cancel the "temporal energy potential" that kept a living or nonliving object anchored in time, thereby casting it controllably adrift three hundred years or more in the past. (*Not* the future; that wasn't even a theoretical possibility.) Time travel would have been self-evidently impractical except as a one-way trip if the same requirements had applied to returning the time traveler to his proper time at the location (relative to the local gravity field) from which he had been displaced. Fortunately, temporal displacement was such a fundamentally and outrageously unnatural state that reversing it required negligible energy, and a pea-sized "temporal retrieval device" or TRD that could be subdermally implanted. Until recently, all TRDs had been set to activate at a pre-set time, so extratemporal expeditions were committed to the past for a fixed time and reappeared on the Authority's displacer stage at a predictable moment, thus assuring that the stage would be clear of any other objects with which the returning time travelers might find themselves occupying the same volume. But the new Special Operations Section required more operational flexibility than that. So, in yet another outrage to the governing council's conservative instincts, a special "controllable" TRD had been devised which the mission leader could activate at will through direct neural interfacing when the mission was complete. Such missions were, of necessity, of short duration, for the displacer stage had to be kept clear at all times until the expedition's return. There could be no dawdling in the past.

It was the way Jason preferred to operate. But then he had been forced to revert to the traditional way of doing things when a wrecked spacecraft in Haiti dating from the 1660s had presented a mystery which offered no narrowly delineated timeframe as a Special Ops target. And now. . . .

"I thought, Kyle, that we had an understanding. I was supposed to be through with this sort of thing when I agreed to head Special Ops for you." It was too much like the nursemaiding of academic expeditions on which Jason had long since burned out.

"I know, Jason," said Rutherford soothingly. "And I wouldn't ask this of you if there was any alternative. But once again you're going to have to find your target before you can even attempt to deal with it."

"All right. Why don't you tell me the details?"

"As you recall, your mission to 1865 Richmond was occasioned by an accidental discovery by Inspector Da Cunha."

"Yes. She informed us by message drop." It was a standard technique. Some out-of-the-way location off the superhighway of history would be specified in advance, and a message on some durable medium would be left there, to wait for centuries before being found in the twenty-fourth century, when the site was periodically inspected. It was one more example of the way the past could be changed but not really changed, and it was the sole means time travelers had of communicating with the Authority.

"You'll also recall that, after planting that message drop and before your arrival, she had discovered the true nature of the threat—a nanotechnological time bomb—by means of the detection features of her recently installed brain implant."

"Yes," nodded Jason, wincing at the recollection of Da Cunha's excitement at receiving her implant. After the Transhuman Dispensation had been extirpated—or, rather, been thought to have been extirpated—a little over a century before, the Human Integrity Act had been passed, forbidding all the nanotechnological and biotechnological and cybernetic techniques that distorted the human genome or blurred the distinction between life and nonlife, man and machine, brain and computer. But the Temporal Service, like certain law enforcement agencies, possessed limited exemptions. One was the tiny but extremely versatile computer implant in the head of any Service officer qualified as a mission leader. Mondrago had gotten one along with his promotion. Pauline Da Cunha had been cleared for it on an accelerated basis, while still only an Inspector. It had been a proud moment for her. "It was sheer good luck that she detected the nanobots."

"Indeed. After her retrieval, the implant's record was naturally downloaded, but since you had evidently put an end to the problem there was no sense of urgency about studying it more closely. But a few weeks ago, while you were on leave, we got around to it. And we turned up a disturbing fact." Rutherford paused as though gathering strength. "After your Special Operations team came and went, Da Cunha evidently felt no need to monitor her implant's detectors any further during the remainder of her stay in the nineteenth century. So she was unaware that, in fact, during that period additional nanobots were detected—"

"—That hadn't been there before," Jason finished for him. "'Disturbing' indeed."

"Naturally we performed as detailed an analysis as the somewhat 'fuzzy' quality of the readings permitted. And the indications are that the time sequencing of these nanobots had commenced at a slightly *earlier* point in time than the ones you had destroyed, suggesting that the Transhumanists have sent—or will send at some point in our own near future—a second expedition back to make a second attempt. But we cannot be precise. The possible time frame involved is too long for us to keep the displacer stage continuously open. Impossible, in fact, inasmuch as we have several expeditions scheduled for retrieval during that period."

"Cut to the chase, Kyle. Just how long a stay are we looking at?"

"The plan is for you to arrive on December 15, 1864, and remain until April 5, 1865. This covers the entire period in which we believe the nanobots could have been emplaced."

Jason leaned forward and held Rutherford's eyes. "You realize what this means, don't you, Kyle? This will make me—and Alexandre, since you're also sending him—contemporaneous with ourselves from April 1 to April 3, which were the dates we were in Richmond on our previous mission."

"I am all too well aware of that. And councilor Kung is *very* well aware of it. Only the gravity of the situation induced the council to approve it. That, and one other thing." Rutherford looked pleased with himself. "I pointed out that on your previous return from nineteenth-century Richmond you reported no untoward occurrences."

"That's true: I never encountered myself while I was there."

"Same here," Mondrago chimed in.

"Just so. This suggests that the concern is illusory."

"Of course, there is another concern," Jason began . . . and then halted, for he couldn't discuss in Dabney's presence the fact that he might encounter Pauline Da Cunha, and have to look her in the eyes knowing her fate and unable to reveal it to her even if—for God knew what reason—he wanted to. Instead, he changed the subject. "What about personnel?"

Rutherford lost a bit of his characteristic self-satisfaction. "Well, er, given the somewhat irregular aspects of this mission, I had to agree that Mr. Nesbit would accompany your party in the same capacity as last time. Aside from him, Dr. Dabney and Superintendent Mondrago, we can allow you two Special Operations officers—*not* chosen from among those who were with you in the same milieu before."

*Yes, that would be pushing things, wouldn't it? I'm lucky they're letting me have Alexandre.* "All right. Let me think about it and I'll give you the names."

Dabney had been looking as though he felt left out of the conversation. Now he perked up, as if desiring be helpful. "You know, Commander, it occurs to me that Inspector Da Cunha would be an ideal choice. After all, she already has experience in. . . ." His voice trailed to a miserable halt as he saw the look in Jason's eyes.

"I regret to have to tell you, Doctor," said Jason in an absolutely expressionless voice, "that Inspector Da Cunha is dead. She was lost on our next extratemporal expedition."

"Oh." Dabney swallowed hard. "I'm very sorry to hear that, Commander." He paused as though waiting for an elaboration.

None was forthcoming. There was only dead silence.

"Well," said Rutherford, a little too briskly, "I think that concludes our business for today. We'll meet again tomorrow to discuss details."

# CHAPTER THREE

The two Temporal Service men Jason had picked were already on hand in Australia when the suborbital transport carrying Rutherford, Jason and Mondrago landed.

It would have simplified things to be able to use people who had accompanied Jason to the collapsing Confederacy before and thus already had the basic orientation for the period. But it was out of the question, of course, with himself and Mondrago going and the council smarting from repeated outrages to its cautious instincts. Fortunately, there were a couple of suitable men currently available.

One was Inspector Adam Logan, a charter member of the Special Operations Section. In fact, he had been with Jason on his brief return to 490 B.C. Athens to scotch the Transhumanists' Pan cult, before the Section had even officially existed. He was of average size and medium Caucasian coloring, nondescript enough to pass unnoticed in many historical milieus. Terms like "the strong silent type" and "a man of few words" might well have been coined with him in mind. But on those occasions when he spoke, what he said invariably made sense.

The other man was a striking contrast to Logan. Constable Angus Aiken was soon due for promotion to sergeant, but his relative lack of experience had still caused Jason some misgivings, as did his tendency to youthful cockiness. However, as usual, beggars couldn't be choosers when it came to finding people who could blend. Aiken was a small man, which was helpful in most past eras. His coloring was not, for his blue eyes and fiery red hair limited the settings into which he could fit without attracting attention. It shouldn't be a problem on this expedition, though, given the large Celtic element in the seceding American states' populations. And he had acquitted himself well on his one Special Ops mission, to his native Scotland around the turn of the thirteenth century to counter Transhumanist machinations involving Templar refugees from Philip the Fair's suppression of the Order in France. But a fixed-duration expedition like this one would be a new experience for him.

Jason lost no time in confronting that issue, at the Service team's preliminary meeting, with Rutherford sitting in. "Angus, I assume that you, along with everyone else, have already been told that on this mission we are not going to be permitted to use the Special Operations Section's unique equipment and methodology."

"I have, Commander." Aiken's manner was scrupulously correct. Like so many other Special Ops personnel, he had been recruited from one of the military "free companies" that had proliferated to fill the gap between the armed forces' chronic underfunding and the demands placed on them by an expanding interstellar frontier. So despite his youth he was not without exposure to a military culture. Besides which, he was addressing a man who was something of a legend in the Service as well as head of Special Ops.

"Good. But I want to make sure you understand the implications of that. We won't have the new controllable TRD's, enabling the mission leader to bring the team back to the present on the basis of his own reading of the situation. No, we're going to be committed to the target milieu for exactly three months and twenty days, come hell or high water, after which our old-style TRDs will activate automatically. If you're like most people who have never experienced that kind of retrieval, you may be a little apprehensive at the thought of being suddenly snatched back to the displacer stage without warning. In fact, I'll be able to tell you exactly when to expect it, thanks to the 'clock' that's one of the functions of my computer implant. Incidentally, mine will be the only such implant. Superintendent Mondrago here has recently received one. But it has now been deactivated—"

("The story of my life," Mondrago muttered.)

"—due to the Service regulation that such normally illegal

cybernetics are only permissible for the mission leader, for whom their necessity is self-evident on a number of levels." For the same reason, Pauline Da Cunha's implant had been deactivated on their Caribbean expedition. It was, Jason thought, just another example of the Authority's inflexible, overcautious rules-worship. It was a standing sore point in his relationship with Rutherford, and he permitted himself a quick glare at the older man. But for all his irritation, he grudgingly admitted to himself that the Service could be worse off. They could have had an operations director who *never* said no to the old ladies of both genders who dominated the council.

"Another consequence of this mission's special circumstances of is that we will be accompanied by Dr. Carlos Dabney, an historian of the period, and Mr. Irving Nesbit, an administrative assistant to the council." Jason smiled thinly at Logan's and Aiken's expressions, which spoke eloquently of what they thought of having two civilians to nursemaid. "Let me assure you that these gentlemen are not without experience. Dr. Dabney has already spent time in the target milieu, as part of a research expedition led by the late Inspector Da Cunha." Like everyone else in the Service, Logan and Aiken knew Pauline Da Cunha was dead; but that was all they knew, for the details of her death had been strictly suppressed. Jason and Mondrago had sat, tightly bound, in a jungle clearing and watched those details in the firelight; now they exchanged a quick eye-contact before Jason hurried on. "And at any rate, his detailed knowledge of the period is indispensable to achieving our objective. He understands that this is not an academic jaunt." *I hope*, Jason mentally hedged before continuing.

"As for Mr. Nesbit, he was with me and Superintendent Mondrago on our recent expedition to the seventeenth-century Caribbean, of which you may have heard a few things, so you know he came through some harrowing experiences. I'm confident he will be able to withstand the relatively civilized milieu of nineteenth-century North America." Jason did not elaborate on the reason for Nesbit's presence, and he was glumly certain he didn't need to. From his own experiences in the twentieth century, the term *political commissar* came to mind. "Are there any questions regarding what I've said so far?"

"Just one, sir," said Logan in his slow, deliberate way. "We've been told the dates of this mission. Don't they overlap the time you and Superintendent Mondrago were in the target milieu?"

"That is correct. For that period he and I will be contemporaneous with our own slightly younger selves. As you know, this is contrary to normal operational doctrines." Rutherford frowned as though he felt Jason was indulging in understatement verging on flippancy. "But, as you also know, it isn't completely without precedent. I've been in this situation twice. In fact, you were with me the first time, in fifth century B.C. Athens."

"I remember it vividly, sir."

"Still, I don't plan to make a habit of it," Jason continued, with a smile that caused Rutherford's frown to intensify. "And we don't expect it to be a problem, for two reasons. In the first place, Alexandre and I were only there for three days, all of which we spent in the city of Richmond. With any luck, our party will be elsewhere at the time. Secondly, and more to the point, during those three days I never saw myself. So we seem to be covered by the Observer Effect."

"But sir, what about Dr. Dabney?" Aiken wondered. "If I recall the dates correctly, Inspector Da Cunha's expedition had a significantly greater overlap with ours." A new thought seemed to occur to him. "And then there's Inspector Da Cunha herself. . . ."

"That could be difficult," nodded Logan, who had known Da Cunha well. "Seeing her, and knowing she's going to die."

*You have* no *idea,* thought Jason sickly. *"Difficult" is not the word for seeing her alive and whole when the last time I saw her she was tied down to the top of a coffin and I had to helplessly watch the things being done to her.*

*Will I be able to handle it, if I have to? I think so. But what about Alexandre? He watched it all too, until a Transhumanist goon knocked him out to stop his screams and curses.*

Jason glanced at Mondrago. The Corsican's expression was very, very controlled. Then he glanced at Rutherford, and his eyes asked a question.

Logan and Aiken looked puzzled, as though dimly understanding that they were watching a byplay in which they had no part.

Rutherford ended the moment with a harrumph. "Here again, the Observer Effect gives us cause for confidence. Dr. Dabney assures me that he never interacted with a second version of himself. And as for Inspector Da Cunha, she mentioned no peculiar incidents when she was debriefed following her retrieval."

"A debriefing for which I wasn't present," Jason interjected. "I was off-world at the time, in transit to and from Hesperia." *Where I'd barely disembarked before learning that my leave had been cancelled,* he silently added, with a glare in Rutherford's direction.

"That debriefing," continued Rutherford, ignoring him, "also provided us with the basis for planning this mission. Inspector Da Cunha had, while in Richmond, encountered certain slaves and ex-slaves who apparently belonged to some kind of secret organization, and evidently wanted to be helpful—although she wasn't certain exactly why."

Mondrago snapped his fingers. "That's right. I remember Pauline saying something about that in the short time we were with her there. She also mentioned that she wasn't able to learn much about them. They were very cautious and secretive, as you'd expect."

"Nevertheless, as she explained in the course of her debriefing, she was able to learn the identity of one member—or, more accurately, associate—of the group, who she could use as a contact: a certain Mary Elizabeth Bowser, who under the pseudonym Ellen Bond was a servant in the household of Confederate President Jefferson Davis . . . where she acted as an undercover agent for the Union side."

Aiken let out a low whistle. "She must have been one very nervy lady!"

"Actually, there were a surprising number of female spies for both sides in that war. Or, on reflection, perhaps not so surprising. Given the social attitudes of the nineteenth century, it must have been easy for women to avoid being taken seriously—a useful attribute for an espionage agent."

"And that must have been doubly true for a woman of African descent, especially in the South," Jason speculated.

"Indubitably. But, to resume, as things turned out Inspector Da Cunha never had an opportunity to make contact with her." Rutherford chuckled. "This was intensely frustrating for Dr. Dabney, who as an expert on the period knew of Ms. Bowser and would have given a great deal to meet her. He should get his chance this time, because our plan is for you to use the information Inspector Da Cunha obtained in order to establish contact with her."

"For what purpose?" Jason asked.

"To persuade her to put you in touch with the shadowy

organization of blacks of which Inspector Da Cunha had tenuous knowledge. You see, one other thing emerged in the course of her debriefing." Rutherford paused, as though neither understanding nor liking the implications of what he was about to say. "You must understand, she had no hard evidence of this. But she could not avoid the impression that that organization was somehow aware of—and opposed to—the Transhumanists."

"But how . . . ?" Aiken began, and then trailed off.

"How, indeed." Rutherford let his listeners chew on that for a few seconds, then turned brisk. "Tomorrow, at the first full meeting of the expedition, Dr. Dabney will provide us with more detailed information on Ms. Bowser."

It was a very subdued and puzzled group that filed out. Jason was the last to leave. Just before he followed the others out the door, Rutherford caught his eye and smiled. "At least, Jason, since we know Pauline Da Cunha did *not* contact Mary Bowser, the plan should minimize the chances of you encountering her."

"Maybe," said Jason without much conviction.

"And, to reiterate, she said nothing in her debriefing about any inexplicable sightings of you, aside from the, ah . . . version of you that was—how to put it?—legitimately in that milieu in the course of your previous Special Operations incursion."

"I know. But while she may not have seen me in the new 'version', that doesn't necessarily mean *I* won't see *her*, knowing her fate and also knowing there's not a damned thing I can do to change it."

Rutherford had no reply to make. Jason departed in silence.

# CHAPTER FOUR

"Director Rutherford is quite correct about female spies in the American Civil War," declared Dabney. He was addressing a full meeting of the expedition, including Nesbit as well as himself, and he was settling happily into what Jason recognized from long experience of similar types as lecturing mode. "Not only was Mary Elizabeth Bowser a woman, but so was her 'control,' a certain Elizabeth Van Lew. The whole story is full of obscure and contradictory elements. This was, to a great extent, intentional; Bowser deliberately concealed and even falsified certain elements of her story—possibly even her real name, which may have been Mary Richards. Besides which, after the war the United States government destroyed the records of many of its Southern spies, to protect their lives from retaliation."

"Typical of the kind of paper trails left by clandestine espionage agents," Mondrago commented.

"Yes. I'm hoping to be able to clear up some of the mysteries. Although," Dabney added hastily, catching sight of Jason's expression, "I do realize that's not our primary objective."

"Doctor," said Logan slowly, "we've all gotten the basic orientation, through sleep-teaching and the other standard means, concerning the facts and figures and issues of the American Civil War era. But can you tell us the specifics concerning Mary Bowser?"

"Certainly, to the extent that the story can be pieced together. She was born in Richmond in or about 1839 as a slave to one John Van

Lew. After his death, his daughter Elizabeth, who had strong anti-slavery opinions, freed the family's slaves. Mary remained with the family as a servant until Elizabeth, recognizing her exceptional intelligence, sent her to Philadelphia to be educated in the Quaker School for Negroes. It turned out she also had a photographic memory. She returned to Richmond just before the Civil War began, to marry a free black man and resume working in the Van Lew household.

"Early in the war Elizabeth Van Lew, who was already considered eccentric because of her anti-slavery and anti-secession views, became positively unpopular with her neighbors by taking food, medicine and other items to the Union officers being held in Richmond's notorious Libby Prison. She would have been even more unpopular had they known that she was helping some of those prisoners escape, and providing safe houses. She also got information from them about Confederate dispositions and smuggled it out of Richmond to the Union high command via her household staff of freed slaves, written in a code she had devised and hidden in things like shoe soles and hollow eggs."

Aiken looked perplexed. "Wasn't she sort of bringing suspicion on herself by openly being a Union sympathizer? I would have thought she would have wrapped a Confederate flag around herself and sung 'Dixie' at the top of her lungs."

"That would have been suspicious in itself, since her views were already well known. Instead, she turned her reputation for eccentricity to her advantage. She made sure she wasn't taken seriously by talking and humming to herself and generally acting demented at every opportunity, so much so that she came to be known as 'Crazy Bet.'"

"Hiding in plain sight," said Mondrago approvingly. "Still, surely the Confederates must have suspected that *something* was going on." The naiveté of earlier eras in matters of counterintelligence was a never-ending source of wonder to him. He had declared himself unsurprised when Dabney had told them that Antietam (or Sharpsburg, as the Confederates called it), one of the most decisive battles of the war, had been lost because secret orders had been found in a field along with the cigars they had been used to wrap.

"Oh, yes. Her home was searched repeatedly. But they never found anything incriminating. She kept all her materials, including a detailed journal of her activities, buried in a hole in her backyard."

"A hole in her backyard," Mondrago repeated with a dazed headshake.

"Eventually Elizabeth Van Lew was running a spy ring that included clerks in Confederate government departments and a high-ranking officer at Libby Prison. And her lines of communication with General Grant had become so routine that she was sending him a daily copy of the Richmond newspaper! But her greatest coup was inserting her former slave Mary Bowser into the 'Confederate White House.' Through a friend, she had Bowser brought in as an illiterate, somewhat dim-witted servant named Ellen Bond—"

("Another alias!" Aiken groaned.)

"—to help Jefferson Davis' wife Varina with social functions. Soon she was taken on full-time. You must understand that servants were effectively invisible, and were assumed to be unable to read and write, or to understand anything beyond simple commands. So there was no attempt to prevent her from reading the state papers lying around Davis' office, and listening in on meetings and conversations."

Mondrago gave an even more incredulous headshake-and-sigh.

"With her phenomenal memory, Bowser was able to retain information verbatim, and being educated could write it down. She then passed it on to another of Elizabeth Van Lew's spies, a baker named Thomas McNiven who made regular deliveries to the Davis household. Eventually, it became obvious that there was a huge leak in the Confederate White House, and McNiven was caught. It was only then that Bowser began to come under suspicion. She was aware that her position had become precarious, and after unsuccessfully attempting to burn the Confederate White House down she fled in January, 1865."

"The month after we're due to arrive," Jason nodded. "Where did she go after that, Dr. Dabney?"

"I cannot say. As I mentioned, both she and the Union authorities did their best to obscure the facts about her. After the war, she simply vanishes from history. There are indications that she moved north, which certainly would have been prudent. But no one knows when or where she died."

Nesbit spoke up. "Nowhere in what you've told us is there anything about any connection between Mary Bowser and some secret organization of African-Americans in that period."

"No, nor is any such organization known to history. I was quite taken by surprise when we of Inspector Da Cunha's expedition learned, if only in vague terms, of its existence."

"Sounds almost like the kind of things the Transhumanists are trying to fill the 'blank spaces' of human history with," Logan remarked.

"Except that, according to Rutherford, Pauline's impression was that they were opposed to the Transhumanists." Jason gave a dismissive gesture. "There's no point in speculating on that until we have some hard data. For now, let's concentrate on completing our orientation."

That orientation, and the rest of their preparation, was not as time-consuming as it would have been for earlier epochs, such as those Jason had recently visited. One example was the elimination from their bodies of forcibly-evolved microorganisms to which people before the twentieth and early twenty-first-century era of reckless antibiotics overuse had no immunity. It wasn't as much of a problem as it had been when he had gone back into the Bronze and Iron Ages of ancient Greece. Since those eras, the microorganisms had had additional thousands of years of natural evolution. And as always, the subcutaneous implantation of their TRDs under the insides of their upper left arms was merely routine.

But the orientation involved, among other things, the acquisition of mid-nineteenth-century American English—and, specifically, its Southern variant—by Nesbit, Logan and Aiken. They did so by direct neural induction, as Jason, Mondrago and Dabney already had. It was another area in which the Temporal Regulatory Authority had successfully argued for an exemption from the Human Integrity Act on the basis of sheer practicality. In this case, the language in question was sufficiently similar to twenty-fourth century Standard International English as almost to constitute a different dialect of the same tongue. This simplified the process, but was not altogether a good thing. They would have to constantly be careful not to let familiarity cause any of their own century's neologisms and loan-words to slip into their speech.

Of course the imposition of a language directly on the speech centers of the brain did not magically confer the ability to speak it like a native of the locality. Thus time travelers, wherever they happened to be, always claimed to be from somewhere else, so oddities and eccentricities of pronunciation were only to be expected. Fortunately, in this case they had a perfect opening, as Dabney explained to them.

"At the time we will be arriving, there were. . . ." He trailed to a halt at the realization of the mixed tenses.

"Everyone has problems like that when discussing time travel," Jason assured him.

"Thank you. At any rate, there were units from the Deep South in Lee's army of Northern Virginia—specifically, in the cavalry." He manipulated controls, and an organization chart appeared on the briefing room's viewscreen.

"As you can see, the Cavalry Corps, under the command of Major General Wade Hampton, consisted of three divisions, one of which was commanded by Brigadier General Wade Butler. Butler had two brigades, of which the one we are concerned with was led by Brigadier General Pierce Young."

Mondrago studied the chart. "I don't see any numerical designations for these units."

"They had none; they were referred to as 'Hampton's Corps' and 'Butler's Division' and 'Young's Brigade,'" explained Dabney, eliciting a disapproving headshake from Mondrago. "But to continue, Young had four regiments, one of which was called the Jeff Davis Legion." A cursor flashed, indicating a box on the screen. "The men of its ten companies were drawn from the states of Georgia, Alabama and Mississippi."

Dabney's listeners nodded. In the course of their orientation they had absorbed enough of the political geography of the old United States of America to follow him. In fact, Jason was already fairly familiar with it from previous expeditions. "None from Louisiana?" he inquired. "When Alexandre and I were in this milieu before, we were prepared to claim to be from there. As it turned out, we never needed to. We were only there for a bare three days. And in the middle of the Confederacy's final collapse, people had other things on their minds besides making searching inquiries as to our origin."

"That was just as well, for in fact there were no Louisiana units in the Army of Northern Virginia at that time; they were all with the Army of the Trans-Mississippi."

"Too bad. Alexandre and I both have the Mediterranean kind of looks that the Virginians of that era would have automatically associated with French or Spanish Creoles, who incidentally had a very different way of speaking."

"It happens I can accommodate you," said Dabney with a smile. "Of the three Mississippi companies in the Jeff Davis Legion, two were from Chickasaw County and Kemper County, which were in the northeasterly parts of the state, well away from the Gulf coast. But the third company, known as 'The Natchez Cavalry,' drew its men from Adams County, on the lower Mississippi River around the town of Natchez—hence the name—where there was a significant Creole element."

"So," said Mondrago, "you're telling me that these people not only had regiments associated with particular states, but that on the company level they were sometimes associated with a particular *county*?" He turned to Jason. "This is starting to remind me of the time we were in fifth century B.C. Athens. Remember the way the army was organized around the ten tribes that the citizenry was divided into?"

"Yes," Jason nodded. "Very beneficial from the standpoint of unit solidarity, but damned inconvenient for us. These men all knew each other, and each other's relatives. We'll have to be very careful not to fall in with the 'Natchez Cavalry' we're claiming to be a part of."

"That shouldn't be a problem," Dabney asserted. "The Army of Northern Virginia, as of our arrival date in December, 1864, was pretty much tied down in the defense of Petersburg, to the southeast of Richmond." The organization chart vanished, replaced by a map. "This included the cavalry, which was used in a variety of roles—patrols, skirmishing, scouting, reconnaissance, and dispatch duty, among others."

"But not, er, charges against the enemy?" Nesbit ventured, romantic images visibly fading in his eyes.

Dabney shot him an irritated look but replied with scrupulous patience. "No. Half a century earlier, Napoleon's heavy shock cavalry had ridden down unshaken infantry a few times—as, for example, at Eylau against the Russians when a snowstorm had soaked their gunpowder—although they failed abysmally at Waterloo. But by the period we are discussing, it was no longer practical. The reasons will become apparent when we get into an in-depth discussion of the revolution in firearms that had occurred since Napoleon's time. At the moment, the point is that we should not encounter our alleged comrades of the 'Natchez Cavalry' as long as we avoid the Petersburg battlefront, as I sincerely hope we do." Dabney gave a rather nervous laugh. Academic curiosity had its limits, Jason decided.

# CHAPTER FIVE

Their transformation into reasonable facsimiles of Confederate cavalrymen came in several stages.

Names were the easiest. Logan, Aiken, Nesbit and Dabney (whose first name wouldn't seem eccentric in one hailing from the Spanish-influenced Gulf coast) could keep their own. Mondrago had done the same on his brief previous jaunt to 1865, while Jason had adopted the surname "Landrieu" along with the rank of captain, and they would do the same this time. It would avoid the need for awkward explanations if anyone saw them in both of their versions.

Uniforms were almost equally simple, for the Authority's workshops had vast experience in turning out period clothing as well as subtle techniques for giving it a well-worn look. The last part was especially important, for they would be posing as soldiers in the last year of a grueling four-year war—soldiers on the losing side, whose supply facilities had always been chronically inadequate. In fact Jason, as an officer, and Mondrago, as a sergeant, were the only ones who would have something resembling the regulation uniforms of gray with yellow cavalry facings. Jason's sleeves sported the Confederate officer's distinctive, elaborate gold braid "Austrian knot" (artfully tarnished and faded), while Mondrago's had yellow chevrons. The others would wear the light "butternut" brownish-gray shade that was the closest most of the South's facilities could come to the regulation "cadet gray." For headgear they all had the "stag hat" that the Confederate cavalry always preferred to the regulation kepi. All the uniforms were of heavy cotton denim. Likewise of cotton were their undergarments, for whose heaviness they would be grateful on their arrival in December. Their boots were as high-quality as they could be made without arousing suspicion in a famously footgear-short army.

As cavalrymen, they would of course be expected to be able to ride horses. Temporal Service personnel learned equestrianism as part of their training, and Dabney proved to be their best rider—he had long done it for recreation, as well as having gone through an introduction to it as part of the course in low-tech survival that the Authority required all would-be time travelers to pass. But that latter course was Nesbit's only exposure to it, and Jason could only hope he would be able to keep up.

But while they could all ride, they would have no horses to do it with. The energy expenditure necessary for temporal displacement, always staggering (at least using the Authority's technology), was a function of two factors: the length of time separating the target date from the present, and the total mass being displaced. For a displacement of five hundred and sixteen years, the total combined mass of six men yielded a reasonable energy cost. But six horses complete with tack were out of the question—Rutherford had experienced heart palpitations at the mere thought. They would have to arrive on foot and obtain mounts locally, by hook or crook. It oughtn't to be necessary to resort to the "crook" part, for Jason was bringing a supply of gold dollars which should serve to purchase practically anything in an economy brought to its knees as much by the hyperinflation of the Confederacy's paper currency as by the Union blockade. Of course, no amount of money could buy what wasn't available to be bought, and Jason doubted they would get prime specimens of horseflesh—which, in Nesbit's case at least, might be just as well. And it would provide them with a cover story to explain their presence in Richmond: they would be there to obtain mounts for their company, the "Natchez Cavalry."

They would, however, carry their own weapons, manufactured to the Authority's uncompromising standard of authenticity. For familiarization with these, they went to the armory, where Dabney, very much in his element, began with general background.

"The American Civil War was fought in the midst of a revolution in firearms. The French historian Jean Colin once said, referring to the advent of gunpowder in China around the year 900, 'More than a thousand years were needed before the invention of gunpowder really transformed war.' That's an extreme position, but there's a grain of truth in it. Up to a couple of decades before our arrival date, the infantry were armed with a muzzle-loading smoothbore musket whose flintlock ignition missed fire one in six times and which was reasonably accurate only out to forty yards."

"We had some experience with primitive slow-loading, single-shot firearms when we were in the seventeenth-century Caribbean," Jason affirmed. "Edged weapons still played a big role."

"Yes. Under such circumstances, a single foot soldier in the open was pretty much at the mercy of a horseman. So the infantry were massed in dense formations designed to maximize volume of essentially unaimed fire, followed by a bayonet charge."

Mondrago, who often surprised Jason with his knowledge of military history, spoke up. "Wasn't there a general of the British Indian army who, when he was told the ammunition was running out, said, 'Thank God! I'll be at 'em with the bayonet!'"

Dabney nodded. "General Gough, at Sobraon during the First Sikh War—a battle which, incidentally, he won. But that was in the 1840s, just as the great change was beginning." He reached behind him to a shelf holding a variety of small arms and held up a longarm. "The British Pattern 1853 Enfield rifled musket, widely used in the American Civil War alongside the very similar American Springfield. It's still a single-shot muzzle-loader, and at first glance it looks much like the good old flintlock musket. But there's a world of difference. In the first place, instead of a flintlock it uses percussion ignition: the hammer strikes a copper cap full of fulminates fitted over a little steel nipple, so it was a near-certainty that it would actually fire when you squeezed the trigger.

"But the most important change was reflected in the name *rifled* musket. Unlike the old smoothbores, it has spiral grooves along the inside of the barrel. This puts a spin on the projectile and give it far greater range and accuracy."

Logan looked perplexed. "Then why hadn't they rifled the barrels of the old flintlocks?"

"They sometimes did, for hunting weapons like the 'Kentucky long rifle.' But it wasn't practical for the military because it was even slower-loading than the smoothbores; it took time to ram a round lead ball down a rifled barrel from the muzzle if the ball was large enough to grip the rifling. What brought about the revolution was *this*." Dabney picked up an object so small that they had to lean forward to see it. "It's a French invention called the Minié ball."

"It doesn't look like a 'ball' to me," said Aiken skeptically. "It's shaped more like a stubby bullet."

"Precisely the point. This established the form and function of the bullet. The flat base is expands when the gun is fired, forcing the lead of the bullet into the rifling grooves. It also confines all the expanding gasses of the exploded powder behind the projectile where they belong, further enhancing range and hitting power.

"The horrific casualties of the war resulted in part from the fact that the generals, as young cadets at West Point, had been taught to study the campaigns of Napoleon. When they tried to use that era's tactics in the new combat environment, the result was the slaughter of thousands of men. They didn't fully grasp the consequences of the revolution in firepower that had occurred. The soldiers, however, caught on by the second half of the war. They had a tendency to 'lose' their bayonets, but were very careful to keep their spades. They dug earthworks without orders, and by the time of our arrival the ten-month deadlock in the trenches at Petersburg had become almost a foretaste of World War I's Western front."

Mondrago examined the Minié ball critically. "So you still had to load the gunpowder charge separately?"

"Yes. The self-contained brass cartridge was still in the experimental stage. Some were used, and by late in the war there were a number of breechloaders and even repeaters like the Henry rifle, which the Confederates called 'that damn' Yankee gun that can be loaded on Sunday and fired all week.' But they were plagued by the problem of fouling of the breech and bore until smokeless powder was invented in the 1880s, and at any event they were few. The masses of infantry continued to use rifled muskets like this one. But those were enough to render the classic Napoleonic tactics obsolete. For example, the artillery was surprisingly ineffective on the battlefield; gun crews could not survive if they got close enough to the enemy's infantry to use antipersonnel case shot ammunition."

"I'm beginning to understand what you told us before," Jason mused. "By this period, a cavalry charge against disciplined infantry fire must have been just an unnecessarily dramatic form of suicide."

"Well put. We cavalrymen—" (Dabney permitted himself a smile) "—had other functions. Scouting, for one, and screening the army's movements from the other side's scouts. Another was long-range raids against the enemy's supplies and communications, tearing up railroad tracks and cutting telegraph lines—a primitive wire-electricity system that was the only means of instantaneous messaging they had in those days. This sort of thing could also unnerve the enemy commander, as in the case of J.E.B. Stuart's famous 'ride around McClellan.' And finally, of course, countering all of this when the other side was doing it. There were a fair number of cavalry-against-cavalry action."

"What sort of weapons have we got?" It was Mondrago's usual question.

Dabney took up a sword from the shelf and drew it from its scabbard. "This, of course, is the traditional arm. Specifically, it's the Model 1860 cavalry saber. Despite the name, it doesn't bear much resemblance to what's used in the sport of sabre-fencing; it's intended for slashing from horseback when level with your opponent."

"That could ruin your whole day," said Aiken, eyeing the wickedly curved blade.

"Yes: they had, as you've observed, a certain intimidation value. But by 1865 their day was pretty much over, although they continued to be issued to cavalry—whose officers, at least, felt naked without them—as late as World War I."

"So what sort of firearms are we talking about?" Mondrago persisted.

Dabney held up a longarm smaller than the Enfield. "Sometimes the cavalry fought as mounted infantry, dismounting to fight. For this they used carbines like this, the Sharps. It's a breechloader, even though at that technological level it was hard to prevent gas leakage at the breech. By the very end of the war the Union cavalry was starting to use the Spencer carbine, one of the experimental repeaters I mentioned earlier, which made them *very* effective mounted infantry—or would have if the Union commanders had employed them in this role as well as the Confederates did.

"But even for close cavalry-on-cavalry melees, the saber was being superseded by this." He produced a large handgun. "The Colt Model 1860 .44 caliber Army revolver."

"I've heard of Colt revolvers!" Aiken piped up happily. "Cowboys and Indians!"

"I'm not surprised that you have. Samuel Colt—who may or may not have had the right to style himself 'Colonel' Colt—didn't invent the revolver; he just turned out good ones on a mass production basis. But the ones you're thinking of, the fully developed double-action revolvers of gunslinger fame, came later, after the war, when brass cartridges had been perfected. This is a single-action revolver, which means you have to cock the hammer with your thumb every time you fire." Dabney demonstrated. "Also, it's what is known as a front-loading revolver. To load it, you remove the cylinder. For each of the six chambers, you take a paper cartridge like this one, tear it open and pour the powder into the chamber, then insert the bullet. After loading all the chambers, you tamp the bullets in using the hinged loading lever under the barrel. Then you grease the heads of the bullets to prevent sparks. Finally you put a percussion cap into the rear of each chamber, where the hammer strikes it and ignites the powder."

"It seems a frightfully complicated and cumbersome process," Nesbit observed dubiously.

"By later standards, yes. But once you've completed it, you can fire six shots without interruption. That gives you a terrific edge over an opponent who has to ram powder and ball down the barrel after every shot. Needless to say, cavalrymen went into battle with at least one revolver already loaded."

"May I?" Jason took the revolver by the rather elegantly shaped grip of its walnut stock. "Pretty long and heavy."

"At two pounds eleven ounces, and fourteen inches in length, it seems that way to anyone used to modern handguns. But the weight has a certain steadying effect which enhances accuracy, as does the single-action feature. It still has a tendency to shoot high, but for close action it is deadly. And, as you know, ours incorporate certain special features."

"Yes, I know." In particular, the handgrip of Jason's revolver held a sensor that could detect functioning bionic enhancements, short-ranged as the inevitable price of extreme miniaturization, and linked to his implant display.

They went through repeated exercises in the loading process before going out onto the firing range for target practice. Jason, Mondrago and Logan all had experience in the field with low-tech handguns. Aiken hadn't yet had occasion to acquire that, but he had a knack for firearms in general. Nesbit, as Jason already knew, definitely did not. Not even the extremely miniaturized laser target designator embedded in the loading lever under the barrel of his otherwise authentic Colt helped much.

As for Dabney, he proved as good as his word regarding his expertise with these weapons. But Jason knew the difference between unhurried, undisturbed target shooting and the terrifying chaos of battle, where marksmanship counted for less than coolness under fire. That was especially true of close cavalry action, where there was no leisure to draw a careful bead.

He broached the subject to Dabney afterwards, in private. "I understand, Commander," the historian assured him, sounding a bit nettled, like one stating what ought to be obvious. "I don't think I'm in any danger of falling into cockiness."

"Good. It is my hope that you won't be exposed to that danger. I do not intend for us to get into any fights unless we're in a position where we have no other choice."

"I understand," Dabney repeated. But something in his eyes bothered Jason.

# CHAPTER SIX

"There's one thing I've never entirely understood, Commander," said Nesbit diffidently. "I know it seems a little late to be mentioning it. I've hesitated to bring it up, since *surely* it must have been thought of by Director Rutherford and yourself. But. . . ."

"But what, Irving?" Jason prompted from across the long rectangular table in the conference room adjoining Rutherford's office, where the team members sat for their final pre-displacement meeting. Rutherford sat at the head of the table. To his left was a small, slender, rather plain woman, fairly young, with straight dark-brown hair pulled severely back. Nesbit looked around the table and finally overcame his apprehension at the possibility of seeming foolish.

"Well . . . these nanobots that Inspector Da Cunha's brain implant detected after your Special Operations team had departed. . . ."

"Yes?"

"Why can't you simply lead another quick Special Operations incursion back to April of 186—or even some later date—and destroy them as well? Of course," Nesbit hastily added, "I realize you can't do so *before* the date at which she detected them; the Observer Effect prevents that. But it seems you should be able to arrive at a date *subsequent* to that and—"

"Yes, we could do that. But the result would be inconclusive." Seeing Nesbit's puzzled look, Jason explained. "Remember, these

41

nanobots' activation sequences suggested that they had been emplaced earlier. What if the second Transhumanist expedition, the one that went back further than the first, planted more of them . . . which Pauline *didn't* detect?" He saw he had gotten through to Nesbit. "If so, the very fact that she didn't detect them means the Observer Effect won't preclude us from destroying them at an earlier date. And as for the ones she *did* detect . . . well, that's why we're remaining until April 5, 1865, one day after her implant detected them, because you're quite correct about the restriction the Observer Effect puts on us when it comes to destroying those. This gives us a short period when we can destroy them, and also any others we discover if we haven't already."

"In short," said Rutherford, "if possible we want to nip the problem in the bud, as people say, by being present when the Transhumanists arrive and foiling *all* their plans."

"Besides which," said the small woman at his side in a voice whose mildness went with her pale, delicate features, "killing Transhumanists is always a worthwhile goal in and of itself."

"Too goddamned right!" growled Mondrago with tightly controlled vehemence. The other two Service men nodded, Aiken with youthful enthusiasm and Logan with mature deliberation. No one found the sentiment incongruous coming from the slight, professorial-looking woman. They all knew Chantal Frey had her reasons.

She had been with Jason in fifth century B.C. Athens as an expert in alien life-forms, when they had made the shattering discovery that Transhumanist time travelers were there, in alliance with the surviving Teloi "gods" they had come to seek. Captured by the Transhumanists, she had been defenseless against the genetically-engineered charisma of their leader, and had sacrificed her loyalties on the altar of an imagined love. But in the end the snarling face behind the smiling Transhumanist mask had revealed itself, and Jason had accomplished a feat unique in the annals of time travel by bringing her back to her proper time without the TRD that had been cut out of her.

Now she was in a kind of limbo, confined to the Authority's Australian facility to conceal her existence from the Transhumanists, who still believed her to have been left to find death in some form or other in ancient Greece. As a former defector, the cloud of suspicion that hung over her had still not entirely dissipated. But she was indispensable, for she was the only one who knew the mysterious time-traveling Transhuman underground from the inside. She didn't know as much as the Authority might have wished, thanks to the secrecy fetish the underground had spent a century and more cultivating. Nevertheless she had repeatedly proved her usefulness. And she lived for two things: revenge against the Transhumanists who had cynically used her; and expiation of her betrayal so that the Authority would trust her enough to allow her into the past again.

"This, of course, is why our plan calls for you to make contact with Mary Elizabeth Bowser," said Rutherford. "She is our only link with the secret organization of which Inspector Da Cunha learned, and which is in turn our only source of information about Transhumanist activity in this milieu. A thoroughly uncertain source, I hasten to add. But without it you would be simply flailing in the dark."

"Are we sure Pauline's contact information is going to enable a bunch of white guys in Confederate uniforms to gain her cooperation?" wondered Jason. "Remember, we're arriving in Richmond three and a half months *before* Pauline learned about her. And when I saw Pauline in April, 1865 and she spoke briefly about this secret organization, she said nothing to indicate that they had told her Mary Bowser had encountered a 'Captain Landrieu' the previous December. Admittedly, we were a little rushed. But unless there's something you haven't told me, I gather that she said nothing about it in her debriefing either."

"No, she did not." Rutherford spread his hands helplessly. "But, to repeat, it's all we have to work with."

Jason thought for a moment. "Chantal, you were in on Pauline's debriefing, weren't you?"

"Yes, I was." Her eyes met his. She was one of the very few people who knew how Pauline Da Cunha had subsequently met her death on that firelit night in an upland clearing in the mountains of seventeenth-century Hispaniola. Learning of it, she had lost her last illusions that there were some things even Transhumanists didn't do. And they both knew nothing should be said about it in this room. Jason gave Mondrago a warning glance, but the Corsican, who also knew, was still keeping his ferocity under tight rein. He turned back to Chantal.

"In the course of that debriefing, did she say anything suggesting to you that this secret organization might possibly have some kind of connection with the Transhumanists? Perhaps even be a breakaway group? Or, more plausibly, could the leader be a rogue Transhumanist."

"We know that's not impossible," offered Mondrago. "Chantal, you remember what we told you about Zenobia."

"Yes, I do." Her eyes held the faraway look that often came over them at the mention of the seemingly almost superhuman black woman Jason's expedition had encountered in Henry Morgan's Caribbean: a fearsome pirate, a pagan priestess . . . and a Transhumanist renegade. Unable to stomach the cult she had been brought in to establish among the blacks of Hispaniola, had cut out her own TRD and fled to join the Jamaican Maroons and found a kind of counter-cult. "But," Chantal continued, "there was nothing to suggest that. And I find it highly improbable. Remember, all the evidence suggests that the expedition that originally placed Zenobia in the seventeenth century departed from a date prior to the one whose presence in 1865 Inspector Da Cunha discovered. If they already knew that there had been a case of an operative going rogue, they would have taken steps to prevent it from happening again."

"Such as?" Aiken was curious.

"Oh, all sorts of ways. For example, a tiny implant in each member of the expedition which, on a neural command from the leader, kills in a manner undetectable by the medical science of that century. Or maybe the implant would merely inflict excruciating pain at the leader's discretion. Or, best of all, each member could be inoculated with something agonizingly fatal unless he gets periodic doses of an antidote only the leader can provide."

A subliminal shudder of distaste ran around the table. Over and above their inherent unpleasantness, these methods of control violated cultural taboos burned into the human psyche by the Transhuman madness and enshrined in the Human Integrity Act.

"All right, then," said Rutherford, ending the moment. "We must assume that Zenobia was the first, last and only Transhumanist turncoat. But whoever these people are, I repeat: they're all we can turn to, and Mary Elizabeth Bowser is our only link to them, however tenuous. This is the basis of our plan." He activated a map on the viewscreen behind him. A river snaked from left to right near the bottom, dotted with islands and spanned by three bridges. From the northern shore spread an urban gridwork. Jason instantly recognized

Richmond as it was in the mid-nineteenth century. He had studied it thoroughly, for his computer implant, spliced into his optic nerve, could project the map as though it floated before his eyes. The map's scope could be enlarged, narrowed or shifted, and it would always feature five red dots marking the current locations of the other team members, thanks to the micro-miniaturized tracking devices included in their TRDs.

"You will appear here, south of the James River," Rutherford continued as a cursor flashed on the indicated location, "just after dawn on your target date." The last part went without saying; dawn arrivals were standard procedure, to minimize the chance of any of the locals being present to see figures appearing out of thin air. The dead of night would have been even better, but for reasons not fully understood an arrival in utter darkness had disturbing psychological effects, intensifying the inevitable disorientation of temporal displacement to hazardous levels. "This is the most logical direction for you to be approaching the city, from the front at Petersburg." The map expanded to include the entire eastern two-thirds of what was then the state of Virginia (a word still used as a geographical expression). Symbols marked the area to the south of Richmond where the Union and Confederate armies had lain deadlocked from June, 1864 to April, 1865 in a kind of dress rehearsal for the trench warfare of World War I.

Mondrago pointed to the top of the map, where Washington, DC lay just across another river, and seemed to do a mental calculation. "So after seceding from the Union, the Southerners picked for their capital a city about five or six days' march from Union territory—from the Union *capital*, for God's sake! They must have had a lot of chutzpah." The Corsican actually pronounced it correctly.

"You're not the first to make that observation," Dabney acknowledged. "But the choice of Richmond wasn't as insane as it seems at first glance. For one thing, it was the industrial center of gravity of the South, with practically the only iron manufacturing facilities south of the Potomac, so its security was vital. And those five days' march led through some very good defensive terrain, with all those eastward-flowing rivers. And given the level of communications technology at that time, there was something to be said for putting the seat of government close to the main theater of war. And finally, there was an element of sheer politics. Virginia only seceded late, after much deliberation; an informal promise to move the capital there was a kind of bribe to induce the state to join the Confederacy."

Rutherford contracted the map to Richmond again. "You will proceed into the city via the easternmost bridge—the other two are railroad bridges. You shouldn't attract any particular attention, as there were undoubtedly no end of men in Confederate uniforms entering the city for one reason or other." He glanced at Dabney, who nodded in confirmation. "Once over the river, you should proceed to the vicinity of the 'Confederate White House' where Mary Bowser was employed but did not reside. Beyond this point, Jason, you must use your justly renowned genius for improvisation. All I can offer you is the one authentic image of her from life." The map vanished from the viewscreen, replaced by a full-length black-and-white photograph, stiffly posed (as was unavoidable given the limitations of that era's cameras), of a woman wearing the era's floor-length dress with the full-sleeved "Garibaldi shirt". She seemed on the slender side, although the narrowness of her waist probably owed something to one of the period's corsets. She was looking directly at the camera, but the broad-brimmed hat she was wearing caused her face to be partly shadowed. What could be seen of her features revealed nothing except her obvious African descent, although the longer Jason looked the more he thought to detect a certain quiet determination.

"Not exactly very much help," he grumbled.

"No, but I repeat that it is all you have. Incidentally, one place you will *not* want to go is Belle Isle." Rutherford caused the cursor to flash over the largest of the islands in the river. "It is, after all, where you found and destroyed the nanobots and apparently where the subsequent ones were also placed . . . and your earlier remarks about the Observer Effect were well taken."

"Also," Dabney added, "when you were there in April, 1865 it was pretty much abandoned. But for a good part of the war it served as a POW camp for captured Union enlisted men, while the officers went to Libby Prison in the city. At its height there had been a large tent city there with thousands of prisoners packed into it, although they were periodically shipped out. But by December 1864 the last of them had been gone for a couple of months."

"Very well, then. Your displacement will occur tomorrow morning. I suggest you all get a good night's sleep."

"First, though," said Jason, "according to my unvarying practice, I'm going to go to the lounge for a last drink or two or three. Everyone's welcome to join me."

"Mint juleps?" queried Mondrago.

"We're going to Virginia, not South Carolina," Dabney chided. "I suggest bourbon."

# CHAPTER SEVEN

"I still think that uniform suits you, somehow," said Chantal Frey, who had pronounced Jason "dashing" looking on his last return from the past in Confederate garb.

"It must be the hat," said Jason with a grin, as they entered the vast displacer dome. He had stuck an ostrich plume in his cream-colored stag hat, which Dabney had told him was a typical touch of vanity on the part of Confederate cavalry officers. He accompanied the grin with what he hoped was a properly raffish stroking of his new goatee. None of them had had time to grow anything like the truly astounding beards to be seen in some Confederate photographs, but Dabney had pronounced their facial hair adequately in-period.

They descended the steps that led down through the terraced concentric circles of control panels and assorted instrumentation to the displacer stage at the dome's exact center, a featureless circular platform thirty feet in diameter. Another expedition had just returned. Jason recognized the fellow Service member who was their mission leader and called out a greeting. "How did it go, Huan?"

"Very well!" enthused the man dressed as an early seventh century Chinese court official with wide-sleeved knee-length turquoise robe and a purely ornamental soft fabric simulation of old-fashioned *liang-tang* armor. "Doctor Shuo, here, was able to conclusively establish the *real* facts about the founding of the T'ang dynasty—and, in particular, how Li Shih-min went about becoming the Emperor T'ai-tsung. And unless I miss my guess it's going to set a cat among the academic pigeons."

Jason lacked any large interest in whether the received story of how Li Shih-min had sent his father into retirement and assumed the throne was true or just an exercise in Confucian hypocrisy. But he made a politely affirmative-sounding response. He and the others continued on down to the stage, where Rutherford was waiting to dispense the traditional pre-displacement handshakes. Chantal also added her farewells.

"As usual," she said ruefully, "I wish I could have been more help."

"You've been a great help with general background," Jason assured her. "Nobody expected you to have any specific information about this Transhumanist expedition, which seems to have originated from a date long after that of the one you spent time with."

"I suppose not." But she didn't appear notably cheered.

"It seems unusually cold in here," Nesbit remarked, rubbing his hands together.

"I ordered them to lower the temperature setting in the dome," Rutherford explained. "I didn't want the instantaneous transition to December in the northern hemisphere to be too much of a shock to your systems."

Dabney nodded. "December weather in Virginia is unpredictable. The previous winter had been a brutally severe one, and the one we're going into is believed to have been not much better. And we're arriving just after dawn." Nesbit looked alarmed and hastily put on his gloves. They all mounted the stage, while Rutherford and Chantal turned and walked toward the transparent-walled mezzanine that overlooked the control center. Then they waited, as the countdown crept toward zero and a harshly buzzing rumble of power transmission could be heard as the great antimatter reactor prepared to provide a prodigious energy surge.

But when it came, temporal displacement provided no spectacular "special effects" from the standpoint of the time travelers. It wasn't even a matter of the interior of the dome being instantly replaced by a new setting. Instead, in a timeless instant, the dome was gone without them having any recollection of it going, as though it was a dream from which they had awakened, rapidly receding from memory, leaving them with the usual bewildering adjustment that accompanies awakening from a very believable dream.

In this case, though, the transition was sharper than most, for the first thing of which they were clearly aware was the chill that abruptly bit into them through their heavy uniforms and the long underwear beneath. That, and the fact that they were all experienced—even Dabney and Nesbit had been through this once before—enabled them to recover their equilibrium more quickly than usual. After only a few moments of disorientation, they were able to look about them at the scene revealed by the sun that was only just clearing the eastern horizon and laying a molten trail on the James River as it flowed toward Hampton Roads and the sea.

The young day was actually a mild one, even for these latitudes; Jason estimated that it was in the upper thirties (although it seemed colder after their transition), and there was only a light frost on the ground, melting almost as fast as the sun's rays touched it. But of course the leaves were long since off the deciduous trees; there were none of the glorious autumn colors that had clothed this land a couple of months before. As hoped, there was no one in sight, and they stood on a dirt road south of the James with the roofs of the suburb of Manchester visible to their left as they looked northward in the direction of the city.

"Let's go," said Jason as soon as he was sure everyone had recovered. "Before people start to get up and about."

People were in fact stirring by the time they skirted the northern edge of Manchester, but no one paid them any attention; as Rutherford and Dabney had foreseen, Confederate uniforms were no novelty here. This was especially true around the field fortifications that guarded the Richmond & Danville Railroad. They passed a detail of gray and butternut clad infantry whose lieutenant saluted Jason. They drew a few quizzical-seeming glances from the men which caused Jason to worry if something unforeseen had gone wrong. Then he heard Dabney mutter something under his breath.

"We're all simply too well-fed-looking," the historian explained in an undertone. "By this point in the war, the South was starving. Malnutrition was becoming common in the army."

"They do look like scarecrows, don't they," said Jason, glancing back at the men who had passed. "Well, there's no help for it. If anybody asks, our regiment captured a Yankee supply train or something."

Then they passed through a cut in the bluffs s and set out across the Mayo Bridge. To the north, across the river, the city stood spread out before them.

Rutherford sometimes took prospective time travelers on tours of their target locales in the twenty-fourth century. In this case there would have been no point. Richmond, after first being burned in 1865 and later swamped by urban bloat in the Great Crowding of the twentieth and twenty-first centuries, had been one of the urban areas practically destroyed during the convulsions attending the extirpation of the Transhuman Dispensation in the mid-to-late twenty-third century. There was a city of the same name here on this river in Jason's time—quite a large city, and a crucial node of the conurbation that was the center of gravity of the twenty-fourth-century North American continent—but it bore essentially no resemblance to its historical ancestor. Thus it was that Dabney had been so motivated to secure a place in Pauline Da Cunha's expedition, and so eager for a second look at what had been lost.

But Jason had studied the historical reconstructions embodied in the virtual tours they had taken, and in the map his computer implant could provide. Now he compared those abstractions to the real thing.

Richmond covered a series of hills rising from the curving bank of the river. To the left was a string of wooded islands and two railroad bridges, beyond which whitewater rapids could be glimpsed. Overlooking them on the northern shore was Gamble's Hill, with its large cemetery. At its foot alongside the river was a series of large brick buildings from whose stacks smoke was already rising—the Tredegar Iron Works, whose output of artillery was one of the things that had enabled the Confederate States of America to keep up an unequal fight as long as it had. To its right, the riverfront was crowded with warehouses, tobacco factories, flour mills and other establishments. Behind them rose the slope of Council Chamber Hill, holding the better commercial and residential districts along Main Street and Franklin Street and crowned by the classical Capitol building designed by Thomas Jefferson in imitation of a Roman temple, currently the seat of the Confederate Congress as well as the state legislature. To the right the land fell away into a valley where Shockoe Creek flowed into the James. More modest residential areas covered the slopes of Church and Union hills beyond that, getting modest indeed near the mouth of Shockoe Creek. Visible to the extreme right was the suburb of Rocketts, location of the principal navy yard of a government that barely had a navy. Behind that, a hill was covered with scores of barracks-like buildings. Dabney pointed toward it.

"Chimborazo Hospital," he explained. "The largest military hospital in the world at this time. In fact, it's quite an enterprise, growing food for the patients and selling the surplus, so successfully that at the end of the war the Confederate government will actually owe the hospital $300,000 in repayment of a loan."

"The hospital might have a little trouble collecting," Mondrago remarked drily.

As was Jason's unvarying experience in past eras, a mélange of subtle, unfamiliar odors pervaded the air. Particularly unidentifiable— but far from unpleasant—was the one which he would later learn was leaf tobacco. A more prosaic one was the smoke of burning coal, some of which wafted eastward from the Tredegar foundries. Another source of it became visible as a train chugged very slowly across the bridge of the Richmond & Petersburg Railroad to their left.

"It's not moving much faster than we are," Aiken commented, watching the train.

Dabney chuckled. "It can't. By this point in the war, these bridges had become so rickety from constant use and inadequate repairs that the trains had to crawl across them and trust to luck." His voice took on what Jason thought was an unmistakable note of sadness. "It's symptomatic. We're going to be seeing a lot more symptoms of the Confederacy's terminal illness."

They proceeded on across the bridge, passing over an island ("Mayo's Island," said Jason's map) and encountering more and more military and civilian traffic. Mule-drawn wagons rumbled, and a file of black men in rough undyed homespun shuffled along under guard as they went south to work on entrenchments. Jason was glad this was an all-veteran group, without any first-time academics. Slavery was a grim constant of the human condition for most of history; time travelers simply had to deal with it.

Beyond the island the bridge continued on its stone piers over a relatively narrow stretch of river to the city side, then passed over a canal. There had been little waterborne traffic on the river, just a few small steam- or sail-driven craft. Here a procession of barges were being raised or lowered from one level to another in locks.

"The James River and Kanawha Canal," Dabney explained. "It was built to bypass the rapids and waterfalls. This city got started as a transshipment point in the eighteenth century, when oceangoing ships could get this far upriver but no farther."

Then they were in the city, walking north along Fourteenth Street. Passing through the cluttered establishments of the canal-front and Exchange Alley, they turned left on Main Street and entered more genteel surroundings, passing various substantial banks, newspaper offices and other businesses as well as the prestigious Spotswood and American hotels. At Ninth Street they turned right and walked north with the well-landscaped Capitol Grounds rising to their right and various government offices on their left. But even in these precincts, there was no escaping the miasma of a city under siege and a failing polity. It went beyond the underfed look of everyone they saw, and the shabbiness of the clothing—little better than that of the slaves, in most cases. No, it was a psychic miasma, as though the Confederate capital was dimly aware that no further sacrifices on its part could be availing. An unspoken realization that, after four years of defeating or stymieing armies twice the size of his own, Robert E. Lee was finally out of miracles. Jason remarked on it to Dabney. The historian nodded again with evident sadness.

"Perhaps these people understand that the Confederacy lost its last hope a month ago."

"In November?" Jason was puzzled. "But I thought the armies were still deadlocked in the trenches before Petersburg, and will be until—"

"I'm not talking about a loss on the battlefield. I mean Lincoln's victory in the United States presidential election. George McClellan, a dismissed general, was running against him on a platform of negotiating a peace settlement on the basis of Southern independence. If he had been elected, and carried through on his promise, the South would have won the war politically after having already effectively lost it militarily."

"Sort of like North Vietnam, a little over a century from now," Mondrago commented.

They crossed Broad Street, pausing for a train that clanged and clattered by on the tracks running along the center of the street. They took care not to flinch at the smoke and cinders it belched, for no one else did. Then, two blocks further north in an area of handsome homes, they turned right onto Clay Street, which, after three short blocks, ended in a cul-de-sac. Here, to the right, was the White House of the Confederacy.

It was a handsome three-story mansion in the "Italianate" style, overlooking the valley of Shockoe Creek to the east, although the terraced gardens in that direction were partially concealed by a carriage house and other outbuildings behind a wall. Smoke rising from one brick outbuilding suggested that it was the kitchen.

"So the Confederate president is in there?" asked Nesbit, gazing at the mansion.

"Probably not, at this time of day," said Dabney. "Jefferson Davis has his working office in the Treasury building, which is on the far side of Capitol Square. But he sometimes works in his private office here when he is ill, as he frequently is."

Jason's intention had been to reconnoiter. Now he began to think about organizing a system of watches by which they could keep the mansion under constant observation while seeking food and lodgings. "Alexandre," he began . . . and then paused, for a slim, youngish Black woman had emerged from the kitchen and was walking briskly along Clay Street in their direction carrying a shopping basket. She was dressed in the long-skirted style of the era, obviously cheap but seemingly adequately warm, especially now that the late morning sun had brought the temperature up into what felt like the high forties. That sun was behind her, which made it hard to see her face very clearly. So did the fact that her face was somewhat downcast under a broad-brimmed hat. But what he could see of that face reminded Jason of one he had seen in a photograph, and as she walked past she raised her head slightly to look at the group of soldiers beside the street.

"Carlos," murmured Jason after she had passed, "is it possible that—?"

"Yes!" said Dabney eagerly. "I think that just might be Mary Elizabeth Bowser!"

# CHAPTER EIGHT

Without pausing for thought or waiting for the others, Jason turned and hurried after the slender female figure that was walking briskly west along Clay Street. "Miss?" he called out to her retreating back. She didn't slow, and showed no indication of having heard. It belatedly occurred to him that she assumed someone else was being addressed—someone white. He put a different tone into his voice. "Girl!"

She halted abruptly and turned slowly to see a man in a gray officer's uniform advancing toward her. She kept her face downcast and did not meet his eyes. "Yes, Cap'n?"

"Are you Ellen Bond?" he asked, remembering Mary Bowser's alias in the Davis household.

"Yes, Cap'n. Ah works back there in the Pres'dent's house," she added, clearly expecting Jason to be properly impressed.

"Yes, I know you do, Ellen . . . or is it Mary?"

For a barely perceptible instant, her head jerked up and her eyes met his, and there was something in them that transformed her face. Then, almost too quickly to register, the moment was over and the mask of dull subservience was back.

"Ah don't know what you mean, Cap'n." A note of whiny pleading entered her voice. "Please, suh, Ah gotta go. Miz Davis, she sent me to market, an' she be expectin' me back by—"

"I'm sure she does, Mary—"

"Ah tell you, Cap'n, Ah ain't no 'Mary'!"

"—but others are expecting you as well." Without the aid of his computer implant Jason summoned up from his memory the words Pauline Da Cunha had been told to use if she had occasion to make contact with Mary Bowser. "Gracchus is coming from the south."

She stiffened, and Jason could almost fancy he heard the mask shatter as it hit the cobblestones. There was absolute silence as he held her eyes with his. The others had come up—Dabney was staring with undisguised curiosity at the renowned but shadowy spy—but she ignored them.

"I know you're trying to decide whether to trust me," Jason resumed. "You may as well. As you can see, there's no point in pretending any more. If I really am a Confederate officer, and know those words, and know that *you* know them, then you're as good as dead . . . and so is Gracchus, probably. But in fact I'm not. And I need your help to contact Gracchus."

She glanced around anxiously. There was no one else in sight. She turned back to Jason and her dark eyes bored into his. "Who *are* you?" she hissed. She still spoke Southern American English, but now she spoke it with an educated accent that told of her Philadelphia schooling.

"I can't tell you that, and if I did you'd think I'm either a madman or a liar. Just try to accept the fact that we're friends of yours."

"So you're for the Union?"

"We're certainly not *against* the Union, but we're not taking sides in this war—which you and I both know the Union is going to win anyway." *Without needing time travel to know it*, Jason didn't add. Instead, he took a stab in the dark. "We have our own war, and it's with the people Gracchus and his organization are also fighting. People far worse than the Secessionists. People who want to inflict something even more evil than slavery."

He had no way of knowing how much "Gracchus" had told Mary Bowser. But her expression told him his guess had been right. "Gracchus has told me much the same thing about his enemies, though he hasn't told me much else. He said I wouldn't believe it, and that even if I did it wouldn't mean anything to me anyhow. But I trust him." She visibly reached a decision. "I can't do anything for you today, and we can't be seen together. Come back here late tomorrow afternoon and wait for a baker's wagon to show up."

"Thomas McNiven," muttered Dabney with a nod. Mary Bowser shot him a startled look but didn't inquire as to the source of his knowledge.

"We'll have to find somewhere to stay tonight," said Mondrago.

"I know a safe place—you might get in trouble otherwise." Mary Bowser gave the surroundings a worried look. Still seeing no one taking notice, she motioned them into the shade of a tree at the corner of Clay and Eleventh. She took a pencil and paper from a small reticule tied to her wrist and wrote hastily—a skill she wasn't supposed to possess. Then she handed the paper to Jason. It was covered with marking in what looked like no alphabet Jason had ever seen.

Dabney looked over Jason's shoulder. "Elizabeth Van Lew's cipher code!" he exclaimed.

"*Quiet!*" snapped Mary Bowser, who immediately looked surprised at herself for having used that tone to a white man. She had, Jason thought, probably never done it before. But then she smoothed out her expression as she looked around at the time travelers' faces. "So you know about her, too. Well, then, you probably know she's hidden a lot of men in her house."

"Escapees from Libby Prison," Dabney nodded, eliciting another puzzled glance from Mary Bowser.

"All right. Show this to her. She lives at 2301 East Grace Street."

"I know," said Dabney.

"And I can find it," added Jason without elaborating on just how he could find it. Then he recalled Pauline Da Cunha. "One other thing: don't reveal this meeting with us to *anyone* you encounter from now on. Agreed?"

"Agreed. And now I've *got* to go—there are more people around. Stay here until I'm out of sight. And one other thing: Miss Van Lew doesn't know about Gracchus . . . and she doesn't need to know." Without another word, Mary Bowser readjusted her shopping basket and set off down Clay Street.

"Just as well she's on our side," Mondrago remarked, in a tone Jason knew he didn't use in connection with just anyone.

With the aid of Jason's implant they turned left on Eleventh Street, then left again on Broad Street and followed the railroad tracks a few blocks, then crossed the bridge over Shockoe Creek. There, at the Virginia Central Railroad depot, they turned right on Union Street, then left onto Grace Street. A walk of about a third of a mile eastward up Church Hill brought them to an impressive three-and-a-half-story mansion on the right, across from a church—St. John's Episcopal, Jason noted.

"Wait here," Jason told the others. He stepped up to the front door and rapped with the brass knocker. A young black woman opened the door and stared at him in apprehensive silence. He recalled that Elizabeth Van Lew's house servants were former family slaves she had freed.

"Please tell Miss Van Lew that I have business that requires her personal attention," he said in what he hoped was the appropriate tone for a Confederate officer.

"Yes, suh," the servant said quietly, and closed the door. After a longish wait, the door was flung open to reveal a tiny, angular woman in her mid-to-late forties with faded dark-blond hair worn in ringlets. She had the kind of looks that suggested she had been pretty in her youth, in a birdlike, high-cheekboned, sharp-nosed way. But now she had become what this era called "spinsterish," with thin lips and a chin perhaps most charitably described as "determined." Her most striking features were her vividly blue eyes, which were currently incandescent with indignation.

"Good day, ma'am," said Jason, inclining his head and touching the brim of his hat. His attempt at Southern gentility fell flat. When she spoke, her voice was pure acid.

"Well, Captain, is my home to be searched yet again? Have they sent you and your ruffians here in the hope you will discover something that escaped Provost-Marshal Winder's odious detectives?"

"No, ma'am. I just—" Jason tried to interject. But "Crazy Bet" was in full tilt.

"It is intolerable! I am a loyal Virginian, persecuted and ostracized because I follow my state's highest tradition of opposition to human bondage." She pointed theatrically across the street at St. John's. "Do you see that church, Captain? That is where Patrick Henry delivered his 'Give me liberty or give me death' speech ninety years ago. There spoke the true Virginia! But now...." She trailed off and lapsed into a mumbled, unintelligible conversation with herself, head bent to one side, in true Crazy Bet style as Dabney had described. It gave Jason his opportunity.

"Rest assured, Miss Van Lew, I and my men are not here to search your house or offer you any other indignity. But I wish to deliver a communication from an associate of yours."

"What 'associate'?" she inquired as though barely hearing him.

"Mary Bowser, otherwise known as Ellen Bond." The blue eyes abruptly lost their unfocused vagueness and froze into ice-shards of sharp concentration. Wordlessly, he handed her the paper. At the sight of the code-writing, the last traces of Crazy Bet vanished. She read rapidly, then met his eyes again.

"I recognize Mary's hand, and she has identified herself in ways no one besides she and I could possibly know," she stated in a level, expressionless and perfectly sane voice. "Who are you? I gather you are not really a captain in the Confederate army."

"No, I'm not, nor is the name I'm currently using my own. It is necessary for me to assume a false identity—a notion that should come as no novelty to you. I could not reveal my true identity to Mary, nor can I to you. But she trusted me, and while I don't know exactly what she wrote, I believe she's asking you to provide us with a safe place to spend tonight."

"So she is. And I trust her." Elizabeth Van Lew reached a decision. "Come in. And be quiet. My mother is asleep upstairs; she hasn't been well for a long time."

She waved them in and ushered them hurriedly through the house. They passed along a wide hallway, past fireplaces with marble mantles, and open doors through which the brocade silk-covered walls of chandeliered parlors could be glimpsed. But for all the architectural splendor and scrupulous cleanliness, there was a worn, threadbare look. Jason recalled that Elizabeth Van Lew had spent much of her inherited fortune freeing slaves and, more recently, operating her spy network, not to mention providing safe houses for escaped Union prisoners.

They ascended several flights of stairs, finally reaching the attic level. Elizabeth Van Lew touched a panel, which slid back to reveal a chamber concealed beneath a sloping roof.

"You're fortunate that no one is here," she said matter-of-factly. "The privations at Libby Prison have become so unbearable that more and more of those poor men are escaping out of sheer desperation, and they know they can come here. I must admit," she added, "those privations are really no one's fault. The entire city is in want of everything; the people with friends and relatives on farms in the country who send them food are the lucky ones. The prisoners are being provided for as well as possible. Which means that the daily ration is a small square of cornbread and a piece of bacon so small that the vermin in the cornbread probably contain more meat."

Nesbit's color didn't look particularly good. Elizabeth Van Lew didn't notice. "I'll try to do slightly better than that by you men. It happens that we've been able to obtain a little meat for a change. Wait here."

"Thank you, ma'am," sighed Jason with feeling. They had all eaten a hearty breakfast before their temporal displacement, but had had nothing since then, and now in late afternoon, they were all feeling hungry.

They made themselves as comfortable as possible in the cramped quarters. "She hasn't pressed us about who we are," Logan observed. "She must really trust Mary Bowser."

"Remember, she doesn't know about Gracchus & Co.," said Jason. "So she has no reason to think we're anything more exotic than Union spies. I'm sure she takes for granted that that's exactly what we are."

Elizabeth Van Lew returned with small portions of food, including some kind of meat Jason couldn't identify. They all mumbled their thanks, and Dabney ventured to elaborate. "God bless you, Miss Van Lew. It is fortunate for us and others like us that there is an abolitionist we can come to for aid in this citadel of secession."

"Please do not refer to me as an abolitionist! I have always been opposed to slavery—it is a cruel, arrogant institution which crushes all freedom, especially freedom of speech, for it cannot permit dissenting opinion. It oppresses everyone, not just the slave. But the abolitionists are fanatics like that madman John Brown, willing to stoop to any ends, including violence and murder. I am as opposed to war and bloodshed as I am to slavery. I am no more an abolitionist than I am a 'Yankee.' I meant what I said earlier: I regard myself as a true Virginian, born in this city, where I intend to die!"

It occurred to Jason that, by the military intelligence she supplied to the Union command, she was enabling the Yankees to more effectively apply the war and violence which she so deplored. But he held his tongue. She was hardly unique in the accommodations she'd had to make to the moral ambiguities of espionage. And he was in no position to nitpick her reasoning as he ate her food.

"Well," he said, "thank you for everything. I know how difficult it must have been to obtain the meat, especially."

"Yes, indeed. The butcher shop was all out of the dog they generally pass off as lamb. But there was a fairly ample supply of dressed rats, for anyone who could pay for them. These cost $2.50 apiece, can you believe it?" She departed, shaking her head and clucking over the effects of inflation.

If Nesbit had looked queasy before, he looked positively ill now.

# CHAPTER NINE

Luckily, a certain amount of warmth seeped up from the floors below to the hidden chamber. But they were all stiff and sore after sleeping in cramped positions on the hard floor with nothing but a few tattered old blankets whose aroma suggested that they had been used by numerous Libby Prison escapees. They were also hungry. Jason assumed that eventually their stomachs would shrink to the point where the pangs would subside.

Elizabeth Van Lew waited until an hour when the street was most likely to be deserted before sending them on their way. Just in case, though, she berated them in fine Crazy Bet style as they left, proclaiming her innocence and mocking them for their failure to uncover any evidence of wrongdoing in her house. Jason went along with the gag, doing his best Simon Legree (short of twirling his mustachios, which he decided would be overdoing it) and sneering, "*This* time!" But he permitted himself a wink at her before turning on his heel and leading his men west along Grace Street.

"We're early," said Mondrago.

"Yes. But yesterday I spotted a place where we can hang around and wait without being too conspicuous."

Jason led them to the Virginia Central Railroad depot at Sixteenth and Broad. There, amid constant comings and goings, often of men in uniform, they were able to kill time until late afternoon, always seeming to be waiting impatiently for some train or other. They were even able to step across the street in shifts to a tavern and obtain some of the meager fare available. Finally, when Jason deemed the afternoon to be far enough advanced, they retraced their steps of the previous day, retuning to Clay Street.

There was no baker's wagon in evidence, and they prepared to wait. After a while, the slender figure of Mary Bowser slipped out from the brick kitchen and stepped along the sidewalk as though on an errand. Coming abreast of Jason, she looked furtively around and paused.

"McNiven is late," she whispered. "And I can't stay out here. The president isn't feeling too well today, so he's working here instead of at the Treasury building. And . . ." All at once her voice trailed off and her eyes bulged as she looked down Clay Street. A carriage was approaching, its two horses' hooves clip-clopping on the cobblestones. "Oh, *Lord!*"

"What is it?" Jason demanded. But she was too agitated to reply.

"I've *got* to get inside. Just . . . just wait here." Without another word, she scurried back to the kitchen.

*Now what got into her?* Jason wondered, as the carriage came to a halt at a soft "Whoa!" from the elderly black driver. There was one passenger: a white-bearded man whose gray uniform bore the three-starred insignia of a Confederate colonel on its collar. Jason decided he'd better display a little military punctilio.

"Ten-*hut!*" he said quietly to his followers, and came to attention and saluted as the colonel alighted with a murmured "Thank you" to the black driver. Jason glanced quickly sideways to make sure the others were at attention . . . and saw that Dabney's eyes were bugged out even further than Mary Bowser's had been. In fact, the historian's jaw was literally hanging open. He wondered why.

Jason looked straight ahead again, to meet a pair of eyes as deep-brown as his own. The colonel was strongly built and of Jason's height, or perhaps half an inch taller, and those dark eyes looked out of a careworn face that must have been outstandingly handsome in youth, although in fact the man wasn't really as old as the beard made him look at a distance—late fifties at most. Jason felt he ought to recognize that face . . . it seemed awfully familiar . . .

Then, with almost physical force, it came to him. And he recalled Dabney having said something about a certain vow to continue wearing the insignia of the wearer's prewar rank of mere colonel until the South won its independence.

All at once Jason's position of "attention" and his salute stiffened into a rigidity they had not attained since he had been a young trainee in the Hesperian Colonial Rangers.

Robert E. Lee returned his salute with grave courtesy.

"Put your detail and yourself at ease, Captain," he said. He gave Jason a keen once-over. "I don't recall seeing you here before."

"Captain Landrieu, sir," Jason rapped out. "Of the Jeff Davis Legion."

"Ah!" Lee nodded graciously. "You men from Mississippi have performed noble service, Captain. But what is your mission here in Richmond?"

"We're just here briefly, sir, to obtain remounts."

"I see. This is fortunate. I have a message for Major General Hampton, and since I'm going to be in Richmond for another few days I was going to have to send a special courier. But since you'll be going back to Petersburg anyway, you can carry it for me and deliver it to your brigade commander, Brigadier General Butler. He can hand it up to Cavalry Corps headquarters."

"Yes, sir." A captain—even if he had been a real one—didn't say much more than that to the army commander. Certainly not to *this* army commander.

"And we will of course want to expedite your departure. I'll write out a requisition for you to take to the remount facility near the railhead on the west side of the city. Or, better still, take it to the Government Stables on Broad Street, which I believe currently holds about a hundred horses, exclusive of those reserved for ambulance use. My signature should enable you to secure horses and tack without undue delay."

*I'll just bet it should!* "Thank you, sir."

Lee reached into an inside pocket of his coat and pulled out a pad of paper. But before he could write anything, an annoyed frown crossed his face. "Actually, Captain, I'm very nearly late for an appointment to see the president. It shouldn't take long. I'll give you the dispatch and write out the requisition afterwards." He started to turn toward the mansion, then seemed to have an afterthought. "You may accompany me inside to wait, Captain, as it's somewhat chilly out here. I'm sure your men can wait in the kitchen, for the same reason."

"Thank you, General. That's most considerate." Jason turned to Mondrago. "Sergeant, see to it." He could hardly bear to meet Dabney's stricken eyes. He was certain the historian would literally have given an arm for the opportunity that he, Jason, was about to have. But he couldn't think of a good excuse for "Private Dabney" to accompany him into the precincts he was about to enter.

As he followed Lee toward the steps leading to the front entrance, Jason belatedly remembered to activate the recorder function of his implant by direct neural command. Now everything his eyes saw and his ears heard would be preserved on a minute disc that would be extracted from a slot in his right temple on his return to the twenty-fourth century. That disc's storage capacity, though vast beyond the conception of earlier eras, was of course not infinite, so the recorder didn't function continuously. So far on this expedition, Jason had used it only intermittently—to record the faces and voices of Mary Bowser and Elizabeth Van Lew, for example. Now he simply left it on.

They were ushered into an oval entrance hall with two niches containing life-sized plaster statues of ladies clothed in styles Jason had seen in fifth century B.C. Athens, holding gas-jet lamps that were cutting-edge technology for this milieu. Through a door straight ahead, Jason glimpsed a parlor elaborately decorated in the "Rococo Revival" style. But Lee turned through a door to the right and ascended a circular staircase whose well, like the entrance hall, featured marbleized wallpaper and niches from which Classical ladies gazed. Emerging onto the second floor, they turned right into a stair hall which functioned as a waiting room, judging from a fanciful mahogany hat rack and several chairs. Here, the furnishings were relatively plain and functional. Under the stairway leading up to the third floor was a kind of pass-through connecting to a tiny office where a handsome but overworked-looking man could be glimpsed. Lee led the way around a corner to the door of that office, and the man immediately rose to his feet.

"Good afternoon, Mr. Harrison," Lee said. "I believe I am expected."

"Of course, General," said the man, who Jason gathered was

Jefferson Davis's secretary. "The president will see you at once." He turned to a door immediately to the left of his, opening onto a much larger office. "Mr. President, General Lee is here."

From his position behind Lee, Jason could look over the general's shoulder and glimpse a tall man, gaunt to the point of cadaverousness, rising slowly to his feet behind a desk. In contrast to the full-bearded Lee, he had only a tuft below the jaw, with the front of the chin shaved. His cheeks were hollow, his nose sharp, his eyes pale blue-gray. Jason recalled Dabney's verdict on Jefferson Davis: *A brilliant man in many ways . . . but not exactly what is called a "people person."*

"Please wait in the stair hall, Captain," said Lee, adding with a twinkle, "I'll only be a few minutes with your compatriot." Jason recalled that Davis was from Mississippi.

Jason turned back to the waiting room and settled into one of the leather-seated chairs. From only a few yards away, the voices from the president's office were, to normal hearing, only a mumble. But the recorder implant's pickup could be adjusted to amplify them, which in turn made them audible to Jason. At first the conversation consisted of commiseration by Lee over Davis's poor health, and other pleasantries. Then Lee's voice took on a getting-down-to-business tone.

"Mr. President, I asked to see you privately while I am in Richmond so that I can speak freely. We both know that our cause has suffered many reverses in the last few months, beginning with the fall of Atlanta in September, followed by Sherman's devastating march through Georgia—"

"An act of barbarism without parallel since the days of Attila the Hun!" Davis's voice was thick with anger.

"—and most recently the overwhelming disaster suffered by the Army of Tennessee at Nashville, of which the word arrived by telegraph only today."

"Yes. General Hood was too rash."

"However, these are not the only misfortunes to befall us—and the Army of Tennessee in particular. I am thinking of the death of Major General Patrick Cleburne just over two weeks ago at the battle of Franklin."

"Yes. He was a brilliant and heroic soldier—'the Stonewall Jackson of the West,' men called him." Davis's voice took on a shrewd edge.

"But I do not believe it is because of his exploits on the battlefield that you bring him up, General. In fact, I think I see where this is leading."

"You are too perceptive for me, Mr. President." Jason could almost hear Lee's smile. But then his voice grew somber. "Almost a year ago General Cleburne did something which, in my opinion, required more courage than facing an honorable death in battle. He openly declared that we should recruit slaves for our army, offering freedom to any who would serve."

"Yes. I remember all too well the hornet's nest he stirred up. I had no choice at the time but to order our officers to let the matter rest."

"But as you know, it refused to remain at rest. As our military prospects grew—and it must be said—increasingly desperate, other voices were raised. And only last month you yourself had the wisdom to propose a compromise under which the Confederacy would purchase 40,000 slaves for military labor but not for armed service at that time, although possibly at a later date, after which they would be emancipated."

"You will also be aware that the Congress refused to accept my proposal." Davis paused. "I know your views on this matter, General— and, indeed, on slavery itself. I recall that you freed your few inherited slaves."

"I have never been comfortable with the institution. Indeed, I have called it a moral, social and political evil, and I meant it. I have sometimes thought that, if tempered by humane laws and Christian sentiments, it may be a necessary evil, allowing the two races to live together in peace for now in the present state of society's development. But its day is clearly over. To put it bluntly: either we will free our slaves or a victorious North will do it for us. As for emulating George Washington in the Revolution and offering freedom to slaves in exchange for loyal service to our nation . . . yes, I have favored that course for some time."

"And have been urging it on me repeatedly, while pressing for it through other channels as well. Yet you have not spoken out publicly."

"I have not thought it appropriate to do so, Mr. President, especially in light of your earlier ban on discussion of the matter by officers. But now, in our nation's extremity, I cannot keep silent much longer." Lee paused, then continued earnestly. "I have watched, heartsick, as our troops freeze and starve outside Petersburg in the mud and filth and misery of the trenches they have dug to take shelter from the indiscriminate slaughter of today's weapons—hardly war as you and I grew up believing it would be like. Certain wits in the ranks, evidently familiar with at least the title of Monsieur Hugo's celebrated novel, have taken to calling themselves 'Lee's Miserables.'" Even the famously humorless Davis chuckled. But Lee continued in dead seriousness. "For six months they have held at bay an army of inexhaustible numbers and ample supplies. Even when those people tunneled under our lines and ignited the greatest man-made explosion ever seen on God's earth, our men sealed the gap at that monstrous crater and continued to hold. But mortal flesh can take only so much. The odds are too great. Our men *must* be reinforced, or their suffering will have been for naught. But our *white* manpower is exhausted. It is my belief that the Negroes would make excellent soldiers—as, indeed, many thousands of them already have, wearing the uniform of blue—if offered the incentive of freedom. And I am now prepared to say so openly."

The silence lasted long enough to make Jason wonder if there was something wrong with his recorder implant.

"You realize, of course," said Davis at last, "that there are those who will say that the course you propose calls into question just what our secession from the United States was *for*. Some who would rather lose the war than win it by arming and freeing the Negroes."

"Then, Mr. President, our Confederacy must decide whether it wishes to keep its independence or keep its slaves. I fear it can no longer do both. For make no mistake: if the Negro becomes a soldier, he can never again be a slave. I do not presume to dictate your choice in this matter. I merely put the issue squarely before you."

There was another long silence before Davis spoke. "You know that I agree with you. I only wish we had acted as you propose long ago, before Lincoln's hypocritical 'Emancipation Proclamation' that didn't free a single slave in the border slave states still adhering to the Union. That would have taken the wind out of the Yankees' canting self-righteousness! But the political problems . . . !" He audibly drew a deep breath. "General, I will only ask this: maintain your silence for another two months. Then, I believe, the time will be right to propose it to the Congress."

"I fear, Mr. President, that by then it will be too little and too late."

"You do not understand the difficulties of my position!" Davis lowered his voice. "General, I pray you to indulge me in this. Your endorsement, issued at just the right time, will undoubtedly assure the measure's passage."

"Very well, Mr. President," sighed Lee. "Have I your leave to go?"

"Of course. Oh, and General . . ." Davis's voice took on an almost ingratiating quality. "It will not be made official until the end of January, but I have the pleasure to tell you informally that I intend to appoint you General-in-Chief of all the armies of the Confederate States!"

"Thank you, Mr. President." Lee's voice was oddly somber, as though he wondered how long there would be any such armies left. "But I am unworthy of such an honor."

"Nonsense! It is long overdue. And I fancy the announcement will have a heartening effect on our people. As you are no doubt aware, they have come to regard you as their great defender, under whose leadership our arms cannot fail."

"If, indeed, they place such exaggerated confidence in me, I can only do my poor best to justify it. Good day, Mr. President."

Jason shot to his feet as Lee emerged from the president's office and entered the waiting room. As they turned toward the circular staircase, there was a burst of childish laughter from behind them. Turning and looking through a door beside the stairway to the third floor, Jason could glimpse what looked like a nursery. Three children— a girl of nine or ten and two boys, apparently aged about eight and three, came running out, squealing. They were followed by another little boy, obviously of half-African descent. The girl took him by the hands and swung him around, sending him spinning off and causing him to collide with Jason's booted legs. He looked up with round dark eyes. Jason wondered who he could be.

"Children! That will do!" A dark-haired woman of about forty, no beauty but not unhandsome, bustled out of the nursery carrying an infant. "You must excuse Jim, Captain . . . Oh! Good day, General Lee!"

"Mrs. Davis," said Lee with a courtly inclination of his head. "I am pleased to see you and your children are in good health."

"*Excessively* robust health, as some might say! Come, children." Varina Davis, first lady of the Confederacy, hustled her brood, including the biracial boy, back into the nursery.

As they descended the staircase, Jason worried that Lee would be too preoccupied with weightier matters to remember the requisition. But once on the street the general wrote it down and handed it to him along with the dispatch for the cavalry corps commander—which, Jason reflected, General Hampton would have to get along without. He wondered why that troubled his conscience.

"Farewell, Captain Landrieu," Lee said as he returned Jason's salute. "Give my best regards to General Butler. I know you will continue to honorably perform your duty." A shadow crossed the still-handsome face. "As will we all." Then he turned, boarded the carriage, and was gone.

Only then did Jason notice that a baker's wagon was in front of the kitchen. Mary Bowser was there, in furtive colloquy with the driver. In the guise of reassembling his men, Jason walked over as the driver gave a final nod and departed.

"I've got to get back inside," Mary Bowser told them. "But here: this is a note for Gracchus."

"I see it's in Elizabeth Van Lew's code," Jason noted.

She smiled briefly. "Yes. It comes in handy even in ways she doesn't know about."

"But where is he?"

"Rectortown, up in Fauquier County. You'll just have to find him." She handed him another note, this one in plain language. "This is the only address I have that might do you some good. Memorize it, and then destroy the note."

"Right." Jason started to go, but curiosity got the better of him. "Let me ask you something. When I was inside, I saw the Davis children, and there was this little black boy with them. Mrs. Davis called him 'Jim.' Who was he?"

"Oh, that's James Henry Brooks—or 'Jim Limber' as they call him. He's the son of a free black woman. His stepfather was mean to him—*real* mean. Mr. and Mrs. Davis got him out of there and have brought him up with her own children. He's their inseparable playmate."

"I see. That was good of them. But it almost seems . . . well, sort of incongruous . . ."

"Yes. I know what you're trying to say." Mary Bowser sighed. "The Davises are not bad people. There are a lot of slaveowners who aren't bad people." Jason thought of Lee. "But there are those that are. And when you're a slave, all you can do is trust to luck that you'll get the first kind, because there's no limit to what the other kind can do—no real limit, because how can laws against cruelty be enforced when slaves' testimony isn't admissible in court? It's slavery itself that's evil, even when the people aren't."

Dabney spoke softly, as though quoting:

> "Bury the unjust thing
> That some tamed into mercy, being wise,
> But could not starve the tiger from its eyes
> Or make it feed where beasts of mercy feed."

Mary Bowser looked at him sharply. "What?"

"Oh, it's from a poem. You won't have heard of it."

She looked at him, and at all of them in turn. "I don't know who you are, and I don't need to know. I'm not even sure I *want* to know. But good luck in your own war." She turned and vanished into the kitchen.

"What was the poem?" Jason asked after a moment.

"*John Brown's Body*, by Stephen Vincent Benét. The reason she hasn't heard of it is that he'll write it in 1929." Dabney shook himself and turned to Jason with a pleading look that would have melted the heart of an iron statue. "Commander, please tell me what you saw and heard in there."

"You'll have a chance to review it all when we get back and my recorder implant is downloaded," Jason assured him. But he recounted Lee's meeting with Davis. Dabney nodded his head sadly.

"Yes. Lee will go public with his long-standing support for freeing and arming the slaves in mid-February. And in mid-March—about three weeks before the fall of Richmond—the Confederate Congress will narrowly pass a bill to enlist black soldiers . . . but *without* offering them freedom, although Davis will override that part by executive order."

"*What!*" blurted Mondrago. "You mean to say they expect the slaves to . . ." He trailed to an incredulous halt. "Talk about too little and too late!"

"Lee used those exact words, just now," Jason recalled.

"He would," sighed Dabney. "He was always ambivalent at best about slavery. And he was flatly opposed to secession—spoke out against it strongly, in fact, arguing that the framers of the Constitution wouldn't have gone to all the trouble if they'd intended for the Union to be broken up at will by any of its members. But once his Virginia voted to secede despite his advice, that was the end of it as far as he was concerned. He turned down an offer from Lincoln to command the United States army. Only a stern sense of duty induced him to accept a commission from the nation he would come to symbolize, and which he kept alive for four years against impossible odds."

They all turned as one and looked down Clay Street, where a departing carriage could still just barely be seen.

"He was," Dabney said simply, "the last of the knights."

# CHAPTER TEN

Three days later they were riding through Fauquier County, Virginia in steadily worsening weather.

Lee's requisition had worked its expected magic at the Government Stables. Officials had practically fallen over themselves in their haste to provide "Captain Landrieu" and his men with the best mounts available. Of course, that didn't mean as much as it once would have, even though the Confederate government still had agents making the rounds of horse farms and buying all the horses they could with increasingly worthless paper currency and even more worthless promissory notes. There simply weren't as many horses to be had as there had been earlier in the war, and the conditions under which they were raised were harsher. So the agents brought in horses that were too young or poorly nourished or both.

Still, the time travelers had been given their pick of what was available, and they also got tack whose leather was still supple, not dry and stiff. They had even been able to obtain items like bedrolls and rations on the side. The rations consisted mainly of the corn bread which the Southerners generally used in place of the Yankees' hardtack, and which attracted vermin even better than the latter. They had no intention of eating it except as an alternative to starvation.

Then they had departed the city, riding northwestward more or less parallel to the railway tracks, through Gordonsville, Orange and

Culpeper, spending their first night at a very basic inn. Then they reached Warrenton, county seat of Fauquier County, a town of twelve hundred with various amenities, including three small hotels. After a relatively comfortable night (thanks to Jason's gold dollars), they set out along the dirt road to Rectortown, leaving what was called "Lower Fauquier" and entering "Upper Fauquier," west of what were rather exaggeratedly called the Bull Run Mountains, with the Blue Ridge Mountains (more worthy of the name "mountains") looming to the west.

It was a rolling countryside whose richness was obvious even in December. Miles of stone walls marked off farms whose substantial stone, brick or clapboard houses crowned the hills. Water-powered mills were a common sight. Jason wished he were seeing the land in the spring or autumn, but even now it had a wintery beauty.

At the little town of Salem, they could see a railway which Jason's map told him they would have to follow the rest of the way to Rectortown. But he thought it prudent to continue a little further along the road, for the sake of inconspicuousness.

"The Manassas Gap Railroad," Dabney told him. He pointed westward to what appeared to be a notch in the Blue Ridge. "It passes through the Manassas Gap, from the Shenandoah Valley, and continues east through the Thoroughfare Gap in the Bull Run Mountains. It's strategically important in the war, because it made it possible to rapidly transfer armies from the valley to the main theater in the east. That was what enabled the Confederates to win the first battle of the war, at Bull Run. It later got torn up by the Confederates to prevent the Union forces from using it. But back in October General Phil Sheridan, the Union commander in the valley, began restoring it, using it as a supply line for an operation General Grant had in mind. The idea was for Sheridan to move southeast from the valley, take Charlottesville, and threaten Richmond from the west while Grant has Lee's army pinned down at Petersburg on the other side."

"Seems to make strategic sense," said Jason, mentally expanding his map to show all of central Virginia. "Does that mean the Union is currently in control of this area?" He asked anxiously, glancing at the color of their uniforms.

"Well," answered Dabney with a smile as they trotted around a curve in the road, with woods on both sides, "that's always been an interesting question where Fauquier and Loudoun Counties are concerned. You see, we're now in Mosby's Confederacy."

"What does that mean?" Jason wanted to know. But before Dabney could reply, they rounded the curve and came almost face to face with a string of supply wagons, under guard—extremely heavy guard, Jason thought, for the size of the caravan—by cavalry. Cavalry in blue uniforms.

After a second of startled immobility, a blue-clad officer shouted, "Take 'em!" His men whipped out their sabers and thundered forward. Almost immediately, they were upon Jason and his party before the latter could wheel their mounts around and even try to flee. Besides, the bluecoats' horses looked better than theirs.

Resistance couldn't even be thought of. They were too few, and their revolvers were unloaded for traveling. "We surrender!" shouted Jason. "We cry quarter!"

The Union troopers crowded around them, collecting their weapons, which they handed over with expressions ranging from Mondrago's surliness to Nesbit's obvious terror. The Union officer, whose shoulder insignia was the two silver bars of a captain, rode up alongside Jason, who extended his saber hilt-first.

"My sword, sir," he began. But the captain cut him off.

"Silence, you damned horse-thief!" He snatched the saber with a cold grin. "I never thought to take any of you partisans this easily."

"What do you mean, sir? I am Captain Jason Landrieu of the Natchez Cavalry, Jeff Davis Legion, and as an officer of your own rank I expect—"

"I said silence, you lying bastard! You're nothing but a common highway robber dressed up in a uniform, and your kind doesn't deserve any military courtesies. And don't fling the so-called Partisan Ranger Act of your so-called Confederate Congress at me." The captain's anger was of a sort Jason recognized from experience: the kind that had long-standing fear trembling behind it. "Oh, yes, I know: ever since the chieftain of your gang sent that letter to General Sheridan last month, threatening to retaliate on his own prisoners, we're not supposed to hang you as you deserve. But if I had my way—"

A nerve-shattering, ululating yell split the air, and gray-clad horsemen burst from the woods alongside the road, bridle reins in one hand and revolver in the other, their horses bounding like jumpers, almost like deer. At their head was a man on a magnificent gray horse that he rode like a steeplechaser, wearing a red-lined cape and with an ostrich plume in his hat, shouting, "Boys, go through 'em!" in a high-pitched but powerful voice.

The panic that flashed through the Union troopers was almost physically palpable. Clearly this was something that, to them, meant more than an ordinary attack. They tried to line up in correct alignment as called for by standard cavalry tactics, but the headlong attack that crashed into them was more like a horse race than the trot or controlled canter of traditional Napoleonic cavalry charges. The attackers were in among them before they could form up, firing at point-blank range, emptying one revolver and pulling out a second.

Jason had no leisure to wonder how a cavalry unit could possibly have approached so closely without being heard before charging. He spurred his horse against that of the stunned Union captain, reached out, and grabbed his saber back. Whipping it out of its scabbard, he slashed at the head of the captain, who instinctively brought up his left arm. Jason's saber almost severed it. With a scream, the Union officer went over, causing his horse to capsize and Jason's to rear in panic, throwing him. He managed to hit the ground in a roll.

As Jason scrambled to his feet he had an instant to look around him. The fight had dissolved into a maelstrom of noise, smoke, and out-of-control riderless horses. Some of the Union horsemen were trying to ply their sabers, but ineffectually in the face of the momentum and firepower of the Confederates, who when their second revolvers were empty would gasp the heavy weapons by the barrels and use them for pistol-whipping. Most simply scattered, galloping back down the road past the wagons, whose drivers were jumping down and scrambling into the woods. Jason's own men found themselves unguarded, and had all they could do to control their horses.

Incredibly, the Union captain had also gotten to his feet, his face a mask of agony. With his good arm, he brought up his revolver. Jason struck it from his hand with his saber and, bringing the blade around, brought the point up to the man's throat. "Do you surrender, Captain?"

The captain nodded weakly, and sank to his knees with glazed eyes.

The fight was over. Some of the Confederate riders, including the leader, had galloped off down the road, where revolver shots could still be heard as they pursued the fleeing Federals. Others were busying themselves plundering the contents of the wagons. Jason now had the leisure to study these men. By and large, they seemed very young, superb riders, and neatly uniformed. One, who wore captain's insignia and seemed to be the senior officer still present, trotted up and dismounted. He was a conspicuously handsome man no older than his early twenties, with a neat mustache and strikingly blue eyes in a face whose tan hadn't entirely faded in December. He was an inch shorter than Jason (which made him fairly tall for this milieu) and strongly built. His uniform was nattier than most of his men's.

"I see you have a prisoner, Captain," he said to Jason. "And a wounded one. Doctor!"

A Mediterranean-looking man who had only just ridden from the woods approached. "This is our surgeon, Dr. Aristides Monteiro. He will tend to your arm." The Union captain mumbled something as the doctor led him aside, hopefully to get him into shape for his journey to Libby Prison. *From which*, Jason thought, *Elizabeth Van Lew may be able to get him out.*

"And who might you be, sir?" the handsome young Confederate captain asked Jason.

Jason gave his cover identity and indicated his men, who had by now gathered around. "We are in your debt, sir, for the timely arrival of you and your men. Who do I have the honor of addressing?"

"Adolphus Richards, sir. And while I am glad we were able to be of service, you mistake me. I am only second in command here. However, the colonel should be returning shortly . . . Ah. I see him coming now."

The riders were returning, the man with the red-lined cloak at their head. Dismounting, he took off his plumed hat and ran his fingers through his light-brown hair as he approached with the brisk, energetic step of a man who would find it difficult to stay still for more than a few minutes.

He was about thirty, and a striking contrast to the stalwart Richards. Standing no more than five feet seven or eight inches tall, he was so slight—surely weighing less than a hundred and thirty pounds—that his uniform looked a couple of sizes too large. His fair-complexioned, clean-shaven face was as lean as the rest of him, with a slightly cleft chin, thin lips and a long narrow nose. He looked, in short, totally ordinary and undistinguished.

But then he drew closer, and Jason got a better look at his face.

The thin lips were a line of fierce and restless resolve. The nose was like the sharp beak of a bird of prey. And then there were the eyes: dark-blue, piercing, luminous, as though there was a fire behind them that powered the dynamic personality of a born fighter.

*He may be a shrimp*, thought Jason, unable to look away from those eyes, *but I don't think I would want to get on this man's bad side.*

"Who have we here, Dolly?" the colonel asked, after exchanging a casual greeting (but no salute; this was obviously a pretty informal outfit) with Richards. "Dolly" seemed an odd nickname for such a tough-looking customer, but Jason decided something of the sort had to be expected by a man whose parents had burdened him with "Adolphus."

"Sir, this is Captain Jason Landrieu of the Natchez Cavalry in the Jeff Davis Legion, in Young's Brigade. He personally captured the commanding officer of the Yankee escort . . . who had just captured him."

The colonel laughed easily. His smile was actually quite charming, and the blue flame in his eyes died down to a twinkle as the heat of combat ebbed. His voice, high-pitched in battle, was now low and pleasant, and his speech was that of a well-educated man. "A most satisfying turnabout, I'm sure, Captain. And an impressive feat, considering that you were using *that*." He indicated the saber that Jason was still holding. It occurred to Jason that he hadn't seen a single saber among his rescuers. "Those things belong in a museum for the preservation of antiquities! I'm glad to see you also carry a Colt revolver. *That's* what you want for close action!" (*Especially when it has a laser target designator*, Jason did not interject.) "But for the best effect, you should be carrying at least two of them, loaded, into battle. We must also see about getting you better horses, even though yours aren't as bad as most of the wretched plugs our regular cavalry has to make do with these days."

"Thank you, Colonel. Your men are splendidly mounted."

"Indeed! We have the best thoroughbreds the Union army can provide." The colonel laughed again, then the dark-blue eyes immediately grew shrewd. "But what brings you and your men up here from Petersburg?"

"Actually, sir, we came from Richmond. We are on a special assignment for General Lee, about which I am not permitted to speak." The young colonel's eyebrows went up, and Jason pulled out the copy of Lee's requisition he had been careful to get. "That is why the general gave me this, which of course is how we were able to obtain fairly decent horseflesh in Richmond. We are currently enroute to Rectortown."

"Well, that's most fortuitous. I'm on the way there myself. I'm to attend the wedding of one of my men tomorrow, on the twenty-first, two miles north of Rectortown. You will accompany us."

"Again, sir, thank you. And my men and I are most profoundly grateful that you showed up when you did. But you have the advantage of me. May I know the name of my rescuer?"

"Lieutenant Colonel John Singleton Mosby." It was said in the tone of a man who expects his name to be recognized. "Commanding the 43rd Battalion Virginia Partisan Rangers. And now, Captain, I need to attend to a few things—most notably, the fair division of spoils from these sutler's wagons. Come, Dolly." And he and Richards walked toward the captured wagons, leaving Dabney staring after him.

"The Gray Ghost!" the historian whispered in awe.

# CHAPTER ELEVEN

As they rode north with Mosby and his men, wearing rubber ponchos over their uniforms against a light mixture of rain and sleet, Jason noticed a couple of things.

The first took him a while to put his finger on . . . something that seemed not quite right. Then it came to him, for he had encountered other cavalry in various ages, and those cavalry could always be heard hundreds of yards away, with the clanking, clattering and jingling of their swords and scabbards and canteens. These men were *quiet*. Their march didn't seem particularly orderly, but with no sabers or drinking equipment the only sound they made was that of hoofbeats. On soft ground, Jason thought, they must have been practically inaudible. He began to understand how they had seemed to appear out of thin air . . . especially if, as he suspected, Mosby gave commands by hand signals up to the moment of battle. He tried to imagine what it must be like for the Federals, never knowing when an attack would burst upon them without warning. And he recalled the undercurrent of fear he had discerned beneath the Union captain's bluster, and the panic that the attack had ignited.

The second thing Jason noticed, as they passed various farms (at each of which men fell out of the column by twos and remained), was that more and more often the barns and grist mills were burned-out shells. He mentioned it to Mosby.

"Yes," the colonel said grimly. "At the end of November, Sheridan sent Merritt's cavalry division through Ashby's Gap to do the kind of destruction they had already done in the Valley. Oh, they had orders not to burn people's dwelling houses—perhaps Sheridan remembered my standing order that no quarter should be given to house-burners. But they wiped out families' livelihood . . . took away the milk cows of mothers with infants . . . left them hungry, all through Upper Fauquier, and Loudoun County to the north."

"So they punished the innocent families of Confederate sympathizers?" Nesbit asked, aghast in a way Jason (who had seen so much of history) could not feel.

"Not just those." Mosby waved toward the north. "Being from Mississippi, you wouldn't know this, but while Fauquier County has always been solidly pro-secession, there are quite a few Unionists in Loudoun County, especially among the Quakers and Germans there, who as a matter of principle don't own slaves. It didn't matter. The Yankee cavalry burned the barns and stole the livestock of people who greeted them cheering and waving the Stars and Stripes. Thus the United States rewards loyalty!"

"Why?" Nesbit was clearly bewildered.

Mosby gave him an odd look and replied as though the answer should be obvious. "To try to make it impossible for me to operate."

"You mean by depriving you of supplies?" Dabney prompted.

"Yes, but beyond that Sheridan sought to turn the local people against me. He thought they would blame me for bringing these hardships on them, and cease giving aid and shelter to my men for fear of further depredations." Mosby laughed grimly. "He was wrong, even though on the eighth of this month he went a step further and closed all trade across the Potomac under the permits that had previously been issued to Unionists on the Virginia side so they could purchase necessities. In the end, all he did was unite the people here even more firmly behind me. They're not the fools he took them for; they know he is the one to blame for their sufferings. They also know I'm able to give them protection, either directly or by keeping the Yankees busy skirmishing. And as you've seen, they're still boarding my men."

Jason recalled the pairs of men Mosby had left at the various farms. He was thinking about it when Nesbit spoke up again—through chattering teeth, for dusk was coming on and the rubber ponchos, while effective against the wetness, provided little warmth. "Ah, Colonel, if I may ask, do we plan to make camp soon?"

"Make camp?" Mosby laughed. "If we made camps for the Yankees to find, I would have been killed or captured a year or two ago! I don't have a tent to my name—none of us do. No: after a raid the Rangers don't make camp. They vanish."

"Vanish?" Nesbit repeated. "Where?" Dabney looked like he knew the answer but was eagerly waiting to hear it anyway.

"Into the countryside." Mosby gave an expansive gesture. "The people hide my men in their homes until I call a rendezvous for the next raid. Usually two per family, although sometimes as many as eight."

"So as far as the Yankees are concerned, the Partisan Rangers as a unit don't exist except when they're raiding," said Jason. "They can't be found." *I'm beginning to understand why Dabney said this man is called the "Gray Ghost."*

"They almost become part of their hosts' families," continued Mosby, obviously in a discursive mood. "They share their booty following raids, and enjoy many of the comforts of home in between. I know some call them 'featherbed cavalry,' but good food and sound sleep give them an advantage over men who're exhausted and fed only on army rations. And the families who board them provide other services as well, taking care of horses, mending uniforms, and giving us warning by passing the word of approaching Yankees."

"It must be because of such a warning that you're now dispersing your command to avoid being caught by General Auger's men," Dabney began . . . then clamped his mouth shut.

Mosby gave him a sharp glance. "How did you happen to know about that," he inquired.

"Uh, we heard some of your men talking about it," Jason put in, with a surreptitious warning glare for Dabney.

"Altogether too much loose talk." Mosby's blue eyes went as icy as the drizzle. "Ah, well, it's true. Just yesterday Sheridan sent his cavalry corps under General Torbert on a raid down toward Gordonsville, with orders to return through this area in the hope that I'll rendezvous my men in response. In the further hope of catching me if I do, he's also ordered Auger, who's now at Fairfax, to send men through Thoroughfare Gap in the Bull Run Mountains to Middleburg. But they won't succeed. And yes, that's one of the ways the people here help us. In return, we provide the only law and order in this debatable part of the state; I run a kind of informal civil and criminal court where the people can come for justice. And we do our best to protect them from the Yankees, and also from bandits who prey on civilians while falsely claiming to be my men."

*I don't think I need to ask what happens to the latter when you catch them.* "I see why this area is known as 'Mosby's Confederacy,'" said Jason aloud.

"I'm too modest to emulate the Yankees in calling it that," Mosby said with a chuckle. "I prefer to call it 'the Flanders of the South.' The resistance of these people to an invader can only be compared to that of the Flemish people who rallied to Guy de Dampierre against the French armies of Philip IV in the Middle Ages." Out of the corner of his eye, Jason saw Mondrago give Mosby a look of surprised respect.

"But," Mosby resumed, "I haven't yet dispersed all the men. Some of them are helping with the wedding preparations at 'Rosenix,' the home of the bride's aunt. It's a special occasion: our ordinance sergeant, Jake Lavender, is marrying Judith Edmonds, the sister of another Ranger, Johnny Edmonds. But for tonight, I know a place where you and your men can stay. I'll send for you tomorrow."

Mosby dropped them off at a sturdy two-story farmhouse which featured, among other things, a large hidden cellar where, they were assured, Rangers had concealed themselves from Sheridan's men. They ate better than people in Richmond could hope for these days, and the cellar was considerably more comfortable that Elizabeth Van Lew's secret attic chamber.

"All right, Carlos," said Jason after the family had gone to bed. "Tell us about this Mosby."

"Yeah," Mondrago urged. "He's an interesting bird."

"Well, for a start, he has absolutely no military training or background. His education was in literature and history. Before the war he was a lawyer—he must enjoy running that rough-and-ready court of his. Like Lee, he disliked slavery and was flatly opposed to secession. But, again like Lee, he felt he had no choice but to go with Virginia when it seceded. He enlisted as a private, then rose through the ranks as a protégé of Jeb Stuart, Lee's cavalry commander, under whom he got a reputation as a matchless scout and intelligence-gatherer. He even did some spying in Washington as a prisoner of war in 1862, before he was released in a prisoner exchange."

"I'll bet the Federals kicked themselves later for exchanging him," Aiken commented.

"Very likely. At the beginning of 1863, Stuart and Lee decided he was wasted in the regular cavalry and sent him up here to form a unit of partisans."

"So these characters aren't really in the Confederate army?" Logan wondered.

"Legally, they are, under the Partisan Ranger Act, which established special rules for such units—one of which is that in lieu of pay they share in whatever spoils they take. Because of that, and the mystique of the bold, dashing cavalier that meant a lot in the South, so many men wanted to join Mosby that he was able to hand-pick them."

Mondrago looked sidelong at Jason. "Does this remind you of anything?"

"Yes," Jason nodded. "The seventeenth-century privateers of our recent acquaintance. Of course, the Spaniards had other names for them."

"I imagine those names were mild compared to some of those applied to Mosby by the Union forces." Dabney chuckled. "The real making of his reputation was in 1863, when he and a small force entered Fairfax Court House under cover of night, in the middle of the Union army, and got away with a Union general and more than thirty other prisoners—not to mention a herd of horses—without firing a shot or losing a man. That wasn't the only time he captured a Union general. Once, he barely missed capturing Grant. When he sent President Lincoln a lock of his hair and hinted that he was going to come into Washington and abduct him, the Union high command wasn't laughing. For the rest of the war, thousands of troops were tied down in a defensive perimeter securing the capital against Mosby, who never had more than four hundred men under his command at any given time."

"When we had our run-in with those Union troops," said Jason thoughtfully, "I could almost smell the fear."

"That was his true genius. He owned the night. The Union troops in this region could never relax; they never knew when he was going to appear out of nowhere, and their estimates of his numbers were always wildly exaggerated. It is attested that sleep deprivation was a problem among them, and they jumped at every sound and rumor, wasting a lot of effort and energy chasing imaginary partisans. Mosby had become almost a bogeyman figure to them."

"The technical term," said Mondrago rather pedantically, "is asymmetric warfare. He used fear as a force multiplier."

"Less technically," said Aiken, "he got inside their heads. Mao Tse-Tung and Che Guevara said something like that. So did Janos Rand in the twenty-third century wars against the Transhuman Dispensation."

"So did Clausewitz," said Mondrago, not to be outdone.

"And for years Mosby operated with impunity only a day's ride from the enemy capital," added Logan wonderingly.

"Yes," nodded Dabney. "And to the very end of the war he still had the tactical initiative."

"What happened to him after the war?" asked Aiken, clearly fascinated.

Dabney smiled. "Here's where his story gets *really* unbelievable. At first he was a hero in Virginia, and when he went back into the practice of law he flourished. But then he committed social suicide by becoming a friend and political supporter of U.S. Grant, who had once ordered that any of his men who were captured were to be summarily hanged. Then he made it worse by outspokenly defending his old mentor, the late Jeb Stuart, against the charge that he had been responsible for Lee's defeat at Gettysburg. This made it seem like he was criticizing Lee, which was a form of sacrilege. So he went from hero to pariah. His law practice dried up, so he went to work for the federal government. Grant's successor as president, Rutherford B. Hayes, appointed him consul to Hong Kong, where he stirred up a hornet's nest by cleaning up the entrenched corruption that had been victimizing both American seamen and Chinese immigrants. Later he worked for the Justice Department in various capacities, and eventually came to be reinstated in the pantheon of Confederate heroes. He lived into his eighties. By then, silent motion pictures were being made about him—he even had a small part in one of them."

"He sounds like a classic example of a 'contrarian,'" mused Jason. "The type who thrives on being a minority of one."

"'Aginner' was the contemporary term," said Dabney. "For some reason, he felt compelled to never back down from a fight and always take the side of the underdog."

"No mystery there," Aiken asserted confidently. "Just look at him. When he was a boy, a scrawny kid like that in this culture must have been bullied unmercifully. There are two ways to react to that. One is to become shy and withdrawn, which he obviously didn't do. The other is to counterattack—fight back at the drop of a hat, even if you lose the fights."

"Hmm . . ." Dabney considered. "Come to think of it, he was once expelled from the University of Virginia for shooting a bully."

"There you have it. As far as he's concerned, the overwhelming Yankee army is a bully in a blue coat."

"Well," said Jason firmly, "that's enough amateur psychology for now. Tomorrow we ought to see his more peaceful side at this wedding, where I gather we're going to have to put in an appearance. Then we're going to have to slip away to Rectortown. For now, let's get some sleep."

# CHAPTER TWELVE

The weather was slightly better, but with portents of turning wretched again, the next day when they arrived at "Rosenix."

As Mosby had indicated, a number of Rangers were present for the wedding, contrary to their usual practice of dispersing after a raid. He himself was there, conversing on the lawn with Dolly Richards and another captain, whom he introduced as his second in command, William Chapman. He was a little older than Richards, but still only in his early twenties. And he was an even more striking contrast to Mosby than Richards: tall, and dark of hair, eyes and complexion.

"I still call him and Dolly captains," Mosby explained to Jason afterwards, "despite the reorganization General Lee approved early this month. Our battalion is to become a regiment, and the two of them will become battalion commanders, with the ranks of lieutenant colonel and major respectively. But it doesn't officially take effect until January 9. The same applies to my own promotion to full colonel—which, by the way, is why I still wear these." He indicated the two-star lieutenant colonel's insignia on his collar.

"Congratulations, sir," said Jason. "I'm sure the extra star will make that uniform even handsomer." This was not entirely flattery, nor did it refer just to the plumed hat and scarlet-lined cape. Compared to what most of the Confederate army was currently wearing, Jason had been struck the previous day by the superior material of

Mosby's gray coat and trousers, with their yellow cords down the seams. He now said so.

"Yes, Yankee sutler wagons often contain some very fine cloth." Mosby laughed. "But you must not imagine that I normally turn myself out this elegantly for raids. I am wearing my best for the wedding. Speaking of which, let's go in."

Not as many Rangers were actually on hand for the wedding as had previously been about, helping with preparations and running errands for the family. Mosby, unable to ignore the possibility that Augur's Union cavalry from Fairfax might already be present in the area, sent men out on patrol, earning a surreptitious nod of approval from Mondrago. However, the wedding proceeded without a hitch. It was only in the afternoon, during the reception, that one of the scouts rode in. With no appearance of alarm, Mosby took the man aside and spoke to him privately. Then he dismissed the scout and returned to the party, wearing a thoughtful look.

"Tom," Mosby called quietly to one of his men, with whom he exchanged a few inaudible words. The man nodded and departed. Mosby then circulated inconspicuously, speaking briefly to Chapman and Richards before approaching Jason.

"What is it, Colonel?" Jason asked.

Mosby spoke in low tones. "It seems Yankee cavalry have entered Salem. They must be some of Auger's men. I'm going to take Tom Love—he's outside getting the horses—and go reconnoiter." He had a sudden thought. "Why don't you and your men come along, Captain? I may need couriers to carry messages for me. Come quietly—there's no need to disturb the reception."

As Jason unobtrusively mustered his men, Dabney nodded. "Yes. I remember now: Mosby was noted for often doing his own scouting." He frowned. "It seems there's something else I *ought* to be remembering—something about this whole situation that seems vaguely familiar, as though I should know what's going to happen next. But I can't put my finger on it."

"Well, whatever it is, we'll find out soon. Let's mount up."

At Salem, they learned that the Union cavalry—six hundred men of the 13th New York Cavalry, under a Major Douglas Frazar—had departed in the direction of Rectortown. Jason hoped he and his men would have an excuse to get into the town and pursue their mission, but Mosby was intent only on locating the Yankee column. They rode on through a developing freezing rain, to the vicinity of Rectortown. Jason was almost fidgeting—so near and yet so far—but he could hardly get into the town now. For they soon discovered that the Yankees had stopped just outside it.

It was early evening, and they looked down from a hill on a bivouac where the Union troops were building fires. "They must be camping for the night," said Mosby. His predatory eagerness seemed to render him oblivious to the weather, even though by now the wind chill made it seem even more miserable than it was. "But it's too late to organize anything for tonight. Captain Landrieu, dispatch one of your men back to the wedding. Tell Captains Chapman and Richards to prepare to harass their column in the morning."

"I'll go, sir!" blurted Dabney and Aiken simultaneously.

"You, I think," said Jason, indicating Dabney. He wasn't too happy about the prospect of being without whatever forewarnings the historian might be able to provide, but Dabney was the best rider they had. "Are you sure you'll be able to find your way?"

"I'm sure. I'll ride hard and get there before it gets too dark."

Privately, Jason thought that would take some riding. But he held his peace as Dabney took instructions from Mosby and departed with a cocky wave. He obviously regarded this as an adventure straight from the pages of his studies. Jason hoped the disillusionment process wouldn't be fatal.

"And now," said Mosby, almost as jaunty as Dabney, "let's head north to Rector's Cross Roads and spread the word among some of the men who're boarding around there to report tomorrow morning."

But as they rode through a world of hanging icicles, the going grew slower, and eventually cold and hunger began to gnaw at even the seemingly impervious Mosby. Shortly before none o'clock, after they had gone about four miles and were still a mile shy of Rector's Cross Roads they saw lights ahead, in the windows of a middle-sized two-story ashlar stone farmhouse.

"'Lakeland,'" said Mosby. "The home of Ludwell Lake. His son, Ludwell Jr., is one of my Rangers, and his daughter Ladonia is married to Benjamin Skinner, another Ranger. We're sure of a warm welcome here—and Ludwell's wife Mary is a famous cook. I recall especially her fresh-baked rolls."

"And we all know hot coffee is your only indulgence, Colonel," said Tom Love with a grin.

"Exactly. Let's stop and seek the Lakes' hospitality."

"I'll stay outside and stand watch, Colonel," offered Love as they dismounted.

"No, there's no danger. Come with me. You too, Captain Landrieu, and your sergeant. Perhaps your men will take the horses around to the back and wait in the barn—I'll have food sent out to them."

Ladonia Skinner answered the door, greeting her husband's commanding officer enthusiastically, as did her mother and her sister Sarah. The three women, with the aid of slaves, set about preparing a meal in the summer kitchen behind the house while Mosby turned left from the entry hall to a parlor, where he shook hands warmly with the master of the house. The parlor had obviously been converted to a bedroom, and the reason why was equally obvious. Ludwell Lake was one of the most obese human beings Jason had ever seen, and undoubtedly couldn't get up and down his own stairs. Jason's imagination quailed at the task of visualizing the details of how Lake had gone about siring three children; presumably he had been far slimmer in his salad days. Fortunately for his daughters, they took after their mother, who was merely matronly.

Mosby and his companions went back through the hallway to the living room and gratefully warmed themselves by the fire until Lake's daughters began to bring in coffee, spareribs, and Mrs. Love's famous rolls to the dining room across the hallway beside the parlor/bedroom.

"Ma'am," said Jason to Mrs. Lake, "Why don't I and my sergeant go out back to the kitchen and take some food to my men in the barn?"

"Why, certainly, Captain. Sarah, help the gentlemen."

"We'll rejoin you directly, Colonel, if we may," said Jason to Mosby, who gave an indulgent wave.

The dining room had a back door for ready access to the kitchen. There, they obtained food and a pot of coffee, which they conveyed to the barn. There, they discussed plans.

"How about it, Commander?" asked Mondrago. "We're only a mile from Rectortown. Maybe we could slip away now, while Mosby is inside, and—"

"I thought of that. Just two problems. One is that Dabney is at 'Rosenix'—my implant confirms that he made it there—and tomorrow morning he'll be riding with Chapman or Richards, thinking that will be the way to rejoin us. The other is that we may be operating in this part of Virginia for a while yet, and we'd better not make Mosby suspicious of us by running out on him. So maybe we'd better—"

At that moment, the chilly silence was shattered by the clatter and clanking of a conventional cavalry unit, and a column of horsemen appeared out of the darkness. Blue-clad horsemen.

"Down!" hissed Jason. "And quiet!" They all went on their bellies inside the open barn door and began to load their revolvers.

"No shooting unless we're attacked," Jason whispered. But the Union cavalrymen showed no interest in the barn as they surrounded the house and dismounted. One, obviously the officer, trotted his horse around to make sure all was in order, then dismounted and, accompanied by several of his men, walked around the house toward the front door.

"So Frazar's men weren't camping for the night outside Rectortown after all," Mondrago whispered to Jason.

"No. Those fires we saw must have just been to cook food before resuming the march, following the same road we took. They must have stopped here because they saw our horses tied up out there." Inwardly, Jason was cursing himself for sending Dabney off. He would have liked very much to have the historian with him now, because he didn't like what was happening. Mosby was a well-documented historical figure—indeed, Dabney had assured them that he would become the stuff of legend, and live on for half a century after the war. And now he was in serious trouble.

In the stillness, he thought he heard the front door open and close. Through the dining room back door came a mutter of voices, the first sounding like it was issuing a peremptory demand, the second possibly Mosby's, although the words were indistinguishable.

Jason glanced left and right at his men. Nesbit, immediately to Jason's left, was shivering . . . and, Jason thought, not just from the cold. He was the only one of them without military training, and his limited experience in the seventeenth-century Caribbean had not prepared him for this kind of nerve-wracking wait. Jason opened his mouth to say something soothing.

Somewhere nearby, a dog's bark suddenly shattered the quiet. Startled, Nesbit's finger tightened convulsively on his trigger. His colt crashed, jumping in his nerveless hand and sending the shot high. Jason instantly grasped his arm and wrenched the revolver from his grasp. But it was too late.

Pandemonium broke out in the back yard. The Union troops, already keyed to a pitch of tension as they usually were at night in "Mosby's Confederacy," had no idea where the shot had come from. They began firing their revolvers wildly, in all directions. There was a sound of shattering window glass, a female scream, and a shout from within: "I am shot!"

This time it was definitely Mosby's voice.

There was the sound of a commotion from within, and the light was extinguished. The cavalrymen between the barn and the house ceased their shooting and, after a moment's bewildered inaction, ran around the house to the front, where an officer was bawling orders. A new light appeared, in the windows of the bedroom adjoining the dining room.

"Come on," Jason whispered. "Carefully!" he added with a glare at the sheepish-looking Nesbit. In a crouching gait, the time travelers scrambled across the yard and flattened themselves against the rear wall of the house. Jason peered cautiously over the windowsill.

Mosby lay on the floor, the front of his blue flannel shirt soaked with blood in the abdominal area. He was holding back the flow with what Jason recognized as a bonnet Sarah Lake had been wearing. Sarah was hastily stuffing his uniform coat with its telltale rank insignia under the bed. The rest of the family, and Tom Love, stood watching. A sound of stomping cavalry boots was heard from the hallway.

"They're coming back," Mosby whispered. "I have to give an imitation of a man about to die." He put his hand in the blood and smeared it on his mouth, as though he was hemorrhaging from within.

The door crashed open and a choleric-looking Union officer wearing major's insignia stormed in, with several of his men crowding in behind him.

"I surrender," Tom Love said instantly, handing over his revolver. "Don't harm the family."

The major ignored him. The redness of his face suggested that, aside from anger, he had been fortifying himself against the chill night with frequent nips from a whiskey flask. He leaned over the prostrate Mosby. "I am Major Frazar, 13th New York Cavalry. Who are you?"

"I told you before, sir," grated Mosby in tones of agony. "Lieutenant Johnston, 6th Virginia Cavalry."

"Yes, so you did." Frazar definitely sounded a bit befuddled. He kneeled down, examined Mosby's wound, then stood up unsteadily. "The bullet entered his abdomen two inches below and to the left of the navel. No point in taking him in," he added callously to Ludwell Lake. "He'll be dead in twenty-four hours. I'll leave him for you to dispose of." He turned on his heel and departed. A pair of his troopers followed, taking Love with them.

The others were about to leave, when one spoke up in an Irish brogue. "Those are rare fine boots, bejesus. I fancy this boyo won't have much use for 'em." The others evidently agreed, for they removed Mosby's boots—and his trousers for good measure—before departing. The Lakes were left alone with Mosby, silently listening to Frazar's troop remounting and riding off.

As soon as the sound of the cavalry column had receded, Jason rose, motioned to his men to follow him and reentered the house through the back door. Then, just in time he halted, flattened himself against the dining room wall and hastily motioned the others to silence as a lone Union trooper reentered the bedroom, revolver in hand. The Lake family shrank back from him.

"I thought I'd stay behind a minute or two and make sure of this Reb," he man said. "And see what I can . . . collect here." He looked around at the household goods, his eyes finally settling on the two Lake daughters. Then he aimed the revolver at Mosby.

Jason silently slipped through the bedroom door behind the man. Frazar might still be close enough to hear a shot. With his right hand, he grasped the wrist of the Union cavalryman's gun arm and twisted it back and up. Simultaneously, before the man could cry out in pain, Jason's left arm went around his neck, which a sharp, twisting sideways jerk sufficed to break. Jason lowered the limp body to the floor as his men crowded in and the Lake family stared openmouthed.

"Captain Landrieu," greeted Mosby, weakly but without the pain-choked rasp he had simulated for Frazar's benefit. "It seems I owe you my life. And I'm glad to see they didn't get you and your men."

*One of whom is partly to blame for all the blood you're leaking,* thought Jason. *I guess saving your life was the least I could do.* "May I see your wound, sir? I have some experience with such things." He knelt beside Mosby and examined him with an eye trained in twenty-fourth-century first aid.

Drunk or not, Major Frazar had correctly located the entry wound. If the bullet had penetrated the peritoneum, the membrane lining the walls of the abdominal and pelvic cavities and investing the viscera, then peritonitis would soon set in and Mosby would indeed have only about twenty-four hours to live. But Mosby's overall aspect made him think that the colonel must have had a freakish stroke of good fortune. The bullet, after entering the abdomen, must have passed above the fascia, the sheet of fibrous subcutaneous tissue, and been deflected, passing around the abdomen to the right side.

"I think you're going to live, Colonel." *Actually,* Jason's inner voice gibed at him, *you* know *he will. Or at least you'd better* hope *he will.* "But you've lost a lot of blood and need medical attention as soon as possible, to get the bullet removed."

"And in any case, we've got to get him out of here," blurted Ludwell Lake, wattles shaking with agitation. "They'll burn the house down if they come back and find out who he really is. We'll bury . . . that," he added, indicating the dead Union trooper. "Fortunately, there's no blood."

"One of my men, George Slater, is boarding at 'Rockburn,' Mrs. Aquilla Glascock's home," Mosby whispered. "It's only a mile and a half to the southwest of here."

"Sarah, go get Daniel," Ludwell Lake ordered. "Tell him to bring the oxcart around and line it with straw. Ladonia, get some quilts."

"We'll help, sir," said Jason.

"Send one of your men to the wedding, Captain, to tell them where I'm going to be," said Mosby in an increasingly faint voice.

"Private Aiken, you go," said Jason. "And . . . tell Dabney we'll rendezvous at Rectortown. You remember Mary Bowser's description of the place we're looking for there?"

"Yes, sir." The young Service man hurried off. At least, Jason assured himself, he'd be able to keep track of Aiken's whereabouts as well as Dabney's.

Sarah Lake presently returned with a young black boy, presumably one of the family's slaves. They wrapped Mosby in the quilts and carried him carefully out to an oxcart with two calves hitched to it and laid him in the straw. Jason and his three remaining companions mounted up, said their farewells to the Lake family and rode along as the boy led the cart down the farm lane.

"Do you know the way, boy?" Jason asked. He seemed very young.

"Oh, yes, Cap'n." The boy smiled. "Daniel Strother's the name. I can get the Cunnel where he's goin'."

Jason would never forget that mile-and-a-half trek through the wintery night. He and the other time travelers took turns relieving Daniel Strother of the task of leading the calves that pulled the cart with frustrating slowness. But they dared not put the semiconscious Mosby across a horse. Even the bumps in the road—and it seemed to be mostly bumps—might be too much for his wound.

Finally they arrived at "Rockburn." As the Ranger George Slater and Mrs. Glascock's slaves carefully moved Mosby off the cart, the Colonel stirred into consciousness and he spoke to Jason.

"Thank you, Captain Landrieu. You've placed me under a debt which I only hope I live to repay."

"Think nothing of it, Colonel." Then something occurred to Jason. "But there is one favor I'd like to ask of you."

"Name it."

"Remember what I told you about the special mission for General Lee that brought me and my men here? As I intimated, it's rather confidential. It would be best if my presence here doesn't become generally known. So when you relate this night's events, please omit any mention of my part in it."

"My lips are sealed." Mosby managed to smile. "Even if I live to write my memoirs, Captain Landrieu will not appear in them."

"Thank you, sir," said Jason. Behind him, he heard Nesbit's sigh of relief. Then Mosby was moved inside and Jason swung back into his saddle. As he turned the horse away, he saw Daniel Strother looking up at him. "Are you going to be all right?"

"Ah'm fine, Cap'n. And . . . Cap'n, I think you'll be wantin' to head off down the road to Rectortown now."

Jason jerked on his horse's reins, bringing his horse to a whinnying halt. "What did you say?"

"Yes, Cap'n, Ah think there's somebody you want to meet there. An' he wants to meet you."

Afterwards, Jason was sure it was the sheer counter-irritant of the sleet that prevented him from being paralyzed by a sense of unreality. "You mean . . . ?"

"That's right, Cap'n." Daniel Strother looked up, with an expression very different from the cheerful diffidence it had worn up to now. "You see . . . Ah know Gracchus."

# CHAPTER THIRTEEN

Rectortown was a tiny place, only about twenty houses, a few stores, and what passed for a "hotel," all in the angle formed by the Manassas Gap Railroad as it turned southward. The most prominent building, and the place's chief reason for existence, was Alfred Rector's warehouse alongside the tiny railway station.

It was the hamlet's smallness that Jason was counting on—along with his implant's locator function—to enable them to rendezvous with Aiken and Dabney when those two arrived. It was hard to get lost here.

It was almost eleven o'clock when they rode into Rectortown's main street—really its only one—and there was no one about. The sleet had abated, but it was very cold. They rode up to a small building—little better than a shack—beside the warehouse. No doubt about it, this was the place described by Mary Bowser. Jason was too tired and chilled for caution; he dismounted and knocked on the ramshackle door. It creaked open, and a late-middle-aged black face looked out. Within, a youngish black woman held up a lantern, in whose flickering light shadowy figures—two women and a small boy—could be glimpsed.

Jason had expected to have to deal with abject fear at the sight of a white man in a Confederate uniform at the door. What he saw was more accurately described as mere apprehension, with an undercurrent of expectancy. It puzzled him.

"Yes, Cap'n?"

Now Jason threw even elementary caution to the winds. "Are you Gracchus?"

The man laughed softly. "Oh, lord, Cap'n, what a question! No, no, Ah ain't Gracchus. Marcus is my name. But," he added, and in his voice the expectancy trembled on the verge of overcoming the apprehension, "ain't you got somethin' to show me?"

*This simply isn't right*, Jason told himself. *Any more than it was right for that boy Daniel Strother to know about me. What's going on here?*

*But anything's better than standing out here freezing.*

Without a word, he handed Marcus the note Mary Bowser had written in Elizabeth Van Lew's cipher code.

Marcus's eyes grew round. "Ah cain't read, and Ah definitely cain't read *this*. But Ah know what it looks like. And Ah know you're the one Gracchus been expecting."

It was Jason's turn to stare, and again he thought of Daniel Strother. "'Expecting'? What are you talking about? Did Mary Bowser somehow get word up here from Richmond?"

"No, Cap'n, it's not that. It's . . . well, Ah don't rightly understand it. But Gracchus will explain everything."

"Is he here?"

"No, but he ain't far. We'll have to send the boy for him." Marcus stuck his head out the door and glanced anxiously around. Seeing no one, he motioned to Jason. "Y'all come inside."

"Can't you just take us to Gracchus?" asked Jason as they crowded into the tiny room.

Marcus gave him an odd look. "Better not, Cap'n. Even this late at night, there might be *somebody* out an' about. So Ah cain't be out after curfew. But the boy, he can sneak around like a 'possum. And even if he is caught, he won't get in no trouble."

Nesbit spoke up. "Do you mean you people here are . . . slaves?"

Marcus raised his head and met Nesbit's eyes squarely. "No, suh. We ain't no slaves. We be free. But the Black Code . . ." He trailed off as though that should explain everything, and gave muttered instructions to the boy, who looked to be no more than six or so, and handed him Mary Bowser's note. The boy nodded and slipped out the door.

"What about Gracchus?" Mondrago inquired. "What if *he's* seen outside?"

Marcus chuckled. "Don't you worry none 'bout Gracchus. He can *really* sneak around!"

He seemed disinclined to further conversation, and the four time travelers warmed themselves as best they could around a small, crude fireplace. The two women—one about Marcus's age, the other young—stared at them with the same expression Marcus had at first worn. Jason decided that the apprehension was unavoidable, given their Confederate uniforms. But he couldn't understand the element of seeing something long anticipated—almost the fulfillment of a prophecy. At any rate, they were as silent as Marcus, and while they waited Jason mused over the seeming incongruity of some of the names. But he remembered Dabney mentioning that those slaveowners who had the advantages of a Classical education sometimes bestowed Roman monikers on their slaves. And he seemed to vaguely recall that "Gracchus" was the name of a Roman family that had been champions of freedom . . .

A scratching at the door interrupted his thoughts. Marcus opened it, admitting a blast of cold air. The boy hurried in, followed by a man who instantly held all of Jason's attention.

He was medium-tall, well-built and in his thirties, with a thin black beard, tightly curled like his hair. His clothing was of the usual rough sort, made of homespun fabric, but included a warm-looking coat. His skin was a richly deep, dark brown, and his lips were full, but there was a certain quality to his strong, predominantly African face—a straightness of features and lack of prognathism—that suggested European genes. That face wore the enigmatic expression Jason had become used to here, but in his case it held an additional element, a quality Jason could not define, as though this man was seeing something he had longed to see but could scarcely credit his eyes.

"You must be Gracchus," he said tentatively.

"I am known by that name." The speech was not that of the local blacks. It sounded educated, and held a lilt that awakened Jason's memories of Jamaica.

"I'm Captain Landrieu."

"Yes. We expected that you would use that name."

*"Expected" again!* "Did Mary Bowser—?" Jason began, but then halted awkwardly, unsure of how freely he could talk in the presence of Marcus and his family. "Is there somewhere we can go to talk privately?"

Gracchus shook his head. "I already took a risk, coming here at this time of night. I shouldn't press my luck."

"Marcus mentioned something about the 'Black Code.'"

"Yes. If we were slaves, it would be the Slave Code. But we're free." Gracchus laid an ironic stress on the last word. "So we're subject to the Black Code instead. We have a curfew. And at any time of day, any white man who sees us in the street can tell us to go home and stay there. And we can't meet in unsupervised groups. Or bear arms. Or testify in court, except as a party to a civil action. Speaking of courts, there's a different—and harsher—scale of legal penalties for us. And, in general, we can't act 'uppity.'" He checked himself. "But you don't need to hear all that." He turned to Marcus and had a short, muttered conversation. Marcus nodded, and shepherded the women and the boy through a small door beside the fireplace, which gave access to a tiny shed built against that side of the shack.

As the door closed, Gracchus turned to Jason and smiled.

"I trust Marcus completely. But he doesn't need to know everything. And we need to be able to talk freely."

Actually, Jason had been wondering how open he could be even in private. He could hardly say to this man that he was here because a fellow time traveler would, in April, learn of the shadowy organization Gracchus led. But he had to start somewhere. "We do indeed. First of all, I'm very mystified by some things I've been hearing tonight, starting even before coming to this house."

"Feel free to ask me any questions you have, Commander Thanou."

"Well, to begin with, earlier tonight a slave boy named Daniel Strother—"

Then Gracchus's last two words registered on Jason with the force of a sledgehammer.

For several seconds, dead silence held the squalid little room, as Jason tried to collect his shattered thoughts.

"I see I'd better start at the beginning," he finally said. *Whatever that means in the time travel business!* he gibed at himself. "By ways which need not concern you at the moment, I learned of an organization which could be contacted through Mary Bowser. I have done so, as is proven by the cypher note the boy showed you. I went to this trouble because I had also learned that your organization and the one to which I belong might be in a position to help each other, because we may have common enemies. By the way, what is your organization called?"

"We go by many names from time to time—or no name at all, when we can manage it—in the interests of secrecy. A name, you see, is a kind of target which can be aimed at. But our real name is the Order of the Three-Legged Horse."

"Three-Legged Horse?" Nesbit echoed faintly.

"It's an apparition which Jamaicans believe manifests itself around Christmas." Gracchus took on a whimsical smile. "It's considered beneficent—by men. Women have always regarded it with a certain apprehension. So I've often wondered about its origin, since our founder was a woman. But . . . she was a very exceptional woman."

"Speaking of Jamaicans," Mondrago interjected, "you talk like—"

"Yes, I'm from Jamaica. Some of us have come here from time to time, to establish the Order in this country. I'm the most recent, brought in by a blockade runner."

"A Confederate blockade runner?" Mondrago looked perplexed. "But . . ." He gave a gesture that vaguely indicated the color of Gracchus's skin.

"The blockade runners are businessmen. They'll carry *anything* if they're paid." From somewhere in the back of Jason's mind came the recollection of a fictional character named Rhett Butler. "They'll even carry free blacks—not that any want to get into this country, least of all now, with this war on."

"But *you* did," Jason pointed out.

"I had to," said Gracchus simply. "I knew it was necessary for me to be here tonight."

"You and your people seem to know a great many things."

"Yes. We also know about the Transhumanists."

Jason took a deep, unsteady breath. "Do you know where I and my men come from?"

"I know *when* you come from," said Gracchus with a smile. "You come from the future. I don't understand how a man who won't be born for hundreds of years can be here talking to me. But I know it's true."

Nesbit spoke like a man staring the unthinkable in the face. "Do all the members of your Order know about time travel?"

"No. That's why I sent Marcus away. Only one of us in each

generation is allowed to know. The knowledge had been passed down from one to another, through the successors of our founder, for two hundred years."

"You mean to say," said Jason, unable to keep incredulity out of his voice, "that details like the precise night I'd show up here at Rectortown, and the name I'd be using, have been accurately transmitted orally over two hundred years?"

"Oh, no. Most of our Order's knowledge is, indeed, handed down that way—as it has to be, given that most of our members are illiterate. Thus they learn of the Demons who long ago tricked men into believing they were gods—all dead now, although we are warned that more of them, even more evil than the first ones, may come again."

*Demons seven and a half or eight feet tall, with long narrow faces and sharp, cruel features, and paler flesh than that of the whitest white man, and hair gleaming of silver and gold, and huge eyes that are all opaque blue . . .*

*Demons who call themselves the Teloi.*

"Gracchus," Jason heard himself saying, as though from a great distance, "who was this 'founder' you mentioned?"

"She was a woman. Her name was Zenobia."

A door in Jason's memory swung open and the seventeenth-century Caribbean sun came flooding in, to reveal a tall, stunningly beautiful black woman in seaman's garb, with the pistols and cutlass she could use with such deadly effect thrust through her rope belt.

"Then," he said slowly, "it is from her that you know about the Transhumanists." *But do you know that she was one herself? Probably not. I doubt if she handed down* that *bit of knowledge.*

"Well, well!" said Mondrago softly, with a grin. "So she did it after all!" Then the Corsican's features went blank and he clamped his mouth shut, lest he reveal information Gracchus might not possess.

*Such as the fact that his Order's founder was a Transhumanist who went renegade, revolted by the foul cult she had been sent back in time to establish among the slaves and runaways of what was to become Haiti,* Jason thought. *And to undo what she had done, she had cut her own TRD out of her flesh so she could remain and establish a counter-cult. And thus we left her when we returned to our own time.*

"Yes, she left us with that knowledge." said Gracchus to Jason, showing no sign of having heard Mondrago. "Again, it is only those of us who are her direct successors who know the evil ones as 'Transhumanists.' The others know only that they must ever be on their guard against unnatural men, who cannot be told from true men, who will try to seduce them into unholy rites, even including the eating of human flesh, and promise their worshipers foreknowledge of the future in exchange for serving them. But now we have moved beyond combatting evil cults. We exist to protect the human race, of any and all colors, from the plots of the Transhumanists."

"But let's get back to your detailed knowledge of my arrival. You've already said this was not an oral tradition created by Zen . . . by your founder."

"No." Gracchus's face went expressionless. "This was *not* handed down by her. Our knowledge of it comes from a letter that was written just after her lifetime, we know not by whom." He reached inside his coat and brought out a waterproof oilskin envelope, from which he withdrew a sheet of paper. "This is not the original, of course. That exists now only as a tattered scrap of sixteenth-century paper, kept as a holy relic in Jamaica. But it has been painstakingly copied over and over. Its full contents are known only to Zenobia's successors, for they concern time travel. Others, such as Marcus and the boy Daniel Strother, have been told only the barest facts they need to know. I brought this copy that you might see it."

Jason kept his hand steady as he took the paper.

"I'll tell Marcus and his family they can come back in," said Gracchus. "It doesn't matter what they see. They can't read."

Jason nodded without really hearing him. He sat down on a stool and examined the letter. It had the look of having been copied and recopied by people who were determined to preserve every detail, however meaningless—and much of it must have been meaningless even to those copyists who had been literate. It was in a typical seventeenth-century hand, and equally typical seventeenth-century English. But with practiced ease, he mentally edited out the peculiarities of spelling and grammar, and read it as twenty-fourth century Standard International English.

"*This concerns the events of December 21st, Anno Domini 1864, as dates shall be reckoned then,*" it began. Jason was puzzled at the last six words, but then he remembered that in the seventeenth-century England and its colonies had still been clinging to the Julian calendar, and would not go Gregorian until 1752. He read on. *"In the colony of Virginia, which shall no longer be a colony then, a great war will be raging. A captain of horse in that war, who shall go by the name of Captain Landrieu, shall. . . ."* Jason read a detailed description of this night, starting with the removal of the wounded Mosby from "Lakeland" and the presence of the slave boy who would send Captain Landrieu and his men to the hamlet of Rectortown, where the members of the Order must succor them. But then, abruptly, Jason knew he had entered into that part of the narrative that had always been restricted to Zenobia's successors.

*"But in truth, Captain Landrieu will be Commander Jason Thanou, a man from the future, as your founder has explained to you is possible, not by sorcery but merely by mechanic arts yet unknown. And lest all that the Order seeks be in vain, he must be told—"*

Jason read the next four sentences—the last in the letter—then blinked, assumed that fatigue had caught up with him, and read them over again. But, stubbornly and perversely, they still said the same incredible thing.

*"—he must be told that it is necessary that he journey into his own past again. This time he must return to Port Royal on the third of June, Anno Domini 1692. And there he must seek out Zenobia, the founder, who he already knows well, and who will not have long to live. These things he must do to preserve the right order of creation."*

Jason looked up, dazed, and met Gracchus's eyes. "'Not have long to live'?" he queried.

The dark man nodded, and spoke with great seriousness. "Yes. We know that she died soon after that date. Now all your questions have been answered. And yes, we will help you against the Transhumanists. But in return you must pledge to do as the letter calls on you to do . . . and which, in any case, I believe your own duty binds you to do."

# CHAPTER FOURTEEN

"Sir! Wake up!"

Jason shook loose from a sleep filled with troubled dreams. He blinked and looked up into Mondrago's face. A pale early-morning winter sun was lightening the windows.

There had been little discussion before exhaustion had finally caught up with them, for they were all struggling to come to terms with the night's revelations. Logan had been even more taciturn than usual, and Nesbit had been speechless in the face of the staggering last few sentences of Gracchus's letter. So they had finally allowed sleep to overtake them for a few hours, sprawled on the wood floor and wrapped in malodorous blankets against the chill.

"What is it?" said Jason, sitting up and stretching against agonizing stiffness.

"Angus has just ridden in from 'Rosenix.' And he's wounded."

"What?" Discomfort forgotten, Jason looked around and saw the redheaded young Service man sitting slumped in a corner. Marcus's daughter, as Jason assumed her to be, was giving him a steaming cup of the blockaded South's ersatz coffee, brewed from parched or roasted chicory, beans, acorns, seeds and various other substances. Aiken looked in no mood to complain. He accepted the cup with a shaky right hand as Nesbit wrapped a hopefully clean bandage around his bare, bloodstained left arm. He looked too exhausted to feel pain.

"Angus!" Jason demanded. "What happened? Where's Dabney?"

"Captured, sir." Aiken took a gulp of the brew that must have scalded the inside of his mouth.

With a curse, Jason mentally activated his map display. Four of the tiny red dots were clustered at Rectortown. The other was to the northwest. The map didn't show the farmhouses, of course, but Jason recalled the location of "Rosenix" well enough to know that the dot was on the far side of it.

"When I got to 'Rosenix,'" Aiken continued, "Chapman and Richards were still in the process of sending our riders to summon the Rangers for a morning attack here at Rectortown, as Mosby had ordered. When I told them about what had happened to him, and where he was being taken, they started out eastward, toward 'Rockburn.' I told them you had ordered Dabney and me to rejoin you here in Rectortown, and they gave their permission, so we separated from them. We'd only gone about half a mile when about half a dozen cavalrymen came at us from behind some trees. We tried to run for it, but they came after us shooting. I got this—" he indicated his left arm "—and Carlos' horse went down. I know he lived—he was struggling to his feet—but they were all around him. Three dismounted and took him, the others came after me. I got away." The last three words were said in a voice of dull dead self-reproach.

"You did the right thing by getting back here to report to me," Jason assured him. He understood what Aiken was feeling: as a Temporal Service member, he was sworn to protect time-traveling civilians, and he had failed. Being a novice who still had to prove himself surely didn't help. "You wouldn't have done anybody any good by getting killed or captured. Now at least we know what happened, and of course I know exactly where Carlos is now."

"You *what*?" It was Gracchus's deep voice, rising almost to a kind of basso squeak.

"Remember, the letter said that in our future time we have . . . arts that you don't. Never mind how, but at any given time I can tell where any of my men are. And this man is being taken in the opposite direction from here." Jason noted that the dot had moved very slightly since he had looked before, in a northwesterly direction. He expanded the map's scale to take in most of Mosby's Confederacy. "These Union cavalrymen seem to be moving toward the town of Paris, and Ashby's Gap."

"Except," said Gracchus somberly, "that I don't think that's what they are."

"What do you mean?" demanded Jason, who was afraid he knew precisely what Gracchus meant.

"Before I tell you, Commander, you must give me the pledge I spoke of last night."

"All right." Jason took a deep breath. "I am not a free agent—I can't simply travel in time at my pleasure. But if I can possibly arrange to do so, I will return to seventeenth century Jamaica as you—or whoever wrote that letter—requested. That is all I can promise. Now tell me what you know . . . however you happen to know it."

"I have my sources of information, Commander. The Yankee cavalry have moved eastward, to Middleburg." Jason saw the name at the right-hand edge of his expanded map, on the Little River Turnpike just west of the Bull Run Mountains. "There shouldn't be any of them around here anymore—and if there were, they wouldn't be riding west."

Aiken, who had been slipping into the beckoning arms of exhausted unconsciousness, stirred into renewed awareness of what was being said. "Wait a minute. I never said they were *Union* cavalrymen. Even in the dark, I could tell they were wearing uniforms like ours."

"That proves it," said Gracchus grimly. "The only *real* Rebel cavalry in this area are Mosby's men, and they wouldn't attack fellow Confederates."

"I thought they were shooting awfully accurately in the dark," Aiken mumbled. "Superior night vision through bionic eyes or genetic upgrade would account for it, especially in conjunction with laser target designators."

Gracchus blinked with incomprehension, but he restrained his curiosity and turned at once to practicalities. "Commander, this way you have of keeping track of your men . . . can the Transhumanists do something like that? I mean, can they recognize you for what you are?"

"They can recognize *me*, and by the same means I can recognize them." Jason made no attempt to explain the sensor in the handgrip of his pistol by which he could detect bionically enhanced Transhumanists, who naturally had similar devices, often longer-ranged. "But they can't recognize my men in this way."

"I don't understand why they attacked your men, then. It's a mystery to me," Gracchus frowned. "I also don't understand why they're headed for Ashby's Gap, wearing gray uniforms. That's going into the lion's mouth; Sheridan's army pretty much owns the Valley now."

"Well," said Jason firmly, "solving those mysteries can wait. For now, our first priority is to get Carlos Dabney back. If in the process we can learn what these Transhumanists are up to, so much the better. Angus, you're in no shape to travel—"

"I can keep up, sir."

"Like hell you can! We're going to be riding hard. You stay here. Gracchus, sit on him if you have to." Jason softened his tone. "I know you want to help, Angus, but you'd just slow us up. When Gracchus thinks you're up to it, follow us in the direction of Paris, almost exactly due northwest. I'll be able to keep track of you, of course, so if you can't find us we'll find you."

Not for the first time, Jason mentally cursed the legalistic conservatism of the Authority's governing council. He had repeatedly urged—practically begged—that Special Operations personnel be given simple implant communicators by which they could subvocalize to each other at fairly long ranges. But even a passive implant involving no direct neural interfacing arguably constituted a technical violation of the Human Integrity Act, and the council had no stomach to fight for yet another special exemption. So they continued to restrict their agents to whatever tedious forms of communications the locals used, while expecting them to combat Transhumanists who were *not* thus limited.

They ate as much of the South's verminous cornbread as they could stomach, and washed it down with the by-courtesy-so-called coffee. Then, very cautiously lest they be observed by any early risers, they slipped out the door and around to the back of the shack, where Marcus had tied up and blanketed their horses. Once out in the open and away from the shed, they rode openly along the street, acknowledging friendly greetings from the few people abroad, who assumed them to be Mosby's men. Then they set out on a very secondary road—which, in this time and place was saying a great deal—toward the northwest.

They were all suffering from inadequate sleep and even more

inadequate food, but the knowledge of Dabney's plight drove them onward. And at least the weather had turned dry, although still chilly. Half a mile short of 'Rosenix,' Jason thought they must be passing near the site of Dabney's capture. They continued on past the site of yesterday's wedding and pressed on, trying to overcome their quarry's long head start. But Jason's map showed that they were not going to catch up short of Paris. He wondered if they would have to press on over the Blue Ridge Mountains into the Shenandoah Valley.

After they had ridden about seven miles, with the crest of the Blue Ridge looming up ahead, they turned north toward Paris, nestled at the foot of Ashby's Gap. They rode past estates with names like 'Belle Grove,' 'Mount Bleak' and 'Hill-and-Dale,' whose stately houses undoubtedly served as safe-houses for Mosby's men. In fact, on a couple of occasions they encountered Rangers heading for the assembly that had been called, and had to pause to explain that they were not doing the same because they weren't part of Mosby's command. It wasn't difficult—most of the Rangers knew each other by sight—but it meant delay.

Paris itself was no larger than Rectortown, and less prepossessing despite its setting. They paused to water their horses, gulp a swift lunch at the one "hotel" and inquire as to the passage of a group of about seven cavalrymen earlier in the day, one of whom seemed to have the aspect of a prisoner. Yes, people had noticed such a cavalcade. All the while, Jason watched the little red dot denoting Dabney's TRD moving steadily westward.

They bolted their food, mounted up, and began to ascend Ashby's Gap. Even though it was now later in the day, it grew chillier as they climbed to higher altitudes, with forest-covered, snow-dusted slopes rising all around them, and the air was slightly thinner. Still Jason urged them on, for their cluster of red dots on his neural map seemed to be gaining a little on the westward-moving one.

*We have one advantage,* Jason told himself as they rode around a blind curve in the road. *We know their location, and they don't know ours.*

He was still telling himself that when a tiny blue light began blinking urgently at the lower left corner of his field of vision, telling him that bionics which had no business in this century were nearby. Very nearby.

The discrepancy between that fact and the still-distant red dot of Dabney's TRD had barely registered on his mind when they rounded the curve and saw a man in a Confederate uniform with yellow cavalry facings, standing middle of the road just ahead, smiling an irritating smile.

Jason reined his horse to a halt and opened his mouth to speak.

His mouth stayed open.

*Capture field!* flashed through his brain, which could still function although none of his voluntary muscles could.

It was a fairly common security device in Jason's world, activated either by sensors or remote control, the latter seeming to be the case here. Anyone within it was paralyzed as long as it remained powered. It was normally built into buildings, but Jason had heard of compact, very short-range portable models. And given the Transhumanists' superior temporal displacement technology, and their utter lack of scruples about using that technology to take anachronistic devices into the past . . .

He could feel a very faint trembling between his thighs as his uncomprehending horse, mad with terror, frantically tried to struggle against its paralysis. He himself knew better.

The man standing in the road gestured and three other seeming Confederate cavalrymen emerged from the trees. *Yeah*, thought Jason with sick self-reproach. *The other two are riding along west of us with Dabney, letting his TRD lure us into this trap.*

*But how did they know we were coming?*

The four Transhumanists, who evidently were wearing the tiny devices that neutralized the capture field, proceeded to walk around them, removing their weapons and then lifting them down from their horses and tossing them on the chill ground in a row like logs, with bruising impact. The one who had been standing in the road looked them over dispassionately. Then he took what looked like a contemporary Bowie knife—although Jason suspected that twenty-fourth-century techniques had given it a monomolecular edge—and without any change of expression proceeded to cut the throats of their horses. Blood gushed forth, steaming, and there was a very faint sound as the animals' paralyzed vocal apparatus tried to scream. The stench of death filled the air.

The leader gave another gesture, and the capture field switched off.

Jason's entire body felt like a limb that had gone to sleep. He could only twitch feebly as he looked up into the face that looked down at him.

In fifth-century B.C. Athens and seventeenth century Hispaniola, he had seen leader-caste Transhumanists whose appearance had been genetically engineered to fit a local culture's godlike ideal, the better to found cults. This one, on the other hand, had clearly been designed to blend. He was medium tall and reasonably well-built by local standards, and his features were so nondescript that, in spite of having dark-brown hair and hazel eyes, he could have been taken for a relative of John Mosby. Nevertheless Jason, who knew the subtle signs to look for, knew him for what he was.

And his smile had grown even more irritating.

# CHAPTER FIFTEEN

Jason was in no mood to appreciate the view as they topped the crest of the Blue Ridge and the Valley spread out below, with the river the Indians had named Shenandoah, or "Daughter of the Stars" gleaming in the distance like a narrow, winding stream of mercury under the afternoon winter sun.

As soon as they had been able to walk, their captors had bound their wrists behind them and marched them a little further along the road and then off to the left, following the ridge line on a trail that looked like it would be just barely accessible by horses. Presently they came to a level clearing below an overhanging crag. A crude but substantial and surprisingly large log building nestled under the crag, almost seeming to grow out of the mountainside at the rear of the ledge. A smaller, rickety shed where a row of four horses were stabled stood to the side. They were unceremoniously prodded forward, into the log building.

The room they entered was a study in incongruities: crude wooden tables flanking the rough stone fireplace held a variety of compact high-tech devices. Jason was glumly sure he recognized the functions of some, but he had no time to examine them closely, for they were shoved through a heavy inner door into a smaller room sunk into the semi-subterranean rear of the building; only the left-hand wall had a small window, and it was sturdily boarded up, admitting only narrow shafts of sunlight. There were no furnishings save a scattering of filthy blankets on the dirt floor. While the Transhumanist leader watched, one of his underlings cut their bonds while the other two stood by with leveled Colt revolvers. They were what the Service called the goon-caste types. Naturally they didn't belong to the Transhuman castes whose obscenely visible bionics and grotesque genetic modifications shouted their divergence from the human norm—those would have been too conspicuous in past ages, and even in the twenty-fourth century the Transhumanist underground had to keep them carefully concealed—but Jason could recognize the subtle indicia.

"Your other man will be brought shortly," said the leader, addressing Jason for the first time.

*Other* man, *singular,* thought Jason. *Does that mean he doesn't know about Aiken? Maybe he assumes the man who got away last night when they captured Dabney is one of us here.* He automatically activated his map display and saw that Dabney's TRD was, indeed, nearing their present location. Aiken's was still at Rectortown.

*And how* did *he identify the two of them as time travelers?*

*I'd better not try to draw him out on that. I might inadvertently say something that would let him know Aiken is still at large. His ignorance of that is the only card I have left to play.*

"May we know your name?" he asked.

"Captain Esau Stoneman, CSA . . . or USA, depending on which uniform I find it convenient to wear at any given time, in this typically pointless brawl among Pugs."

*"Products of unregulated genetics,"* Jason automatically translated the acronym—the Transhumanist term for all humans other than themselves. *So he's not taking the trouble to conceal what he is.* Aloud: "I mean your *real* name—or, rather, designation."

"It would mean nothing to you. You'll have to be content with 'Stoneman.' Not very original, I admit; it was the name of a Federal cavalry officer who led a raid through Virginia last year. But it tickled my fancy." The Transhumanist turned on his heel to go.

"Why did you kill the horses?" Nesbit suddenly blurted.

Stoneman (as Jason decided he must think of him) paused, turned, and gave Nesbit a puzzled look, as though he didn't understand the question. "Why not?" Then he was gone, motioning his men after him, and the door closed, leaving them in semi-darkness.

✧✧✧

It wasn't long before the door was opened again and Dabney was shoved through, clearly weary and famished. The food they were given—more of the cornbread that Jason was coming to heartily detest, and scummy water—did little to alleviate the latter. And Jason couldn't let him sleep just yet.

"Did you tell them anything?" he demanded.

"Nothing," declared Dabney with a woozy headshake. "They didn't ask me anything." His head drooped. "I'm sorry I got taken, Commander. I'm the cause of all this."

"Don't blame yourself. You clearly didn't stand a chance. Did they happen to say how they recognized the two of you for what you are?"

"No. They hardly said *anything*." But Jason's question seemed to cause something to occur to Dabney, and he looked around the semicircle of faces. "Where is Ai—?"

Jason hissed through his teeth and gave a surreptitious shushing motion with a one hand. A search by him and Mondrago had failed to turn up any surveillance devises in the crude room, but he saw no reason to take chances. Dabney understood, even through his haze of exhaustion, and shut up. Jason also shot Nesbit a look that he hoped would be self-explanatory. He knew he didn't have to worry about Mondrago or Logan.

Dabney fell asleep. For the rest of them, time dragged excruciatingly by, with no acknowledgment of their existence from their captors. After a while, boredom was aggravated by hunger. Stoneman was, of course, trying to wear down their morale; in Nesbit's case Jason was afraid he would be successful, and Dabney also began to show the signs after he awoke. He himself at least had the distraction of periodically checking his map display. He forced himself to show no reaction when the red dot of Aiken's TRD began to move northwestward from Rectortown.

Finally, the heavy door was opened with a startling suddenness which Jason was sure was intentional. Two goons with drawn revolvers entered and flanked the door, followed by Stoneman. The latter wore the look of arrogant contempt that Jason had learned to associate with the leader castes, although he wasn't as blatant about it as Franco, Category Five, Seventy-Sixth Degree, or Romain, Category Three, Eighty-Ninth Degree had been. It was impossible to avoid the impression that, while Stoneman might be no more intelligent than those other two Transhumanists of Jason's acquaintance, his intelligence was less banked down by conceit.

"I'm sure I needn't tell you why you are still alive," he said without preamble. "You should be a useful intelligence asset. We have a number of questions to put to you."

Jason kept his voice level. "First, I've got one for you. When you captured Dabney, here, how did you know that he and this man—" (he indicated Logan) "—were time travelers?"

This was a crucial moment. To Jason's inexpressible relief, Nesbit revealed no reaction. His relief deepened as he watched Stoneman's face and saw no reaction there either. The Transhumanist's expression reflected nothing but a moment's hesitation before concluding that the information could do no conceivable good to a man already condemned to death.

"We are well aware of your ability to keep track of your personnel by means of the tracking devices incorporated in their TRDs—we naturally use the same technique ourselves. By the time my expedition was temporally displaced—and I believe we come from a point slightly in the future of your own departure time—we had developed a sensor that can detect those devices. It can only do so at a range of a few yards, unfortunately. But it still has its uses."

Jason kept his face carefully expressionless. The Transhumanists' possession of such a capability was bad news indeed. But Stoneman had just confirmed that he didn't know of Aiken's existence—and he wouldn't be able to detect him unless the young Service man came practically cheek by jowl with him.

"So," Jason said, "you could emplace this thing by the side of the road you knew we'd come along, following Dabney, and know it was us . . . which is why you've now captured all of us." (*No harm in reinforcing that last misconception,* he told himself.) "But I'm curious: how did you know what road to emplace it beside the other night, when Dabney and Logan rode by?"

"We can detect the energy surge accompanying temporal displacement," said Stoneman, and Jason unconsciously nodded, for he already knew this was true. "We've been aware in general of your movements since you arrived. By good fortune, we were operating in this area, and some of my men—wearing their blue costumes—were with Frazar's cavalry. Your face is a well-known one among us. Unfortunately we had no opportunity to do anything at the time, but had to lie in wait. And now I think I've allowed you quite enough questions. Soon it will be time for *my* questions. I expect you to be a fruitful source of information on all aspects of the Temporal Service, especially the Special Operations Section that you head."

"Torture," Jason stated rather than asked. "It's been tried on me before."

"I wonder if it's ever been tried on subordinates of yours—especially non-Service personnel for whom you're responsible—while you were forced to watch. But set your mind at rest. I've always been skeptical of the value of torture. It's inconclusive and unreliable. And I don't need it. I have drugs and devices that can obtain the information I need despite any quixotic efforts by you to withhold it. The basic field-model mind probe I have available will take a great deal of time, especially inasmuch as I have other matters to engage me and will only be here at intervals. But we'll have plenty of time." Stoneman smiled as though at some obscure jest. Then he gestured at the room beyond the door. "You doubtless noticed a number of items there."

"Yes: blatantly anachronistic technology that you lunatics are reckless enough to bring into the past."

Stoneman's façade of rational equanimity vanished as his eyes went incandescent with fanaticism. "'Recklessness is what you Pugs always call boldness! You were afraid to use to the fullest the godlike tools that biotechnology and nanotechnology had placed in your hands by the late twenty-first century. But our ancestors were willing to follow these developments out to their ultimate logical conclusion."

"Carrying any idea out to its 'ultimate logical conclusion' regardless of consequences is a form of insanity. The only people who do it are totalitarian fanatics: the Nazis, and the Stalinists . . . and the Transhuman Movement."

"Those others were merely confused, half-hearted precursors of ours. While you, in your fear, crawled back into evolution's womb, our ancestors reinvented themselves as a rationally designed race of superbeings."

"I can tell," Mondrago muttered drily.

"And instead of accepting extinction and passing the torch on to your successors," Stoneman went on, showing no sign of having heard him, "you sought to exterminate them. You nearly succeeded. Now we have to hide in the shadows . . . until The Day."

"Ah, yes," nodded Jason. "*The Day*, when all your plots you're riddling the past with come to fruition simultaneously, sort of like a time-on-target salvo." He cocked his head. "Since of course you have no intention of letting me return to my own time alive, it wouldn't do any harm to share that date with me, would it?"

"I see no reason why I should. In fact, I demean myself by talking to a randomly evolved primate that would make such a suggestion. And besides," Stoneman added with a tight little smile, "you're quite wrong. I have every intention of letting you and your men be retrieved alive—as mindless husks, after we have wrung from you all the information you possess. Oh, yes, we also have the capability of performing mindwipe. It is a small, portable unit like all our equipment—even our temporal displacement technology has limits—but the technology can be miniaturized."

"I know that much about selective memory erasure," said Jason, recalling the single-shot unit he had taken back to the seventeenth century to excise from Henry Morgan's mind memories it could not be permitted to retain. "I also know you're lying about it. It doesn't do what you claim it does. It only erases certain memories."

"Ah, but do you know that it is 'selective' only because of the safety thresholds built into it? Our device has the option of removing all those restraints—*all* of them. When on this setting, it is uncontrollable: it obliterates all memories, all personality, reducing the subject to a blank-minded moron. This process takes practically no time at all. But, at any rate, we'll have plenty of time."

"You've used that phrase before."

"Yes." The Transhumanist's smile grew crafty. "You see, when we return the drooling mass of non-sentient flesh that was formerly Jason Thanou to the Authority, we will do so with an additional twist."

"And what might that be?" Jason could see that Stoneman, while he might be a cooler article than the other leader-caste Transhumans he had encountered, shared their inability to resist an opportunity to hold forth to someone—even a Pug—other than their own yes-men.

"You are naturally familiar with temporal stasis bubbles," said Stoneman with seeming irrelevance.

"Naturally," Jason echoed, although he didn't pretend to any in-depth understanding of the theory. It was fairly new technology in the late twenty-fourth century, generating a field within which the passage of time was retarded, so that a second within the bubble might equal a very long time indeed in the outside universe—an all-or-nothing process that caused time to practically stop. It was expensive, but it had its uses—various medical applications, and also the preservation of extremely ancient sites which the pollution of the Hydrocarbon Era had almost eaten away. Jason recalled the view of the Acropolis from Kyle Rutherford's Athens office.

"In the seventeenth-century Caribbean," Stoneman continued, "you prevented us from achieving our planned technology exchange with the Teloi battlestation that was passing through the Solar System at that time—destroyed the battlestation, in fact. Nevertheless, the surviving members of our expedition had overheard enough generalities from Ahriman, our Teloi liaison, to be able to provide us on their return with certain hints—pointers, if you will. In the world of research and development, knowing for certain that a thing is possible is often half the battle. And the Teloi had learned to fine-tune the temporal stasis bubble phenomenon . . . and even to *reverse* it."

*Yes,* thought Jason, who in the Aegean Bronze Age had spent time imprisoned in a Teloi "pocket universe" with its own customized time-rate. *That would explain how the Teloi were able to pull off that particular trick. I'm not likely to forget it, since it caused me to be the first and so far only time traveler in the history of the Authority to return late—a distinction I could easily have done without.*

*But . . . wait a minute! What was that about* reversing *it?*

As a horrible suspicion awoke in Jason's mind, Stoneman's smile took on a gloating look.

"I see you've grasped it," said the Transhumanist. "Within this building, we can set up a reverse-stasis effect, so that time is speeded up. It has its uses. It enables us to get work done at a faster rate than those outside. In point of fact, we have activated it now. It is difficult, and the time rate cannot be speeded up by a very great factor. Still, the atomic decay in the microscopic 'clocks' inside your TRDs is proceeding at a time rate slightly more than two and a half times that on which the outside universe—including the Authority—operates. They're going to have a bit of a surprise at a considerably earlier date than the one on which they expect you to appear on their displacer stage. With luck, that stage will be empty at the time you materialize . . . although it *does* get an awful lot of traffic, doesn't it?"

"But what about *you*?" Jason heard Logan ask in his usual calm way. "It also applies to you. How can you people operate this way?"

"Oh, it's quite simple. Whatever our retrieval time works out to be, we send prior notification of it by message drop, at a site that is constantly checked in our own time. Thus our displacer stage can be cleared when necessary."

*It really* is *simple.* Jason mentally kicked himself for never having thought of it as a solution to the problems involved in the "controllable" Special Operations TRDs. *I'll have to write Rutherford a memo on it when I get back,* he thought sickly.

Still not really believing it, he summoned up his display. The red dot denoting Aiken, which had been moving slowly along the road from Rectortown appeared to have slowed still further, so that there was no perceptible movement at all.

Beyond the ghostly, translucent outlines of the optically projected map that filled his field of vision, he could see Stoneman's infuriating smile.

# CHAPTER SIXTEEN

"Yup, I seen 'em," nodded the elderly man, rocking back and forth in a chair on the porch of the "hotel" in Paris. "Come through around noon yesterday—a captain and three men, looking like you say. In fact, I talked to the captain. He was asking about some other cavalry that had passed through. I told him they'd headed over the Gap, and he thanked me kindly and rode on, in an awful hurry."

"Thanks," said Angus Aiken, and mounted his horse.

The old fellow gave him a narrow look. "Your color don't look none too good, young feller. Why not rest a bit?"

Aiken shook his head. Gracchus had been skeptical about letting him set out so soon. But his wound was a minor one, and he didn't want to get even more separated from Commander Thanou and the others than he already was. "No. I've got to rejoin my command."

He turned the horse's head and started out toward Ashby's Gap.

A week later, he was back in Rectortown, entering the town at night so as to avoid being seen seeking out Marcus's shack.

"So you never did find Commander Thanou?" asked Gracchus as Aiken warmed himself at the fire and sipped ersatz coffee. Marcus and his family were out of earshot. They seemed to understand that there were things they were better off not hearing.

"No. More to the point, *he* never found *me*."

"That's right: he somehow always knows where you are." Gracchus shook his head slowly. "But you can't find him in the same way, can you?"

"No. But, I wanted to stay as close behind him as possible, to make it easy for him to make contact with me. So after hearing he had passed through Paris I pressed on, over Ashby's Gap into the valley.

"But then the trail went completely cold. I spent four days in the nearby parts of the valley." Aiken recalled those days with no fondness. He'd had to cope with the lower temperatures at higher altitudes, and also with the stress of having to find his way without the commander's optic map display as a guide. Nor had that been his only source of stress. *My second mission*, he reproached himself bitterly, *and I've made a hash of everything.* "I stayed on the Ashby's Gap Turnpike, crossing the Shenandoah River at Berry's Ferry and proceeding to the town of Millwood. But nobody I could talk to there had seen any groups that resembled the Transhumanists with Dabney, or the Commander and the others following them. It was as though they had vanished off the face of the earth."

"I'm surprised you didn't vanish into a Union prison camp," said Gracchus drily. "Before you changed, that is," he added, indicating Aiken's rough farm-hand civilian outfit.

"Oh, I remembered what you'd said about the Valley crawling with Sheridan's troops. I was very careful, until a farmer who put me up— I took a chance and claimed to be one of Mosby's men—let me have these clothes. I kept going, along the road toward Winchester . . . and got to see some of what Sheridan had done to the valley. It's worse than Merritt did over here." Aiken scowled. He noticed that Gracchus's expression was carefully neutral. "Anyway, nobody had seen either of the two parties, so before I got to Winchester I decided that the commander wasn't in the valley; he must have circled around and gone back east through Ashby's Gap, somehow missing me."

Aiken paused, as a cloud crossed his mind. Turning back had been a difficult decision, for he'd been deeply perplexed. Surely Commander Thanou, who knew where he was at all times, wouldn't simply have left the Valley and abandoned him there without trying to retrieve him! His perplexity had deepened when he'd recrossed the Blue Ridge at Ashby's Gap and found that no one at Paris had seen "Captain Landrieu" and his men returning eastward. But he'd been disinclined to press his luck by returning to the Union-occupied valley.

"So you came back here," prompted Gracchus, interrupting his thoughts.

"Right . . . and I've been dodging Yankees ever since. People tell me that Torbert's cavalry came through on their return march on the 27th, just when I was on my way back from the valley."

"Yes. By that time, Sheridan had learned that Mosby had been wounded—in fact, Northern newspapers were reporting he had been killed—and he wanted conformation. But they didn't find him. The next day, Major Frazar came back, in disgrace for letting Mosby slip through his fingers and determined to find him. That was three days ago, and he's been looking up every chimney and into every chicken coop in the county. But Mosby, even though he still has to be carried around, has stayed one step ahead . . . as usual." Gracchus shook his head and gave a tongue-click of reluctant admiration. "Word is that Frazar got orders yesterday to give up the search, and that he'll be court-martialed before long. They'll get him for being drunk on duty, most likely."

"So there shouldn't be any Yankees around here now."

"No, not right now. Oh, Sheridan will keep sending raids through here. And just yesterday, on the first, he stationed Devlin's cavalry brigade at Lovettsville, in northern Loudoun County, where there are lots of pro-Union Germans."

"That's right: yesterday was New Year's Day, 1865, wasn't it?" It brought home to Aiken how thoroughly he had lost track of time; Christmas had come and gone while he had been skulking about west of the Blue Ridge. It also brought home to him the excellence of Gracchus's sources of information. "But anyway, none of them are operating here in Fauquier County at present."

"No. And Mosby's men are taking advantage of it to get him out of the county. Dr. Monteiro, who cut the bullet out of him, is taking him to his family's home in Amherst County so he can convalesce. But in the meantime, this county alone isn't going to be able to support the Rangers through the winter. I've learned that they're rendezvousing at Salem under his second-in-command Captain Chapman to decide what to do."

"Then that's where I ought to go. In fact, maybe the commander will be there."

"Maybe." Gracchus gave him a look that was not unkind but completely uncompromising. "If, that is, he isn't lying dead somewhere in the valley. I'm sorry; that hurts me more than it does you." (Aiken wondered what he meant by that.) "But it would account for his failure to link up with you."

"In fact, it's the most obvious explanation," Aiken admitted miserably. "I just haven't let myself think about it. I've *got* to go on the assumption that he's still alive."

"But if he isn't," Gracchus persisted, "where would that leave you?"

"It would leave me stuck here on my own until April 5, when at some point in the small hours of the morning I'll be snatched back to my own proper time. So I've got to stay alive until then. Which is yet another reason for me to put my uniform back on and head for Salem. I'll need all the friends I can get, and I've got a ready-made group of them there. And there are certainly worse friends to have than Mosby and his men!"

"I suppose so." Gracchus had gone expressionless to the point of coldness.

Aiken recalled what he had learned about the issues of the current war, so remote from those of the twenty-fourth century as to be barely comprehensible. He knew he could never feel, on an emotional level, what Gracchus felt. "According to Dr. Dabney, our historian," he said carefully, "Mosby is no supporter of slavery."

"Maybe not, by personal preference. But if the side he fights for wins the war, slavery will remain, so he might as well be. And don't think he can't be mean. Last November, right here at Rectortown, he selected several prisoners by lot to be hanged." Gracchus paused, and his expression changed to one which Aiken could not read. "Uh . . . Mr. Aiken . . ."

"Angus."

"I still have trouble getting used to that." Gracchus shook his head slowly. "Angus . . . I know you come from the future. So just like I know who won the Revolutionary War, I suppose you know . . ." He trailed to an embarrassed halt, and his expression grew almost pleading.

*Nesbit would have a stroke*, Aiken thought. *But what the hell—my career in the Service is probably wrecked anyway. And considering how much this man already knows . . .* He drew a deep breath and spoke words that violated one of the Authority's most sacrosanct rules.

"Remember what I said about me returning to my own time on April 5? Two days before that, Richmond will fall to Grant's army. And the day after that, President Lincoln will enter the city."

When Gracchus could finally speak, he said only, "I sure intend to be there to see that!"

Salem was easy to find. The next morning Aiken simply rode south, following the Manassas Gap Railroad, for a little less than four miles.

The town was a good deal more substantial than Rectortown, with around three hundred people. Its half-mile-long main street was lined with homes, churches, around half a dozen businesses, and some kind of private academy. As Aiken rode in, it was obvious that the resident population was outnumbered at least two to one by the Rangers who had mustered here. He recalled Dabney mentioning that this was the nearest thing Mosby had to a center of operations; there were many homes in the surrounding country where his men boarded, and it was here that Mosby would, in late April, gather the Rangers for the last time in a field north of town and disband them, undefeated.

Riding along the main street, Aiken passed a nattily uniformed rider and recognized a familiar face. "Captain Richards, sir!" he called out.

Adolphus "Dolly" Richards gave him a perplexed look, then his handsome features formed a smile of recognition. "Oh, yes, you're one of Captain Landrieu's men, aren't you? I'd recognize that red head anywhere! What's your name? Is your captain here?"

"Private Aiken, sir. And no, I don't know where Captain Landrieu is." Aiken launched into a highly edited account, omitting all mention of the Transhumanists and the Order of the Three-Legged Horse, beginning with an honest description of the events of Mosby's wounding, and then stating that he had been wounded and Dabney captured (by Yankee cavalry, in this version) and that "Captain Landrieu" and the rest of the detail had set out over Ashby's Gap to try to effect a rescue.

"The captain left orders for me to follow him at best speed, but I couldn't find him," he concluded on an accurate note. "The valley was too hot to hold me, so I thought I ought to come back here and try to make contact with the Rangers."

Richards looked glum. "I wish Captain Landrieu well in his gallant attempt, but I fear he may have come to grief in the valley. From your account, we owe him a great debt for saving Colonel Mosby's life. That obliges me to do what I can for you, who may be the last survivor of his command. Come with me; I'm on my way to meet with Captain Chapman."

They rode a short way north of town, more or less retracing Aiken's steps. "Bill Chapman is in command in Colonel Mosby's absence," Richards explained as they rode. "He and I are still officially captains, because the reorganization of the Rangers that the Colonel worked out with General Lee almost a month ago still hasn't officially gone into effect. When it does, the battalion will become a regiment, and Bill and I will command its two battalions, him as a lieutenant colonel and me as a major. As a practical matter, we've gone ahead and organized the battalions; I've got Companies A through D, Bill's got Companies E through G. Ah, here we are."

They turned off the road at the most imposing mansion Aiken had yet seen in "Mosby's Confederacy." The sign at the gate read "Glen Welby." A number of Rangers were visible on the front lawn.

"The owner is Richard Carter, one of the wealthiest men in the county," Richards explained. "He's often let Colonel Mosby use it as a headquarters." As they dismounted and tied up their horses, the tall form of William Chapman descended the steps.

After initial greetings, Richards repeated to Chapman the story Aiken had told him. Chapman thoughtfully stroked his black beard—surprisingly thick for a man only in his mid-twenties—and regarded Aiken with somber dark eyes.

"I'm afraid, Private Aiken, that I must regretfully agree with Dolly. We can't cherish too much hope for Captain Landrieu." Chapman's expression lightened slightly. "Normally, no one is allowed to join the Rangers without first being interviewed by Colonel Mosby. But that's not exactly practical at the moment; he's now at his family's house, and Dr. Monteiro says it will be weeks before he can resume command. So I'm going to allow you to attach yourself to us."

"Thank you, sir."

"Now, Dolly and I have decided to separate before dispersing for the winter. His battalion will stay here in Fauquier County, from which it will be conducting raids into the valley, against the Baltimore & Ohio

Railroad. I'm taking my battalion to the Northern Neck." Aiken still had trouble with the local geography, but he seemed to recall that the expression referred to the area to the east, between the Rappahannock and Potomac Rivers. Going into winter quarters at the doorstep of the enemy's capital city, he reflected, would have seemed a rather remarkable thing to do, had one been talking about any outfit other than Mosby's Rangers.

"Sir, if I may, I request to be assigned to Captain Richards' battalion. As long as there's a chance that Captain Landrieu has in fact survived, I should stay here against the possibility of his return."

"I understand. And I respect your loyalty." Chapman turned to Richards. "Satisfactory, Dolly?"

"Perfectly." Richards smiled. "Welcome to the Partisan Rangers, Private Aiken."

# CHAPTER SEVENTEEN

For all its ear-shattering shriek of brakes, the locomotive couldn't stop short of the break in the tracks. It veered off the tracks, pulling the train of freight cars with it, toppling over the right side of the embankment and crashing onto its side with a roar and a scream of escaped steam. Then the car immediately behind it rammed into it and its boiler exploded, spewing red-hot cinders.

The yells of the sixty waiting Rangers split the frigid mid-January night as they spurred their horses from the trees along the southern side of the tracks. The few Union guards were still trying to hold onto the tops of the now wildly canted freight cars. Most of them simply threw away their rifles and surrendered, or else fled into the darkness, down the slope toward the upper Potomac River. Most of the shooting consisted of Rangers discharging their Colts into the air to emphasize the ill-advisedness of resistance.

Angus Aiken blazed away with the best of them, just as glad that he wasn't having to actually shoot anyone as an alternative to being shot himself. Not that he was unwilling to do so, after some of the things he had seen in the last two weeks.

He had lived as the other Rangers did, boarding with pro-Southern families. He'd been constantly on the move, for Sheridan had continued to send cavalry raids through Mosby's Confederacy and nearby areas of the valley. Aiken had seen the results when a Ranger was found at a farm. The fences of such a farm were destroyed, all livestock except one milk cow were confiscated, and a warning was issued that if partisan activities continued the entire area would be devastated and all civilians relocated elsewhere. Aiken was not unaware that such things, and worse, had happened before in Western warfare, but it still seemed to him like a grim foretaste of the total war of the twentieth century. Perhaps the fact that it was happening to people who had befriended him made a difference.

Between these raids and Mosby's absence, Sheridan had become convinced he could economize on security for the Baltimore and Ohio Railroad in the northern reaches of the valley, a long-standing victim of Mosby's raids. So he had dismissed the Maryland 2nd Eastern Shore Infantry regiment from Duffield's Depot, leaving only Colonel Marcus Reno's 12th Pennsylvania Cavalry near Charlestown, south of the B&O, and infantry pickets along the Winchester and Potomac Railroad that joined the B&O at nearby Harper's Ferry.

The reorganization of the Rangers as the 43rd Virginia Cavalry regiment had become official on January 9, with the still convalescent Mosby as a full colonel. Due to some bureaucratic snag, Chapman's and Richards' promotions had still not been authorized. But they continued to command their battalions as captains. Richards, operating in the Valley almost as freely as in upper Fauquier County, had excellent intelligence of Sheridan's moves, and knew of the new weakness. He had crossed the Shenandoah River and slipped past Reno to this spot, a mile and a half east of the now undefended Duffield's Depot. And now the Rangers whooped it up as they ransacked the derailed freight train.

"Lookee here!" someone yelled. "Canned food! This one here reads 'oysters.'" The watering of the Rangers' mouths was almost audible.

"And here!" someone else called out. "Coffee beans! Millions of 'em."

"If only Colonel Mosby were here!" cried Richards. "You know how he loves his coffee." Amid the laughter and cheers of the Rangers, he curveted his horse in the light of the burning coals that had spilled from the wrecked locomotive. He was superbly turned out as usual (his men loved to relate the story that once, when Union troops had taken his uniform while he had hidden in a secret room of a house where he was boarding, he had collected some men, pursued the

Yankees, routed them, and recovered his finery), and with his feathered hat he might almost have been Mosby himself. The resemblance ran deeper. He had assimilated the colonel's methods so thoroughly that the Union high command often mistook him for Mosby; the word "clone" might have occurred to them if it had existed. At this moment, on his rearing horse, waving his hat, he embodied the mythos of the "Rebel Raider"—the last flourish of the Cavalier that the world would ever see.

More and more, despite everything, Aiken found himself regretting its passing. Grant and Sherman and Sheridan were forerunners of the next century, when Winston Churchill would say, "War, which used to be cruel and magnificent, has now become cruel and squalid." Aiken knew he was seeing it in the last few months it could still occasionally be magnificent.

Richards turned to him, face flushed. "We'll have to call this the 'Coffee Raid.' Like the 'Greenback Raid' last October, just two or three miles west of here, when we captured the strongbox containing the payroll of Sheridan's army."

"Sheridan's troops must not have been amused."

"Neither was Sheridan. He's not a man noted for taking misfortune philosophically." Richards was, Aiken suspected, understating matters considerably. "It is, I know sinful to take as much pleasure as I do in causing him distress." Richards' expression grew grimmer. "It was even more of a pleasure to outwit Reno tonight, if only because I understand he's an associate of Custer."

"Custer?" Aiken thought the name was somehow vaguely familiar.

"George Armstrong Custer." Richards grew grim indeed. "He's one of Sheridan's right-hand men, and the cold-blooded butcher who last September executed six of our men he had captured. I don't know how much you heard about that. Colonel Mosby was forced to retaliate, lest more of our men be so treated. In early November, at Rectortown, he assembled men of Custer's we had captured and held a lottery to select seven of them to be hanged."

"I've heard some mention of it," said Aiken, remembering Gracchus.

"No one's heart was really in it. And in the end, we only hanged three of them. Four escaped, which the colonel told me actually pleased him, for they took the word back to Sheridan. Afterwards, he wrote to Sheridan and proposed that such things cease on both sides. And in fact there have been no further executions of prisoners. So, however disagreeable the business was, it was necessary to prevent further barbarities." Richards' expression turned compassionate. "So even if Captain Landrieu and his men have fallen into the hands of the Yankees, and even if the Yankees regard them as Partisan Rangers despite their membership in a regular cavalry unit, there is every reason to hope that they have received the treatment due to prisoners of war."

"Thank you, sir." Aiken knew Richards was trying to encourage him, after two weeks in the valley and Fauquier County just over the Blue Ridge from it, during which there had been no contact by "Captain Landrieu." But Richards, who meant well, hadn't mentioned the appalling conditions under which prisoners of war lived in this era. For the same reason, he hadn't mentioned the obvious alternative, which was that "Captain Landrieu" lay dead in a ditch somewhere in the valley.

He also hadn't mentioned the *other* alternative—that Commander Thanou and the others had been captured by the Transhumanists— for the simple reason that he couldn't imagine it.

*I'd better face it,* Aiken told himself. *I'm stuck here on my own until April 5.*

*And whatever Gracchus might say,* he thought, looking around at Richards and the other Rangers, *there aren't many better men to be stuck with.*

For long stretches, time ceased to have any meaning for Jason, or for any of them.

Stoneman had meant what he said about his long absences, during which they were left in the care of the goon-caste guards, fed inadequate rations and otherwise left to their own devices (and their own gradually accumulating excreta) in the inadequately heated room. Jason put them all on a regular schedule of exercises, partly for the obvious reasons of health (including the fact that it helped combat the inescapable, merciless chill) but mostly to give a certain structure to their lives. But they couldn't exercise constantly, especially in their weakened state. The rest of the time they had no barriers against the mind-destroying boredom.

Ideas for escape naturally consumed their thoughts. But Stoneman never took more than two of his subordinates with him in his absences; there were always at least three guards, and their untiring vigilance and careful procedures never left open any realistic possibility of a breakout.

At one point, during one of those absences, Nesbit cracked and started pounding uselessly against the heavy boards that prevented all but a little sunlight from seeping into the room. That merely brought in the goons, one of whom gave him a dispassionate beating while the two others held revolvers on Jason and the rest. The tedium resumed, varied only by Nesbit's moans.

Jason couldn't help feeling guilty because his implant gave him a distraction the others lacked. He could keep track of Angus Aiken's movements—unnaturally slow, of course—as the young Service man moved back and forth in Fauquier County and the valley, passing tantalizingly near this very spot when he ascended Ashby's Gap. As long as that little red dot was moving at all, he knew Aiken was still alive.

He could also watch the optically projected digital clock tick down toward their retrieval, more rapidly than it should have in terms of the universe outside this cabin.

"Well," Mondrago once remarked, "now we know why we never encountered ourselves—this current version of ourselves, if you know what I mean—when we were in Richmond in April, 1865."

"Right," Jason had nodded dully. "We won't be in this time then, like we're supposed to be. We'll have been retrieved." He didn't add *prematurely*. That was a realization that never left any of them.

The dreary, empty time dragged on and on. Jason found himself actually looking forward to Stoneman's presence, simply because it would be something new.

The Transhumanists' very basic portable mind-probe equipment could only operate upon one subject at a time. Stoneman started with Jason, who had a pretty good idea why, and as he was led out of confinement into the outer room and tied into a heavy chair, he taunted Stoneman about it.

"Aren't you worried that we'll all go *poof* and vanish without warning before you can get your information, much less wipe our minds? Remember, you don't know when we're scheduled for retrieval."

"No, I don't," the Transhumanist admitted as he attached electrodes to Jason's head. "And I lack the equipment for actually reviewing the mind probe's recording media—that will have to wait until we return to our own time. But I'm not unduly concerned. Our analysis of the Authority's operational practices—very predictable, in the case of such a hidebound organization—suggests that your stay in this era should last several months. This will give us ample time to extract the information we want. And, as I've already indicated, the mind-wipe is a very brief process." He completed his work, and a thought seemed to occur to him.

"We have a limited supply of advanced explosive devices here," He explained, gesturing toward a small packing case in a corner, "but unfortunately we have no facilities for surgical implantation of them, or for triggering them to explode immediately following retrieval from temporal displacement. Otherwise we could send you back to the Authority as a living booby trap, resulting in a damaged displacer stage covered with a substance resembling chunky tomato paste—a denouement which you could contemplate as you awaited retrieval, watching the clock tick down." Stoneman nodded like a man making a note to himself. "Yes. I must suggest the idea to my superiors, for expeditions on which we anticipate encountering and possibly capturing Temporal Service personnel. But now . . . to business!" He held a pneumospray hypo to Jason's arm and injected him. "For this very rudimentary field-model mind probe to function, it is better if the subject is in a semiconscious state and therefore incapable of mental resistance. So the process will unfortunately be painless."

That was the last Jason heard as the drug took hold and robbed him of his will, if not of his soul.

It was now January 30, and Dolly Richards was once again leading them into the Valley.

The wags claimed the raid was to celebrate his promotion to major, which was finally official as of this date. Richards of course denied it, although he had, characteristically, had the one star of his new rank sewn onto his collars for the occasion. Thirty rangers had rendezvoused at Bloomfield, a tiny hamlet just east of the Blue Ridge and halfway between the turnpikes leading west to Ashby's Gap and Snicker's Gap. Avoiding the massive forces—two cavalry divisions and strong infantry support—that he'd learned Sheridan currently had concentrated around Winchester, Richards led them north toward their old stamping ground: the B&O track between Harper's Ferry and Martinsburg.

*One more train to rob*, Angus Aiken had thought, an obscure quote bubbling up in his mind.

But now he lay on the roadbed at midnight, watching a Union mounted patrol passing along the tracks. Another had done the same half an hour earlier.

"So," muttered Richards, who like his mentor Mosby believed in doing his own scouting, "they're *really* patrolling this stretch of rail line now."

"Not to mention the infantry details we saw encamped along the line," said Aiken, trying to keep his teeth from chattering in the cold.

"I reckon us derailing their trains along here got a mite tiresome," opined Hern (nobody seemed to know his first name), the other Ranger Richards had brought along. He expelled an eloquent squirt of tobacco juice to emphasize his point.

"All right. Let's get back." Richards led the way as they scrambled down the embankment and scuttled into the woods to the clearing where the Rangers were waiting, standing around holding their horses' heads. There was also a civilian, accompanied by a pair of blacks and talking animatedly to Bartlett Bolling, one of Richards' most trusted men. At their approach, Bolling walked up to the major.

"Sir, this man—a sympathizer I know well—tells me there's a small Yankee cavalry camp near here—he can lead us there—and that they're not being any too watchful."

"All right. The railway is too well guarded. We're going to change our plan and hit that camp—we could use some horses. Let me talk to this man." Richards and Bolling strode off, leaving Aiken to reclaim his horse. As he untied the animal from a tree, he heard a voice—unmistakably one of the blacks'—behind him.

"Don't y'all remember dis darkie, Massa?"

"What?" said Aiken irritably, in a tone he had over the weeks, unavoidably picked up from the men among whom he'd lived. But then recognition of that voice hit him, and he whirled around and stared into the dark face of Gracchus.

# CHAPTER EIGHTEEN

"What are you doing here?" Aiken demanded in a low voice, motioning Gracchus into the trees surrounding the clearing. The other Rangers, crowding around Richards and the civilian informer, didn't notice as they slipped into the darkness. "How did you know I was here?"

"I've got ways of finding things out." The minstrel show dialect was now in abeyance. "I knew Mosby's men were raiding up here, so I had a pretty good idea I'd find you." Was it just his imagination, Aiken wondered, or was there was an undertone of disapproval in Gracchus's voice?

"But why are you looking for me?" Eagerness awoke in Aiken. "Is it news of Commander Thanou?"

"No. Sorry, but there's no word of him and the others. I came for you because I need your help—and it's something your duty binds you to help me with." Gracchus suddenly seemed tense, in the way of a man discussing things that lay beyond his understanding but not beyond his fear. "It happened that one of my men, from the Order, was down near Ashby's Gap. He recognized some Transhumanists—we don't have your means, but we know the signs. He tracked them. He discovered what he thinks is a cache of *nanobots*, whatever those are."

Aiken stared at him. "How could he know?"

"He couldn't be certain. But from descriptions that are part of the oral tradition handed down by our founder, he was pretty sure. I need for you to confirm it . . . and make sure we've really destroyed it." Gracchus paused. "What *are* these things, anyway?"

"They're machines so tiny you can't see them," was the best Aiken could do.

"Then how can they do any harm? And if you can't see them, how did somebody make them in the first place?"

"You'll just have to take my word for it. They're timed to become active on a certain date far in the future. And when they do, they can do all sorts of harm. They can . . . change things, on the molecular level—"

"On the *what*?"

"Never mind. They can change machines so they don't work anymore. They can turn objects into dust, or goo—objects, or living things. Some of them can also . . ." *How do you say, "Resequence the genetic code" to him?* "They can turn people into something that isn't human. Into monsters God never intended."

The whites of Gracchus's eyes showed all around his irises, and when he spoke the Jamaican undertone in his speech was more pronounced. "Mon, you're talking about magic. Evil magic."

"It's not magic, but it is evil. More evil than you can possibly imagine."

"Then let's get going!"

At that moment, Richards stood up from the map, scratched in the dirt, that he had been studying by torchlight. "All right! Let's mount up!"

The Rangers hastened to obey, and Hern noticed Aiken. "C'mon, Angus!"

"I can't leave now, Gracchus," Aiken whispered.

"Can't, or don't want to?" Gracchus's voice was cold.

"Damn it, this is *not* the time!" Aiken forced his voice down. "Look, we'll wait for an opportunity for me to slip away without it seeming like desertion." Without giving Gracchus a chance to reply, he turned to Richards. "Sir, this nigger here says he can help guide us."

"Good." Richards swung up into his saddle. "Have you got a horse, boy?" he asked Gracchus, who was clearly older than he was.

"Yes, suh," said Gracchus, mumbling sullenly as was expected of him, with a venomous sidelong glance at Aiken.

"Then let's ride!"

It was a letter-perfect horse-stealing raid, up to a point.

Approaching the bivouac site with their trademark silence, the Rangers sent men ahead who captured two unsuspecting pickets. At gunpoint, those men revealed the countersign the sentries were using. Richards then chose nine men to go into the encampment with him, while the others waited in the darkened woods to fall upon any possible pursuers.

Aiken was one of the nine, to his annoyance, as he had thought Richards' absence might afford him an opportunity to go missing in the night. Gracchus looked even more annoyed, but he was forced to admit that it wasn't Aiken's fault.

"I'll station myself somewhere along the tree-line, where I can cover you if I have to," he whispered.

"Cover me with what?" Aiken whispered back.

"Give me your Sharps."

Aiken looked around nervously, making sure that no one was watching, then slid the breech-loading carbine out of its long saddle-side holster and handed it to Gracchus. It was a weapon the Rangers used for fighting on foot, but it shouldn't play a role tonight. He decided he'd worry later about explaining where it had gone. Gracchus slipped off into the darkness as Aiken took his place in the raiding party.

Richards sent a few men ahead on foot, using the countersign to quietly capture several sentries in succession. Then he led the others, including Aiken, Bolling and Hern into the center of the bivouac, a long open area with canvas-roofed cabins lining one side and stables on the other. With soundless efficiency, they untied eight horses and began to lead them away.

At that moment, a guard they had missed stepped around a corner at the far end of the row of cabins. He gaped for only a second before raising his carbine.

"Surrender!" called Bolling, pointing his revolver. But the sentry fired first, yelling an alarm that died in a gurgle as Bolling shot him down.

Pandemonium erupted as the Union troopers boiled from the cabins. The Rangers, captured horses and all, galloped down the thoroughfare with bloodcurdling yells, firing at the cabins and sending the Yankees scrambling back inside.

All at once, Hern's yell took on a different tone as his horse's bit broke and he galloped past Richards, out of control. "For God's sake, catch my mare or I'll go to hell!" he shouted.

"I've been expecting you to travel that road for some time!" Richards shouted back with a laugh, as he spurred his horse to catch up.

They were at the outer perimeter of the encampment when Richards caught Hern's horse. As he did so, Aiken saw, out of the corner of his eye, a Union trooper between the huts and the tree line, drawing a bead on Richards. Reining in his excited mount with his left hand, he aimed his Colt with the help of its laser target designator. But even that was insufficient as the horse bucked again, and he missed. He aimed and fired again . . . but he had come to the end of his six-round cylinder. Cursing, he fumbled for his second revolver, knowing it would be too late.

There was the crack of a Sharps carbine, and the Yankee doubled over and collapsed. Richards, unaware of how close he had come to death, rode on, leading Hern's horse. Aiken, left behind, looked at the tree line, from which the shot had come. Gracchus was lowering the carbine. He looked amazed at himself.

Aiken trotted over to him. "Do you know whose life you just saved?" he asked with a grin.

"I thought he was aiming at you," said Gracchus gruffly, with an air of wanting to make that perfectly clear. Then he got down to business. "Let's go. They'll assume you got killed back here."

"Right. This is our chance."

They slipped into the woods, where Gracchus's horse was tied to a tree. Behind them, the noise diminished. They rode quietly away. It was a clear night, and Aiken could tell from the stars that Gracchus was leading him on a south-southwesterly heading. "You say we're headed for Ashby's Gap? Richards' men will be leaving the Valley by way of Snicker's Gap, so for the first fifteen miles or so we'll be paralleling their route. And, like them, we'll have to avoid Charlestown—there's a major Union concentration there."

"I know. We'll swing a little to the west. Ready for some hard riding?"

They had gone only about three miles, and were crossing the rails of the Winchester & Potomac Railroad only a mile west of Charlestown, when they heard shooting to the east. "That must be Richards skirmishing with the Yankees," said Aiken. For the barest instant, he pulled up on the reins and hesitated. Gracchus looked back over his shoulder and glared. Aiken shrugged, and they rode on.

"What if someone sees us riding together after daybreak," Aiken asked after a while. "I mean, my uniform and your—"

"Don't worry," said Gracchus expressionlessly. "Our story will be that I'm your slave."

Southwest of Charlestown it at least was safe to follow the road to Berryville south of that, they had to strike out across open country again, toward Millwood, before taking the Ashby's Gap Turnpike east. All in all, it was almost a thirty mile ride to Berry's Ferry on the Shenandoah.

Aiken had grown accustomed to all-night operations, for that was the way Mosby's men operated. But by the time they crossed the Shenandoah it was late morning, even though Gracchus had allowed only brief stops for rest, and he was swaying in the saddle. But he forced his fatigue-dulled mind to concentrate on the problem at hand.

"Gracchus, we're going to need explosives. What have you got along those lines?" He thought he recalled Dabney mentioning that dynamite wouldn't be invented until 1867. Here and now, black powder was still as good as it got.

"You may be surprised," said Gracchus with the first smile Aiken had seen on him in quite a while.

Beyond of the river, with the Blue Ridge looming ahead to the east, they turned off the road and worked their way upward through rough, wooded country just to the north of Ashby's Gap, their horses often struggling for footing.

"Where are we going?" asked Aiken.

"To meet some of my men, who should already be there. They're full members of the Order of the Three-Legged Horse, so you can speak freely around them—except, of course, about time travel."

Presently the grade flattened as they entered a swale, and a small meadow opened out before them. Two roughly dressed black men waited there, encamped beside their horses. There was also a pack mule, with a cylindrical burden wrapped in a rubber covering.

Gracchus must have told the men what to expect, for they looked only slightly uncomfortable at the sight of Aiken's Confederate uniform as Gracchus introduced him. He introduced them to him by the obvious pseudonyms of Gaius and Tiberius, presumably on the theory that one cannot be made to reveal what one does not know.

"And now," said Gracchus, "you were wondering about explosives . . ." With some effort, he lifted the cylinder off the mule's back and very carefully set it down on the ground. He then peeled off the waterproof wrapping.

It was a large can made of thin sheet metal. Gracchus removed the lid, revealing the can to be full of black powder. "Twenty-five pounds of it," Gracchus explained. "And this is what makes it work." He pointed to a small box attached to the underside of the lid. It contained what Aiken recognized as a clock mechanism of this era . . . except that in place of the clock's striker was a gun lock.

"A timing mechanism," Aiken breathed. "Gracchus, where did you people get this bomb?" Gracchus gave him an odd look, and he remembered that in current parlance "bomb" meant an explosive shell fired by a mortar. Something like this was known as an "infernal machine."

"Well, the fact of the matter is, we stole it from the Rebels." Gracchus seemed to decide a little background was in order. "About a year ago, Union General Judson Kilpatrick led a cavalry raid on Richmond, intended to free the Union prisoners there. It was a miserable failure. One of his officers, a Colonel Dahlgren, was killed. Papers were found on his body by the Rebels, who claimed they included instructions to kill Jefferson Davis and his entire cabinet. I don't know if they really said that, or if the Rebels forged that part to get their own people good and mad. If so it worked, and the Rebels started hatching plots with Copperheads in the North to assassinate President Lincoln." Aiken recognized the term for Southern sympathizers. "We learned of one of these plots, involving an actor named Booth. The idea was to plant one of these machines under the part of the State Dining Room of the White House where the president sits for formal occasions, set to explode when he was there and collapse the floor under him."

"How did you find out about this?"

"We sort of blundered onto it, thinking we were dealing with some

Transhumanist trick. Anyway, it turned out the Rebels had a spare, which we were able to avail ourselves of. Of course, they can still try it—or try something else." Gracchus gave Aiken a look that could have meant any number of things. "From what you've told me, I don't suppose they'll succeed," he prompted, and then paused expectantly, but Aiken said nothing. He had already said too much.

After a moment's silence, Gracchus sighed. "Well, anyway, will this do?"

"Yes, I think it just might. Now where is this cache?"

# CHAPTER NINETEEN

The stultifying months dragged on, varied only by sessions under the mind probe.

Finally Stoneman had wrung all of them dry of the information their minds held—information he could record but lacked the equipment to review. Now he told them, with unconcealed gloating, the he was prepared to wipe that information—and everything else—from their brains, a process that would take only a few minutes. But he kept putting it off, wanting to give them time to contemplate the impending expungement of their memories and their very personalities.

Jason had never been religious, but he prayed Stoneman would continue putting it off just a little longer, after which it would be too late.

They had entered this prison of distorted time on December 23, and—as Jason knew precisely, from the digital countdown he could summon at will—they had been in it for ninety-seven days. He had no way of knowing what date that translated to in the outside universe, although it must be somewhere around the end of January since Stoneman had said that time was speeded up by a factor of around two and a half, a figure Jason had confirmed by observing the unnaturally slow passage of the sun through the cracks in the boarded-up window. But as far as the microscopic atomic clocks in their TRDs were concerned, it was now April 4.

If Stoneman would only continue playing his sadistic little game one day longer, they would vanish from his enraged sight with their minds still intact. To be sure, they would then face the harrowing uncertainties of materializing on an unprepared displacer stage, but at least they would be free of this chill, stimulus-deprived hell.

They all knew it, for Jason had kept their spirit from guttering out altogether by giving them periodic whispered updates on just how close the light at the end of this nightmarish tunnel was. He knew he was running the risk that one of them would crack under the strain and blurt the information to their captors, precipitating the immediate commencement of the mind-wipe. But he also knew that the repeated reminders were necessary for their morale, and none of them, not even Nesbit, had broken silence. This, despite the fact that on top of everything else they now had to cope with the nerve-wracking suspense of wondering which would come first: their retrieval, or the end of Stoneman's patience.

Jason wished he could risk telling them how proud he was of them.

The mule, with its vital and dangerous load, could barely keep its footing as they scrambled uphill in the direction of Ashby's Gap.

A short ride had brought them to the base of a trail, where they had left their horses tethered to trees and Gracchus had slung Aiken's Sharps over his shoulder. Now Gracchus led the way along the rough trail, with Gaius leading the mule and Tiberius coaxing it. Aiken brought up the rear. The air grew chillier as they ascended the slope, but at least the day was clear and the winter sun gave some warmth as they emerged into its wan light in a clear area. Across a shallow valley, Aiken glimpsed a crag overhanging a rough, largish log building on a level ledge. But he had no time for the scenery, for Gracchus was motioning him toward a kind of cairn—really, just a heap of rough stones which only a second look revealed to be unnaturally symmetrical.

They set to work, using a pickaxe and a shovel strapped to the mule's harness to dislodge the stones and then dig in the freshly-turned dirt beneath. They had not far to dig. Presently the shovel clanged against something solid. Tiberius, who had been wielding the shovel, brushed the dirt away . . . and then recoiled slightly as though at the sight of something unnatural—something that had no business in his world.

*As, in fact, it doesn't*, thought Aiken as he stared at the top of what he recognized as a containment vessel for delayed-action nanobots. The dully gleaming synthetic composite material of which it was made, obviously nothing of this era, caught the sunlight. It was, he knew, very long-lasting—indeed, practically imperishable to the slow forces of nature. But it did not have, and normally did not need, much in the way of resistance to sudden explosive forces. Aiken turned to Gracchus and his men, who were gazing round-eyed.

"We don't need to dig any deeper. Just lower the b . . . the infernal machine down on top of it. Then pile the dirt around it. After we've set the timer and closed it up, we'll heap the stones over it, to further contain the force of the explosion."

They set the clock mechanism for half an hour, giving them ample time to descend the trail to their horses and put some distance between themselves and the blast. "All right," said Aiken, picking up a stone, "let's—"

At that moment, a man in a Confederate uniform appeared on the ridge. With an insect-like swiftness that Aiken knew to be the product of genetic upgrade, he brought up his carbine—which probably incorporated an inconspicuous laser sight—and fired. At the same instant the *crack* reached their ears, Gaius staggered backwards as a soft-nosed slug blew a teacup-sized exit wound out his back with a shower of gore that included the shreds of his heart. He was dead before he hit the ground.

Aiken and Tiberius went flat, Aiken simultaneously drawing his Colt. Gracchus went to one knee and fired back with Aiken's Sharps, but missed. The Transhumanist—doubtless smiling coldly, Aiken supposed—chambered another round.

*Yours isn't the only laser sight around here*, thought Aiken, aiming his Colt and watching the little pink dot. He squeezed the trigger, and the Transhumanist toppled over. Gracchus—who had just witnessed what was, by his world's standards, an extraordinary pistol shot, stared at him.

"Forget the rocks!" Aiken snapped, scrambling to his feet. "The dirt will have to do. Let's go *now!* There'll be others."

"Why?" Gracchus wanted to know. "You got him before he could—"

"Just take my word that he was able to raise an alarm." There was, of course, no time to try to explain about implant communicators. "Let's get out of here. But first, reset the timer so there's just enough time for us to get out of danger before it blows."

He smacked the mule on the rump, hoping the animal would run away in time.

*Oh God, he's not going to wait any longer!* The despairing thought stabbed through Jason's mind as the heavy door was flung open and Stoneman stalked through, flanked by two goons who took up their usual watchful flanking positions beside the door like the automata they were.

But then he saw that the Transhumanist's face was contorted with fury.

"So," Stoneman spat, "you think you're very clever, don't you?"

"Whatever do you mean?" asked Jason in a tone of insultingly bogus innocence on which he got a lot of practice with Rutherford.

With a motion too quick to follow, Stoneman slapped him across the face. "No more lies! One of my men reported, before he apparently was killed, the presence of interlopers where none of the local Pugs would have reason to go. So the five of you here aren't your entire party—you have other men, still at large. And you never told me!"

"Should that surprise you?" asked Jason with unabated insolence, rubbing his stinging face. Actually, he was grateful for the slap, for it had brought him out of the numb lethargy bred by his long confinement. All at once, his mind was in high gear again. And he took note of the word *men*—a misconception of which he wasn't about to disabuse Stoneman. Nor was he about to reveal the existence of the Order of the Three-legged Horse, whose members must surely account for the plural pronoun, whether or not they were—as he hoped—acting in concert with Aiken.

The thought of Aiken caused him to consult his optically projected map. Yes, the red dot of Aiken's TRD was very close. And it was moving at a rate that indicated the reverse-stasis field had been turned off.

"Not at all," said Stoneman, taking a deep breath and looking annoyed at himself for letting his self-control slip in the presence of Pugs. "And it's of no great moment. We will simply track them down and—"

The floor trembled beneath their feet, and a roar smote their ears. Stoneman, his restored superciliousness forgotten, rushed to the window and peered through a crack between the boards. Then he whirled and gave Jason a glare whose concentrated and distilled venom was new even to Jason's experience.

"I will be back shortly," he hissed. "And when I do, I believe I will dispense with my original plan, which was oversubtle. I will simply kill you . . . except that it won't really be 'simple' at all. Quite complicated, actually." He strode out through the door, followed by the goons.

"What's happening, Commander?" asked Nesbit.

"I wish I knew." Jason went to the window and squinted at the crack. Across a shallow valley, in a clear area on the opposite slope, smoke was still rising from what had clearly been a black-powder explosion. As he watched, four horsemen galloped away from the stable and descended into the small valley, headed in the direction of the smoke.

Mondrago joined him at the window-crack. They looked at each other.

"Stoneman said one of his men had been killed . . ." Mondrago began.

"Which leaves a total of five," Jason finished for him. "And four just rode away." He left unspoken the obvious corollary: Stoneman, in his angry haste, had for the first time left them with only one guard. Instead, he turned to Nesbit. "Irving, here's what I want you to do . . ."

When the guard heard a blood-curdling scream through the door, followed by a cry of "He's trying to kill me!" he thought of only one thing. His leader-caste commander had ordered that the prisoners were to be kept alive. Without pausing for the reflection for which his caste was not noted anyway, he drew his revolver and pushed open the door to the inner room.

Nesbit was supine on the floor, with Jason on top apparently throttling him, and Dabney stood to the side yelling, "Stop him!" The tableau was startling enough to make the guard momentarily forget that there was no one else in his field of vision. As he stepped across the threshold Mondrago, standing behind the door to the right, swung the door sharply into his right arm, knocking the revolver from his hand. Simultaneously Logan grappled him from the left.

With the strength of his genetic upgrades, the guard flung Logan from him with his left arm, sending him sprawling. But as he did so, Mondrago grasped him around the neck with his right arm while delivering a short, sharp knuckles-first jab to his left temple. He sagged to the floor.

"Was it necessary to be *quite* so realistic, Commander?" wheezed Nesbit, rubbing his throat as Jason hauled him to his feet.

"Had to be convincing, Irving." Jason scooped up the guard's revolver and thrust it through his belt. "Now let's go . . . after doing one thing."

In the outer room, Jason wrenched open the carrying case Stoneman had told him contained explosives. There were a few small, spherical state-of-the-art twenty-fourth century grenades, whose size belied their destructiveness. They could be set for delayed action, but Jason had no leisure to fiddle with timers. He scooped up three of them and handed one each to Mondrago and Logan. Then they all ran outside.

"Keep running—fast," Jason ordered Nesbit and Dabney. When the two civilians were well away, he and the two other Service men simultaneously tossed their grenades back through the door and sprinted. They all knew exactly how many seconds they could sprint before dropping to the dirt and making themselves as flat as possible.

The ground jumped under them and the blast battered their ears. As soon as the small bits of debris stopped falling on them, they got to their feet and looked back. The cabin's roof was fallen in and its walls blown outward. The smoldering rubble held the wreckage of the mind-probe device and its storage media on which their memories had been imprinted. Over the centuries, in this remote locale, the bits and pieces would rust away into meaninglessness and the forest would take over the ruins.

"Now let's move," Jason commanded as they caught up to Nesbit and Dabney. "We've got to try to catch up to them."

They scrambled down into the shallow depression and across the dried-up creek bed at its bottom, then up the sparsely wooded slope on the other side, to the clearing where the explosion had taken place. Nothing was to be found there except a crater, the mangled body of a black man . . . and four horses, tethered to trees. Clearly, Stoneman and his men had left them here because they could not negotiate the heavily wooded downhill slope on the other side of the ridge.

"Here, sir!" Logan pointed to a rudimentary trail leading down the slope.

"That's where they must have gone," Jason snapped. "Let's go!"

They hadn't gone far before they heard the sound of gunfire. Continuing more cautiously, they peered around a curve in the trail and saw Stoneman and his men, concealed behind trees and boulders, firing at other men further down the trail, sheltered behind a large fallen tree, with four tethered hoses beyond. One of the goons was lying still, which doubtless explained the caution Stoneman and the other two were displaying.

Jason thought furiously. He had the only gun among them, and the living hostiles were too widely dispersed for him to simply sneak up behind them and put three bullets into as many backs before they knew he was there, especially given their gene-engineered reflexes. He recalled that Dabney was a crack shot but had no training in unarmed combat. He handed the revolver to the historian.

"Carlos, follow along behind us as we work our way down there, but stay behind and give us covering fire as seems indicated. Irving, wait here. You two know what to do," he added to the two Service men. "But wait for my signal."

They deployed into the trees on either side of the trail and scrambled downhill, unnoticed because of the noise of gunfire and the Transhumanists' fixation on their quarry ahead. As they drew nearer, Jason saw that Stoneman was to the right, with Logan stealthily approaching his back through the trees. *Too bad. I wanted him for myself.* He, and Mondrago to his left, closed in on the two surviving goons. He drew a breath and opened his mouth to shout the signal.

Something—Jason would never know what—alerted Stoneman. He whirled, and for a frozen fraction of a second stared at Logan across a few yards. "Behind us!" he shouted, and simultaneously brought his revolver around and fired. Logan went over with a groan, clutching his abdomen.

The two goons also turned. The one in front of Jason tried to fire, but Jason delivered a circular kick that sent the revolver spinning out of his hand. The follow-through on the kick brought him close enough for a killing solar plexus punch. As the goon went down, he saw out of the corner of his left eye that Mondrago had kicked the other goon in the crotch and, as he doubled over with a shrieking grunt, brought both fists down on the back of his head while bringing his knee up into his face.

Then, out of the corner of his other eye, he saw Stoneman drawing a bead on him. He dropped, trying to use the body of the goon as a shield.

Dabney's revolver cracked. He missed, but his bullet hit a tree beside Stoneman, sending a shower of splinters into his face. With a cry, the Transhumanist fired three ill-aimed shots that caused them all to flatten. Then he dashed away into the woods.

"Don't follow him," Jason commanded, getting to his feet. "He's still got a gun. We'll have to let him go."

"I'd like to see the look on his face when he goes back to his cabin and sees what's happened to all his high-tech goodies," said Mondrago wolfishly.

Jason didn't comment. He rushed over to the fallen Logan, who was moaning with the agony of a gut shot, the most painful of all bullet wounds. The others all gathered around. Nesbit was already trying to stanch the blood flow with a piece of cloth torn from Logan's shirt.

"Irving, you're good at first aid. Keep him alive for a little while, will you?" Jason summoned up his clock display, then leaned over the writhing figure. "Adam, just stay with us until retrieval." If there was a breath of life left in Logan when they arrived on the displacer stage in the twenty-fourth century, the medical team that was always standing by for retrievals would be able to save him.

"I'm sorry I missed, Commander," said Dabney.

"Don't worry about it," said Jason, although it tended to confirm his earlier thoughts about the difference between a combat situation and unhurried target shooting.

"Commander!" came a familiar voice from behind the fallen tree up ahead. "Is that you?"

"It is, Angus," he called out in reply, recognizing Aiken's red head as he and Gracchus stood up. He noted the puzzled look on the two men's faces. Then it came to him.

*Of course. After more than three months of my time, with no opportunity to shave, I must look like Robinson Crusoe, with this beard that, as far as they're concerned, I haven't had time to grow.*

"It really is me, Angus," he repeated. "It's all of us. And it's damned good to see you." He stepped forward and shook hands.

"And it's *really* good to see you, sir. I don't know how much longer Gracchus and I could have held out."

"Angus, we've got a lot of catching up to do, and not much time to do it in." Jason consulted his clock display again. "Not much time at all," he added, to Aiken's obvious puzzlement. "So give me a quick report. Tell me about that explosion on the other side of the ridge. Was that what I hope it was?"

"Yes, sir. Thanks to Gracchus here, we destroyed one cache of nanobots."

"For which," Gracchus added grimly, "two of my men died." For the first time, Jason noticed the body of a black man lying behind the tree trunk, the top of his head removed by a soft-nosed slug. "I hope it was worth it."

"Believe me, it was," Jason sighed. "Thanks. And good work, Angus. And now, tell me: what date is today?"

Aiken blinked. "Why . . . it's February 1, 1865, sir."

"I see." Jason did a quick mental calculation. *The ratio was 2.45 to 1, to be exact.* "Angus, while about forty days have passed for you, ninety-eight days have passed for us." He succinctly explained the Transhumanists' reverse-stasis field to the stunned Aiken and the uncomprehending Gracchus. "So as far as we—and our TRDs—are concerned, this is April 5."

Aiken grew goggle-eyed. "April 5? But sir, that's—"

"—Our retrieval date. That's right. In a few moments, we're going back to our time. You, on the other hand, are going to remain in this era for another two months and five days. Now," Jason continued, overriding Aiken's stammered protests, "it is imperative that you be in Richmond a few days before that date, because I am going to meet you there." *Assuming that the displacer stage is empty at this particular point in the linear present, so that I don't die,* he mentally hedged. "Remember, we're going to have to clean up what Pauline Da Cunha learned about—*after* she learned about it. But we don't know for certain that that cache is the only one left. So in the meantime, your first priority is to try and locate any others. Did you see that man who got away?"

"Yes, sir, I got a look."

"He calls himself Stoneman, and he's a particularly dangerous high-caste Transhumanist. Always be on the alert for him, because you're going to have to stick it out on your own."

"Not altogether on my own," said Aiken with a smile. "I've made some good friends." Jason assumed he meant Gracchus. He turned to the black man.

"Gracchus, it's been a privilege to know you."

"Oh, I think you just may see me again, Commander. As I already told Angus, here, I want to be in Richmond at a certain time—April 4, to be exact." He smiled, then turned serious. "And it sounds like you're going to take another trip to this era, and be there on that date."

"That's right. But first I have to keep a promise and take a trip to a different time and place. An earlier time."

Their eyes met, and Gracchus nodded with understanding. He seemed to want to say something—to want it badly, in fact—but his jaw clamped down on whatever it was.

But there was no time to try to draw him out. "Stand by!" said Jason to the others. "Angus, goodbye and good luck. Gracchus, don't be too surprised by what you're about to see."

"Oh, not much surprises me, Commander. In fact—"

But then he was talking to no one, and there was a faint popping as air rushed in to fill the holes left by five men who were no longer there.

# CHAPTER TWENTY

Even an old hand like Jason, forewarned to the second, could never entirely avoid the dizzying disorientation of temporal retrieval, when the disturbingly unnatural phenomenon of temporal displacement seized him and the world around him vanished, to be instantly replaced by the glaringly lighted, instrument-crowded interior of the displacer dome.

He now discovered that it was even worse when a Waffen SS *obersturmführer* just missed colliding with him.

Admittedly, the man with the death's-head emblem on his peaked cap seemed even more startled than Jason was. With a yelp, he recoiled backwards from the filthy, wildly bearded apparition who had so impossibly sprung into being in front of him, bumping into a woman dressed in an early-1940s-style dress and hat. She screamed, and the pair of enlisted SS types behind her stood paralyzed with shock.

"Murray, it's me!" shouted Jason, recognizing the officer, as pandemonium broke loose under the dome.

"Jason?" said Superintendent Murray Waxman, eyes bugging out incredulously. But Jason had no time for him. He rushed to the edge of the stage and yelled at the medical response team, who stood in ineffectual bewilderment.

"Get up here! We've got an injured man."

That galvanized them. They rushed to Logan's side, pushing Mondrago, Nesbit and Dabney out of the way. Behind them hastened Kyle Rutherford.

"Superintendent Waxman, I believe we will have to slightly reschedule your expedition's displacement," Rutherford said with desperate primness. Then he turned to Jason, face to face with the unprecedented and the inexplicable, both of which were anathema to his orderly soul. "Jason, how . . . why . . . ?"

"Wait a minute!" Jason snapped, and turned to the medics, kneeling over Logan. Their expressions told him all he needed to know, even before their chief looked up and shook his head.

"I'm sorry, Commander. The stress of displacement must have been too much, given the seriousness of his wound."

"Uh-huh." Jason looked down into the still face of one of the most solidly dependable men he had ever known. One more score to settle. He turned back to Rutherford, who he imagined was probably counting the shaggy heads and noticing that none of them was red.

"Constable Aiken should be returning at the scheduled time," he answered Rutherford's unspoken question. "Hopefully he'll return alive, as he was when I last saw him."

"But Jason, the rest of you . . . How . . . Jason? *Jason?*"

"I'm all right." But Jason had to steady himself, and shake his head to clear it. He knew his concentration was wavering, and his legs growing rubbery. The cumulative effects of his months-long captivity, which the adrenaline rush of his escape had held at bay until now, were catching up with him. And, although it should have been the last thing on his mind, he was abruptly aware that he could smell himself, and recalled Benjamin Franklin's witticism. He forced himself to think and speak clearly. "Look, Kyle, I'll give you an informal report in your office. This involves Transhumanists, so Chantal Frey ought to be brought in. But first, let me take a shower and change clothes. And have a medic standing by to give me some kind of stimulant. And it wouldn't hurt if you could order up some coffee."

"Of course, of course," mumbled Rutherford as Jason, followed by Mondrago and Dabney, staggered away, oblivious to the stares of the technicians.

What Rutherford had sent to his office was more along the lines of a high tea. Jason told his story between bites of marmalade-laden toast and gulps of scalding coffee.

Rutherford went into something resembling a low-grade state of shock at the news of the Transhumanists' reverse-stasis field, and was some time coming out of it. Jason could hardly blame him. One of the fundamental, unquestioned assumptions on which the Authority's operational doctrines were based was that time travelers' TRDs would activate on schedule. The only exception to date had been Jason's tardy return from the Bronze Age after his imprisonment in the Teloi "pocket universe." But that had been an unrepeatable fluke, for the pocket universe's only interface with the normal universe had been atomized by the volcanic explosion of Santorini; the genie-lamp could no longer be rubbed. The Authority had heaved a sigh of relief. But now that sigh turned out to have been premature. The old comfortable certainty was gone.

"Well," said Rutherford briskly, hastening to move on to another subject, "at least Constable Aiken was able to destroy the cache of nanobots."

"*A* cache," Jason corrected. "We know of at least one other: the one in Richmond of which Pauline Da Cunha became aware, and which we're going to have to go back there to deal with at a time when the Observer Effect will let us. But yes, Angus did take care of one, with the help of Gracchus."

"Ah, yes . . . Gracchus. Tell me again about him and his organization—this, uh, Order of the Three-Legged Horse."

"Yes!" Chantal Frey spoke up. "You say the Order had its origin in the 'counter-cult' started by Zenobia in seventeenth-century Jamaica after she went renegade?"

"Right. They looked back on her as their founder." Jason smiled. "I use the past tense. But for all I know the Order still exists today in the twenty-fourth century, as secret as ever." Rutherford and Chantal both blinked; they clearly hadn't thought of this. "But there must have been someone else involved in the Order's origin. You see, there's one thing I didn't tell you. I told you we made contact with Gracchus and his people, but I didn't add that they were expecting me."

"I beg your pardon?" Rutherford looked blank. "I must have misunderstood—"

"No, you didn't. And Gracchus explained why. He showed me a

copy of a letter some unknown party wrote around or just after Zenobia's time, setting forth my actual name, and accurately predicting the exact time and place I would show up."

Chantal simply stared. Rutherford, as he often did at moments like this, took refuge in understatement. "Clearly we are dealing with something out of the ordinary here."

"It gets even better," Jason continued. "The letter went on to say that I must go back in time to a certain date—June 3, 1692, to be exact—in Jamaica, and meet Zenobia. It didn't say why, but it stressed its importance. And," he added firmly, before Rutherford could find his tongue, "Gracchus made me promise to do it, as a condition of helping me. I agreed. And he kept his side of the bargain. I intend to keep mine."

"Do you mean to say," Rutherford finally managed, "that you want the Authority to send you back to seventeenth-century Jamaica a second time?"

"I do. And I see no reasonable objection to it." Jason began ticking points off on his fingers. "First of all, as you yourself have indicated, we're faced with a deep mystery here—one which clearly involves time travel in some fashion, and therefore is worth our while to solve. Secondly, we're talking about a target date twenty-three and a half years after I was there before, so there's no danger of any messy situations such as me encountering myself. Thirdly, it should require minimal preparation; I've already acquired the local version of English, and received orientation—not to mention a great deal of experience—in the general period."

"But, but," stammered Rutherford, "it would require authorization by the council!"

"Why? Fourthly, as I was about to point out, you have ample authority as operations director, using your discretionary funds, to authorize Special Ops missions. Especially considering that, fifthly, displacing a single individual less than six hundred and ninety years shouldn't involve a huge expenditure."

"And sixthly," stated Chantal, with the determination that often surprised people when expressed in her quiet voice, "it will involve a second encounter with that fascinating Transhumanist renegade Zenobia. For which reason, Jason, I am going with you."

Both men gaped at her.

She turned her deceptively mild gaze on Rutherford. "You've been assuring me that you're finally prepared to give me the chance to prove myself, but that the right opportunity has never quite arisen. Well, if this isn't the right opportunity, what is?"

"But," Jason protested, "this is going to be a Special Ops mission! You're not a member of the Special Ops Section—or even of the Temporal Service, for that matter!"

"I am, however, the nearest thing to an expert on the Transhumanists you've got. I realize I'm not combat–trained, but this is one Special Operations expedition on which you're not expecting to do any fighting, so that shouldn't be an issue. Besides, the very fact that you're using Special Operations procedures will mean a mission of short duration, so I shouldn't require really extensive period orientation—I won't need to 'blend' for any length of time."

*And you'd really like to meet Zenobia,* Jason thought. *That's been clear ever since I told you about her.* "This may not be one of our search-and-destroy Special Ops raids, but I can't guarantee your safety."

"Understood."

"Well . . . Kyle, maybe she could get more meaningful information out of Zenobia than I did. Let's make that two people, not one."

Rutherford looked at the two of them somberly. "I believe we are dealing here with private imperatives—to which the Authority does not normally cater. However, these would seem to be very exigent ones. And your points are cogent ones, Jason. The first one is particularly compelling." He turned briskly to a speaker on his desk and spoke to his secretary. "Find out if Dr. Roderick Grenfell is still on Earth. If so, ask him to call me as soon as possible." He turned back to Jason. "If Dr. Grenfell hasn't already departed for his home system—Kappa Reticuli, isn't it?—he may be able to provide valuable insights concerning the target milieu."

"Thank you, Kyle." Roderick Grenfell, an authority on Caribbean history, had been with Jason in the 1660s. He had experienced mental trauma from the horrors he had witnessed, but was now completely recovered and had recently been guest-lecturing at various Earth universities. (Time-traveling historians were always very much in demand for that sort of thing.)

"And now," Rutherford continued, seemingly embarrassed by Jason's gratitude, "there's another matter to consider. Don't you want to return to April, 1865 to finish what you began before undertaking this, rather than afterwards? If by chance you should come to grief in Jamaica—"

"—Then Mondrago could do the job in Richmond. So could any experienced Special Ops man, properly briefed. No, Kyle, I have to be sure of fulfilling my promise to Gracchus."

"I see. Well, then, we'll make that *three* people. I'm sending Superintendent Mondrago with you."

"What? But Kyle, that's not necessary. This is a personal commitment of mine."

"True. But I want to make as sure as possible of getting you back alive."

Before Jason could think of anything to say, the speaker buzzed. "Director, I have Dr. Grenfell on the line."

"Splendid. Put him on." They all turned to the comm screen as Roderick Grenfell's face appeared against the backdrop of an academic office.

"Director Rutherford, I was told you wanted me to. . . ." Grenfell gave Jason a puzzled look. "Commander Thanou, isn't it? I didn't recognize you at first. But it is a pleasure to see you again."

"Likewise, Doctor. We wouldn't have disturbed you, but we need to ask you to give us the benefit of your expertise."

"Certainly. I'll be glad to help in any way I can. Do I gather that you're planning another expedition into the Caribbean past?"

"Correct. Specifically, I'm going back to Port Royal, Jamaica, with an arrival date of June 3, 1692. That's almost twenty-four years later than we were there, and I would be grateful for any advice you could provide. For example, any changes that might have occurred in the intervening time . . ." Jason trailed off, seeing that Grenfell was staring at him, and had been ever since he had pronounced the date.

"Well," the historian said slowly, "I can certainly see why that time-frame would hold a certain, er, interest. And I can only admire your courage and wish you luck."

"What are you talking about, Doctor? That sounds a bit ominous."

Grenfell's stare intensified. "You mean you don't *know*?"

"Evidently not. I'm afraid you'll have to spell it out for me."

"Well, the fact of the matter is, four days after your projected arrival date Port Royal ceased to exist. One of the most devastating earthquakes in the history of the Western Hemisphere, together with its accompanying tsunami, sank two thirds of it beneath the sea forever."

# CHAPTER TWENTY-ONE

Their temporal displacement was worse than usual, for the inevitable disorientation was compounded by the abrupt transition from the conditioned air of the displacer dome to suffocating, absolutely windless heat. They were instantly bathed in sweat.

*And this is dawn!* thought Jason, head spinning, as he gasped at the almost unbreatheably stifling air. *What is it going to be like with the sun up?*

The combination was almost too much for Jason and Mondrago, veterans though they were. It was entirely too much for Chantal Frey, who had had only one experience of time travel. She collapsed to the sand. Mondrago was promptly at her side, helping her to her feet.

"Thank you," she gasped, and tried to manage a smile. "I'll be all right."

"That'll make one of us," grunted Mondrago. He looked north, at the bay on whose opposite shore was the tiny village of Liguanea, where Kingston, Jamaica, was soon to be founded as a refugee camp for earthquake survivors. The sun was just peeking over the hills to the east, turning the dawn from violet to blue, and it shone on water that was so absolutely still as to resemble a pane of glass. "Earthquake weather," he stated succinctly.

They stood on the Palisadoes, the long, narrow peninsula—glorified sand spit, really—which separated Kingston Harbor (as it would come to be called) from the Caribbean Sea to the south, and at whose western end Port Royal stood. On his previous expedition to seventeenth century Jamaica, Jason's party had arrived at the eastern base of the Palisadoes and walked the whole way, in deference to the Authority's chronic jitters at the thought of some early-rising local witnessing time travelers appearing out of thin air. But he had managed to convince Rutherford that that had been overcautious . . . and that Chantal might not be up to the hike. So this time they had materialized only two miles from Port Royal.

Of course, that proved to be one hell of an "only" under these conditions. As the sun climbed higher into the cloudless sky, the heat grew more oppressive, and they were tormented by more mosquitoes than Jason remembered here, away from the jungle, for there was no sea-breeze to help. Roderick Grenfell had mentioned that a brief, violent burst of rain in May had failed to relieve the drought, serving only to bring out unprecedented numbers of the obnoxious little bloodsuckers.

The historian had been extremely helpful, altering his schedule to come to Australia and give them a series of in-depth briefings on what they were getting into. So Jason looked at the loose sand of the Palisadoes with new eyes, knowing that Port Royal sat on a thirty- to sixty-foot layer of the stuff, atop coralline sandstone and gravel. And he knew what that was going to mean for Port Royal, four days from now. "Building on sand" was not just a figure of speech here.

Approaching the city, they attracted no particular attention, and given the limited life expectancy of pirates they were highly unlikely to encounter any of their old shipmates from twenty-four years earlier. They could even use their actual names. Jason and Mondrago were dressed as they had been on their last entry into Port Royal, in buccaneer style—coarse cotton shirts, rawhide breeches and broad-brimmed hats—and armed to match, with cutlasses, pistols, and muskets that were flintlocks now rather than the wheellocks they had carried in the 1660s. As before, their cover story was that they were pirates down on their luck. Chantal wore a long colorful skirt and frilly blouse that would cause her to be assumed to be a whore in Port Royal, but if necessary her status as Jason's exclusive property would be forcibly established. (All of this had been explained to her, and she had nodded after just one gulp.) She would be French, from the nascent colony of Saint-Domingue on the island of Hispaniola, so no one would remark on any oddities in her pronunciation of the seventeenth-century English which had been hastily imprinted on the speech centers of her brain. For all these reasons, their preparation had taken less than two weeks.

It soon became apparent that the port was more heavily defended than it had been. There were no less than five small forts, the largest and newest of which was called Morgan's Fort after the buccaneer admiral who had, in 1675, been knighted and appointed deputy governor of Jamaica, with instructions from King Charles II—presumably issued with a straight face—to suppress piracy. According to Grenfell, he had done it with such gusto that Port Royal was now changing. It was still a haunt for privateers, but they no longer owned the place, and outright pirates were regularly hanged on Gallows Point. The sugar industry was the wave of the future, as Morgan had foreseen, and by the time he had died in 1688 at age fifty-three (of dropsy brought on by decades of an alcohol intake that was legendary even among pirates) he had been the richest landowner on the island. The random cruelty of the corsairs was giving way to the organized, industrial-scale cruelty of plantation slavery.

They entered the town, passing the cemetery where, it occurred to Jason, Henry Morgan must lie. *Must look him up and pay my respects,* Jason thought. They proceeded north of the respectable areas on relatively high ground where the affluent in their impractical London-fashion clothes lived in their multistory brick houses—even more impractical, as they were soon to discover. Instead Jason led them to the waterfront district—precisely the area that was going to vanish beneath the waves with the most thoroughness. It was still only midmorning, and the innumerable grog shops had only a few patrons, engaged in desultory gambling that would grow dangerous as the day progressed and more rum was consumed. But Grenfell had mentioned that there were two captured French ships in the harbor, and the privateers had obviously been drinking up their proceeds, for now they lay unconscious in the muck of the stinking alleys between the taverns with equally unconscious whores draped over them. Nearby, they passed the two prisons—the Bridewell for "strumpets" and the Marchalsea for violent criminals—where malefactors were even now being locked into the stocks where they would spend the rest of the hellish day enduring whatever substances passersby chose to throw at them. They also passed Fishers Row, where business was under way and seafood and tortoises and poultry were being slaughtered on the spot just before cooking, lest they spoil.

Jason kept glancing at Chantal, wondering how she would react to the sights and smells of the town known as the "Sodom of the New World." But she seemed to be holding up. And as they proceeded along a cobblestoned street paralleling the dockside, Jason saw that there was one assault to her sensibilities she would not have to endure. There was no lash-driven disembarkation of brutalized Africans from noisome slave ships, as he had been expecting since Grenfell had told them that by this time the island was importing over fifteen hundred of them annually. In fact, the harbor with its huge warehouses and variegated merchants' establishments seemed a good deal less busy than he remembered, although there were plenty of ships tied up at the wharves. A glance out over the unnaturally still waters, with becalmed ships motionless in the distance, showed him why. Those ships couldn't make the dock, and the ships loaded with Jamaica's exports of logwood and sugar couldn't depart, in this stupefying windlessness.

Jason began seeking out dockside idlers and tavern-crawlers, who gloomily affirmed that business was at a virtual standstill. But that was just a conversation opener. As casually as possible, he made inquiries as to a black female privateer captain, leader of a Maroon crew. That got him some uneasy looks, for Zenobia had always been regarded as more than a little uncanny, if not a witch, although no one dared to say it to her face. No one was particularly eager to talk about her, but Jason finally got grudging confirmation that, yes, her ketch *Rolling-Calf* was in the harbor and she had come ashore by boat several times on some mysterious and doubtless ill-omened errands. But no one seemed to know her current whereabouts.

"Isn't it a little indiscreet for her to be here, if not positively dangerous?" Chantal asked Jason. "After all, from what I understand about this society . . . well, she's obviously African, and aren't the Maroons who follow her escaped slaves?"

"Along with a few of the native Taino people of Jamaica," Jason nodded. "Her base of operations is what will later be called Port Morant at the eastern end of the island, near the Maroon settlements in the Blue Mountains. But as for coming to Port Royal . . . you've got to understand that the usual rules sort of go by the boards around here where pirates are concerned."

"'Privateers,'" Mondrago corrected. "Or else 'Brethren of the Coast.' Calling one of them a 'pirate' is a good way to get your throat cut."

"Besides which, this colony passed anti-piracy laws in 1687," Jason affirmed. "These people operate under letters of marque—or 'commissions' as they're called in this period—which aren't all that hard to get. And since the English crown is too cheap to provide naval protection, the privateers are the only defense Jamaica has got against whoever England is currently at war with—France, this year. So however little the respectable element may like a lot of things about privateer behavior—such as their acceptance of any recruits they can get, including runaway indentured servants and slaves—they don't bitch about it too loudly."

Further inquiries yielded nothing but surly uncommunicativeness, and they turned down a side street in search of relatively habitable accommodations for their short stay. They had received the "controllable" Special Operations TRDs; as mission leader, Jason would be able to activate them at his discretion, with the understanding that he would do so in no more than four days, during which the displacer stage would be kept pristinely clear. Rutherford, torn between concern for their safety and the temptation to obtain recorded observations of the great Port Royal earthquake, had agreed to leave the matter up to Jason's on-scene judgment.

"This is the day we're supposed to make contact with her, according to Gracchus' letter, right?" asked Mondrago.

"Right. But before we do any more searching we need to make sure of a place to stay." Jason turned to Chantal. "I warn you, any place we can get is going to be kind of, er, basic. But the further we are from the waterfront—"

"Jason?" Chantal prompted, for he had abruptly fallen silent.

He didn't hear her, for his implant had picked up functioning bionics. Following the sensor readings, he turned a corner . . . and was no longer aware of anything in the street except the back of a figure up ahead—a very female figure, but one dressed in seafarer's garb, and topped with a head of tightly curled black hair under a broad-brimmed plumed hat.

"Zenobia!" he called out, as soon as he could speak.

She froze in her tracks, then slowly turned around. All at once, the sheer impact of her came rushing back.

The genetic engineering that had produced her must have carried with it longevity, for to all appearances she had hardly changed at all since early 1669. But that must have been merely incidental; the real purpose of her masters in the Transhumanist underground had been to give the depraved cult they had sought to establish among the slaves of Hispaniola a perfect founder. They had sought to craft an archetypal African high priestess, if not a living African goddess.

They had, Jason thought, succeeded beyond their wildest expectations.

She was as tall as Jason, who was a tall man in this era, and her figure combined full curves and a slender waist with long, lean muscularity. Her ebony-skinned face featured lips that were full without being everted, and a nose with wide nostrils but a narrow, delicately curved bridge. It was more than a highly individual face; it was a unique one, which rose to a kind of beauty whose universality transcended race and fashion. Jason doubted that even the nineteenth-century white Southerners of his recent acquaintance would have been immune.

No doubt about it, the Transhumanists had achieved their aim . . . in every respect save one. They had never dreamed that their tame goddess would rebel, strand herself in the past by slicing her TRD out of her own bleeding flesh, and devote her life to undoing the foulness to which they had made her an accessory.

"So it's you," she finally said. "You haven't changed." Her voice was low and melodious. Jason knew it could be a great deal more than that if she chose, by virtue of a bionic vocal implant imparting to it a subsonic wave that induced a tendency toward acceptance of whatever was being said. Likewise, her beautiful black eyes were bionic, with various features that included night vision and a capacity to give off a seemingly supernatural glow in the dark. It was all part of her overall design, to fit her for what the Transhumanist underground had created her to do.

By the definitions of Jason's society, she was a cyborg—an abomination. And he now came to the realization that he didn't care.

At the same instant, another realization stabbed him like an icicle through the gut. Or, rather, he belatedly made a connection from which his mind had unconsciously shied despite its obviousness.

Gracchus had told him that she had not long to live after this date. And given what he now knew about what was going to happen in four days . . .

"You haven't changed," Zenobia repeated with a smile, derailing Jason's unwelcome train of thought. He became aware that Mondrago and Chantal had rounded the corner and come to a halt behind him. For a moment they all stood in silence, ignoring and ignored by the passersby. (Minding one's own business was good policy in the streets of Port Royal, and it was too early in the day for many of the local residents to be drunk enough to forget that.)

"I remember you too, Alexandre," Zenobia finally said. She eyed the small pale woman beside him somewhat askance. "And this is . . . ?"

"Chantal Frey, a . . . consultant of ours. And," Jason continued, "you haven't changed either. But of course you know *why* I haven't changed, don't you?"

"Of course. You wouldn't have, even though it's been a long time for me." Zenobia drew an unsteady breath. "So you've come back. Why?"

"Well . . . I promised someone that I'd meet you here in Port Royal today."

"What?" Her bewilderment was clearly not feigned. "What do you mean? How did you even know I was going to be here?"

"Someone in this era is going to write a letter telling me so. It will get handed down by the counter-cult you've founded. I read it recently—in terms of my own consciousness, of course—late in the year 1864, during the American Civil War."

The last term clearly held no meaning for her, nor would Jason have expected it to, even though she was from the twenty-fourth century. The Transhuman Movement regarded interest in the human past as ideologically suspect. So Transhumanists, aside from the leader castes and specialized researchers, generally had very little knowledge of history. *Which also means,* whispered a voice he didn't want to hear, *that she's never heard of the Port Royal earthquake of June 7, 1692.*

But she obviously grasped, and was shaken by, the implications of what he was saying. She glanced left and right to make sure no one was overhearing them. "Let's get to the inn where I'm staying, so we can talk in private. There are two of my men there—everyone else is giving it a wide berth, so there'll be room for you. It's not a nice place," she added in an apologetic aside to Chantal. "In fact, it's pretty squalid. But you'll be safe there."

Chantal's features took on an expression of what Jason interpreted (correctly) as exasperation with being treated as though she was made of spun sugar. He considered telling her that by Zenobia's standards she *was* made of spun sugar, but thought better of it.

As Zenobia led them through the streets, Jason drew abreast of her, matching her long-legged stride with some difficulty. "You never told me what brings *you* to Port Royal at this particular time."

"Well, let's just say you and I may be in a position to help each other again. And for the best of all possible reasons: a common enemy."

"What? Are you saying Transhumanist time travelers are here?" *Hunting me, maybe*, ran his unspoken thought. *If sometime in the future of 1865 they defeat the Order of the Three-Legged Horse and obtain Gracchus' letter . . .*

"Not that I know of. And if they are, you should be able to detect them if they come close. But I have reason to believe there is a Teloi in Port Royal."

# CHAPTER TWENTY-TWO

The inn lived down to expectations, but Zenobia had spoken the truth about its relative privacy. The two Maroons she had left there—one very large African with scars from the slave-lash on his back and no discernible sense of humor, and one astonishingly tattooed Taino— were enough to discourage intrusion by anyone not already frightened off by Zenobia's reputation for witchery. She had paid the innkeeper enough to soothe his pain over the loss of other patronage, but made clear to him that her conversation with her friends was confidential. He kept his distance as she and the three time travelers sat down on benches at a rough wooden table, after bringing the rum she had ordered. It was a particularly ferocious brand of the well-named "kill-devil" which flowed through Port Royal as though from a municipal utility system. Chantal, after nearly choking on one imprudently quick gulp, nursed it along just to be sociable, shuddering at each sip.

"So," said Zenobia as the Maroons kept watch at the door, "tell me about this letter."

Jason related the entire story of Gracchus and the Order of the Three-Legged Horse. He was well aware that such revelation of the future violated one of the Authority's most fundamental rules. But he consoled himself with the thought that this was a special case, and that Zenobia, although self-exiled in the seventeenth century, was hardly the usual denizen of the past to whom the rule was intended to apply.

*And besides,* he concluded the thought, *what Rutherford doesn't know won't hurt him.* Zenobia was gratified to learn that the work she had begun in the 1660s would endure for at least two centuries, but she was unable to shed any light on the letter, or on why its mysterious author had been so insistent that Jason needed to meet her on this date.

"Maybe it has something to do with this Teloi you mentioned," Jason prompted. "Tell us about him."

A shadow seemed to cross her features. "Do you remember the Teloi the *Tuova'Zhonglu* sent to Earth ahead of their battlestation, as advance liaison officer to deal with the Transhumanists?"

"Only too well—the one who went by the name 'Ahriman.'" Jason's eyes met Mondrago's in a moment of shared memory of a night in the mountains overlooking the Bahia de Neiba in Hispaniola, twenty-three and half years earlier to Zenobia but horribly fresh in their own minds.

It had been then that they had learned of the divisions among the Teloi, a race that had ages ago bioengineered itself into a near-immortality whose unanticipated side effects had left them, by human lights, insane. Those who had created *homo sapiens* a hundred thousand years earlier had belonged to the *Oratioi'Zhonglu*, a group or association (as close as English could come to the untranslatable *Zhonglu*) who had exiled themselves on a world where they could reign forever among a race of slaves and worshipers, with no external reality to contradict their pantomime of godhood. But their human creations had turned rebellious, and those of lower Mesopotamia had learned the rudiments of civilization from a stranded spaceship crew of the amphibian Nagommo, inveterate enemies of the Teloi. Meanwhile, elsewhere in the galaxy, the long Nagommo-Teloi interstellar war had ended in a Pyrrhic victory for the former. The Nagommo had won at the expense of their own delayed-action extinction. But the Teloi had been exterminated outright . . . with the exception of the *Tuova'Zhonglu*, a military cadre whose characteristic Teloi madness had taken the form of an obsessive conviction that they had been cheated of victory, betrayed by effete, decadent dilettantes of whom the *Oratioi'Zhonglu* were prime specimens. For millennia they had haunted the spaceways in their grim battlestations, nursing their festering grievances and burnishing their self-image as the chosen survivors of an otherwise unworthy race, destined to restore Teloi glory in due course. God alone knew how much horror they had wreaked on helpless worlds in their wanderings.

Then, in 1669, a battlestation had passed through the Solar System. And the Transhumanists had known it would, having been in contact with the last pathetic remnants of the *Oratioi'Zhonglu* "Olympian gods" in fifth century B.C. Greece. (The *Oratioi'Zhonglu* had reciprocated the contempt of the *Tuova'Zhonglu*, whom they regarded as gold-braided boors, but the two factions had been in fitful communication.) And they had made contact . . .

"Right," Mondrago nodded. "The Transhumanist leader—Romain, Category Three, Eighty-Ninth Degree, wasn't it?—suckered them into a deal with bogus promises of what he could do for them with time travel. In exchange, they were going to give the Transhumanists Teloi military technology. In the meantime Ahriman helped with the creation of their twisted cult by posing as a new and especially powerful version of the Petro, the evil family of *loa*, or gods, who according to African beliefs could be inveigled into giving you your wishes with ritual sacrifice—" He stopped, halted by the memories that the word *sacrifice* had summoned up from the dark recesses of his memory.

"—And promises to serve them," Jason finished for him. "But we queered their little deal when we destroyed the battlestation. And we killed Ahriman, which I should think must have put a crimp in their cult."

"Remember, Romain mentioned a 'small advance party' of them. Ahriman was just the head of a party of three. After you sent Romain to his death and the rest of the Transhumanists were temporally retrieved, the two surviving lower-echelon Teloi were stranded on Earth and left to their own devices."

"Let me guess," Jason ventured. "Those 'devices' consisted of going into the god business."

"Nice work if you can get it," Mondrago commented.

"They had a ready-made cult to sponge on," Jason reminded him.

"That must have been difficult, with no Transhumanist go-betweens," said Chantal. "As I understand, the *Tuova'Zhonglu* Teloi were too arrogant to learn a human language. How did they communicate?"

"You'd be amazed how mutual self-interest can overcome a language barrier," Zenobia sniffed. "The Transhumanists had chosen *houngans* and *mambos*, or male and female priests, from among their acolytes and left them in charge. They were the ones among the escaped slaves who found the cult most to their taste." She grimaced at the ghastly play on words she had unintentionally committed. "Anyway, they and the Teloi were so obviously useful to each other that it didn't even need to be put into words. The priests had a couple of real live Petro *loa* to put on display, thus strengthening their hold on the worshipers. Which in turn made the Teloi indispensable and assured them of survival. Having to live under primitive conditions among a race they despised soon drove them mad—"

("How did anyone notice the change?" muttered Mondrago.)

"—but at least they were well fed." Zenobia spoke the last two words unflinchingly. "You remember that we saw Ahriman getting the lion's share of—"

"Yes, I remember," Jason cut in hastily, not wanting her to continue.

"Well, his two subordinates eventually acquired a taste that went beyond the requirements of ritual. As time went on, the cultists began raiding the plantations of Saint Domingue . . . harvesting among the slaves."

Chantal took a gulp of kill-devil, looking as though she needed it.

"But you've fought them," Jason stated rather than asked.

"Oh, yes. We've kept Jamaica free of them—the language difference helped—and we've even had some successes over in Hispaniola. A few years ago we caught and killed one of the Teloi." Zenobia smiled at a pleasurable memory. "Since then, the other one has gone even madder, and the cult's atrocities have caused it to be widely hated among the slaves in Saint Domingue, which has given me an opening for spreading my message there."

Mondrago grinned nastily. "I'll bet the Transhumanists will shit rivets the next time they drop in and find that their carefully nurtured cult has been discredited thanks to a pair of crazed Teloi loose cannons."

"Unfortunately, the cult is as feared as it is hated. It's very hard to make any headway against it among the ignorant and superstitious—which of course means all the slaves. Also, a *houngan* called Donnez has arisen who seems to be more ambitious and intelligent than the rest. He's persuaded the one remaining Teloi to teach him enough of the Teloi language to communicate after a fashion. By now, he's become a master at manipulating the hopelessly insane Teloi, who goes by the name of Ogoun Ge-rouge, a Petro death-god. You see," Zenobia explained parenthetically, "the 'Ge-rouge' means he's the Petro version. They tend to have the same names as the Rada, or good *loa*."

"I'm confused," said Mondrago forthrightly.

"You're not the only one to react that way," Zenobia assured him.

"But the point is," said Chantal, attempting to drag the discussion back to practicalities, "according to you, that Teloi is now in Port Royal." She shook her head. "Wouldn't he be a little bit conspicuous here?"

"My sources of information indicate that Donnez has managed to find a ship whose captain was willing, if paid well enough, to bring in himself and a few adepts . . . and a certain large crate. The problem, of course, would be getting the crate ashore and finding a place of concealment. They probably haven't done so yet, in this damned weather. We've been watching the docks."

"But why are they going to the trouble?" wondered Jason.

"They must be making a serious attempt to get their cult established in Jamaica. Also," Zenobia added calmly, "they're probably hunting for me. Ogoun Ge-rouge would have insisted on being in on that, for revenge. He and the other Teloi had become homosexual lovers, you see. I gather that sort of thing works more or less the same way among the Teloi as among us." She dismissed the subject with a toss of her head. "Anyway, Jason, this is just what your Special Operations Section exists to combat. Will you help us?"

"Yes, of course." Jason met her eyes and saw nothing else besides those eyes, not even the sharp looks he was getting from Mondrago and Chantal. "We'll do whatever we can, for as long as we can stay."

*Which,* he reminded himself, *isn't going to be long. After which, the Observer Effect says she's going to die.*

*How much can I justify telling her?*

It was the following afternoon, and Jason and Zenobia stood in the cemetery on the Palisadoes, gazing at Henry Morgan's tomb. The air was as motionless as it had been the day before, and the water in the distance as smooth, and it was all very peaceful. It seemed impossible that the quiet tomb could contain the spirit of the overgrown roaring boy Jason had known.

"I was here four years ago when he died," said Zenobia. "He had been going to a folk doctor among his slaves, and also to the local *obeah* man or spirit doctor. He told me he liked them better than his Western doctors because they didn't try to make him stop drinking. But neither sort could do him any good by that time." She gave a sigh of reminiscence. "For his funeral, the governor issued a twenty-four hour amnesty. A lot of ships flying no flag showed up, and there were so many men with prices on their heads walking around the streets that it was almost like old times. When they interred him, the Royal Navy ships in port fired a twenty-two gun salute."

"I thought twenty-one was the regulation number for a former governor."

"So it is. But this was *Morgan*."

"Yes. He was always an exception to a lot of rules, wasn't he?" For a long moment, nothing else needed to be said. "It must have been quite a funeral," Jason finally continued. "But . . . I imagine you and your Maroons held your own ceremony."

Zenobia gave him a look of new appreciation. "Henri must have told you a few things," she said, referring to Dr. Henri Boyer, the expert in Caribbean folkways who had fought beside her and given his life to save hers.

"He did. He told me about the duppy: the spirit that gives the body power when it is alive, and which can cause much harm to the living if it's allowed to get loose after the body dies, without the restraint of the heart and brain—at least if the duppy is a powerful one." Jason gave her a quizzical look. "You don't literally believe in any of this, do you?"

"After so many years among the Maroons . . . I'm not so sure. At any rate, my men certainly do. And if ever there was a duppy that could wreak havoc, it was Morgan's!" She smiled at memories of Morgan . . . and, Jason strongly suspected, of Henri Boyer. "We couldn't do a proper *Koo-min-ah* ceremony because we didn't have access to the body. But at least we had all nine nights to try our best. With any luck, his duppy will stay in the grave where it belongs."

*But the body won't, according to Roderick Grenfell. His coffin will be last seen floating out to sea, when this ground dissolves.* Jason looked down at the sand, and recalled what was going to happen to it in two days. So many things kept reminding him of that.

"It must have seemed strange, talking to him at the end. After all, you remembered going into space with him, when we destroyed the Teloi battlestation." A thought occurred to Jason. "You didn't—?"

"Oh, no. I didn't tell him anything about the parts of his memory you had told me you were going to come back and wipe. Not that it would have done any harm at that point; he would have thought I was talking nonsense. But it was tempting. He would have thought it was a damned good story."

"But you still didn't."

"Of course I didn't." Her voice dropped. "I had promised you I wouldn't, hadn't I?"

They walked back into the waterfront district. The heat was as stifling as ever, but Jason overheard people commenting that at least there had been none of Port Royal's chronic minor earth tremors lately. He knew what that really meant: the Earth was gathering its forces.

He realized he probably wasn't very good company. He started to say something apologetic about it, but the thought made him realize that Zenobia seemed equally lost in her own thoughts. They walked on in silence to the inn. The interior was deserted, for the others were out taking their turn watching the docks.

Abruptly, Zenobia spoke. "I've never forgotten you, you know. But it's been a long time. Why didn't you come back at an earlier date?"

"I've told you why I had to come here yesterday," he reminded her. *And nothing happened yesterday. So why did the letter specify June 4?* "But I probably should have."

"And of course, you never *will* come back, at some later point in your own lifetime, to a date earlier than this. Because if so, I'd already remember it, wouldn't I?" She shook her head at the perplexities of time travel, then turned and met his eyes. "I wish you had."

A moment passed before Jason trusted himself to speak. "I thought it was Henri that you—"

"Oh, I'll never forget him. But he's been dead for almost twenty-four years of my lifetime. And after he died . . . when we were stranded and took that trek along the southern shore of Hispaniola, and I got to know you . . ." Her eyes shifted away, and her voice dropped almost to a whisper. "I never told you." Then her eyes took his again, and would not let go.

"I never told you either," he heard himself say.

*This is insane,* he frantically told himself. *I'm not some adolescent boy letting his balls do his thinking for him. And this is wrong on every conceivable level. It would be wrong even if I didn't know she's going to die shortly and can't tell her I know. And—*

And then she was in his arms and none of that mattered any more.

# CHAPTER TWENTY-THREE

"Sir, I need to have a word with you in private."

That got Jason's attention. For Mondrago to say "Sir" in that formal tone of voice was unusual, and generally ominous. His facial expression went with it.

"All right, Alexandre." Jason took off his hat and wiped the sweat from his hair, for he had just come into the common room of the inn from the afternoon heat where Zenobia was still observing the docks. "Let's go upstairs."

They left the area of the door, where the Taino Maroon was keeping watch in his usual inscrutable silence. Walking toward the rickety stairs, they passed a table where Chantal sat in stony, tight-lipped silence. She had done that a lot lately. Jason wondered why.

Once they were in the upper room—more like a loft, really—Jason sat down, for his head barely had clearance. He waited for Mondrago to speak up, but the Corsican suddenly seemed overtaken by awkwardness.

"Go ahead, Alexandre," Jason prompted, "you can speak freely." He essayed an encouraging smile. "Besides, I already know you're an insubordinate smartass, so you've got nothing to lose."

Mondrago did not smile back. "All right, I'll say it flat out. What the hell do you think you're doing?"

Jason sighed. He had known this was coming, but had been in no frame of mind to worry about it. "I won't pretend I don't know what you're talking about. And I won't answer your question with any of the bad jokes that spring to mind."

Mondrago drew a deep breath. "Sir, ever since day before yesterday, it's been pretty obvious what you and Zenobia were up to that night—you haven't exactly succeeded in being discreet about it. And you've been at it ever since, whenever you got the chance. How you still have the strength to go out and search for the Teloi is beyond me. Now, don't get me wrong: not for the world would I begrudge any man his jollies. But this is crazy! It's now June 6. You know what's going to happen tomorrow."

"Yes, I know," said Jason miserably.

"Then you know we can't stay any longer than that. Remember the guidelines: you have to activate our 'controllable' TRDs and take us all home as soon as it becomes unsafe for us to stay here and observe any longer. *Are you going to be able to do that?*"

Jason said nothing.

"Furthermore," Mondrago continued inexorably, "you also know that Zenobia is going to die soon. Has it occurred to you that maybe she dies tomorrow in the earthquake? It's sort of the obvious way to go around this time; thousands of others will."

"Of course it's occurred to me!" snapped Jason, guiltily aware that in fact he had been stubbornly pushing it out of his mind.

"But have you carried the thought one step further? If that is in fact the way she dies, maybe you're the *cause* of her death."

"What the hell are you talking about?"

"Think about it—if you're in any shape to think straight just now. There's been no sign of the Teloi. If we hadn't met Zenobia on the third, she might have decided by now that it's just a wild goose chase, and given up and left Port Royal. As it is, ever since day before yesterday she's been in no hurry to leave—thanks to *you*. You're the reason she's going to be here tomorrow morning."

Jason was again silent, face to face with a possibility he had not considered because he had not been in a mood to consider it. His state of denial about Zenobia's impending death and its perfectly logical linkage with tomorrow's disaster had shielded him from it.

"And don't forget," said Mondrago, softening his tone a notch or two, "with that digital clock in your head, you're going to know exactly when it's going to happen."

"Eleven forty-three A. M.," Jason nodded. Grenfell had explained to them that a stopped pocket watch had been recovered from the bottom of the harbor in the 1960s, allowing the time of the catastrophe to be pinned down so precisely.

"So," Mondrago continued implacably, "watching that countdown tick down, are you going to be able to deal with it?"

"I'll tell you in the morning," said Jason, and turned away.

June 7 was the most unbearably hot and stifling morning yet. The oppressive air matched the mood that hung over Port Royal, and, indeed, contributed to it.

For the past three days, they had seen the signs. Half-crazed men wandered up and down Market Street, ranting that God's judgment was at hand. Their message resonated more than it would have most places, here in this town built on privateering and best known for drunkenness and whoring; the various clergymen had been saying the same thing, in their more decorous way, for a long time. And an astrologer had recently added his prediction of impending disaster. Not to mention the usual sorts of rumors—unrest among the slaves, French raids on Jamaica's northern coast. Small wonder that the earliest risers on this enervating morning included physicians, scurrying to dispense "cures" such as rum punches and opium-based elixirs to their patients, notably the high-strung wives of wealthy merchants.

Jason, Mondrago and Chantal rose early, for the heat and their foreknowledge made sleep out of the question. It left them with time on their hands, and also privacy, for Zenobia and her Maroons were still out. So Jason knew certain matters could no longer be evaded.

But he didn't care, for in the course of the sleepless night he had come to a decision. Now he felt the fatalistic calm of irrevocable commitment.

Mondrago and Chantal looked like he was fairly sure he himself did, with puffy, shadowed eyes in exhaustion-hollowed faces. He imagined they also shared his slightly headachy feeling. But Chantal seemed somehow less surly than she had the past couple of days. Perhaps, Jason thought, she was drawing strength from Mondrago, to whom she was keeping almost clingingly close despite the heat. They both looked as though they were expecting him to say something. They also looked puzzled by his seeming serenity.

The silence had grown brittle when Mondrago finally broke it. "Well? How much longer?"

Jason summoned up his clock display. It was 9:31. "A little over two hours to go."

"So at what point do you plan to activate the TRDs?"

"I haven't decided yet. As you know, I have the discretion to determine the exact moment. Of course I'll give you warning. And . . . there's one thing I need to make sure of before I do it."

Chantal began to look apprehensive. "What would that be?"

Jason met her eyes unflinchingly. "I'm going to tell Zenobia about the earthquake. And if it appears that she's in danger of being killed in it, I'm going to save her."

For a time, they simply stared at him, motionless in the unnaturally still heat.

"Are you out of your goddamned mind?" Mondrago finally blurted. "Sir," he added as an afterthought.

Chantal spoke, her voice charged with an urgency that momentarily banished all her earlier resentments. "Jason, you *can't*! The Observer Effect—"

"I'm well aware of the Observer Effect. But we don't *know* that she's due to die in the earthquake. We've just been assuming that, because it's such an obvious way for her to go. *If* she does!" Jason looked back and forth between his two listeners, urging them with his eyes as he extemporized freely. "Think about it: the only proof we have of her death around this time—the only thing that makes it part of 'observed history'—is Gracchus's letter, whose writer is unknown, so we can't exactly verify his reliability. Maybe he was wrong! Maybe she *doesn't* need to die! Maybe—"

"I can't believe I'm hearing this bullshit," Mondrago cut in coldly. "It's the purest kind of rationalization. You're just trying to convince yourself."

That which had been smoldering inside Chantal for two days burst into a flame that glared through her eyes. "And we know *why* you are, don't we?" she hissed.

Jason met her glare with one of his own. "My motives are none of your concern—just as my relationships are none of your business. At any rate I've made my decision. And, over and above the legalities of my position as mission leader, I'm the one with the implant that controls all our TRDs. So what I say goes."

Chantal's expression changed to one of near-desperation. "Jason . . . I'm sorry. I shouldn't have said that. But surely you must understand that you can't do this!"

At that moment, the door was flung open and Zenobia strode into the inn, followed by the two Maroons.

"I can't?" Jason said quietly to Chantal. "Just watch me!" He turned, and he and Zenobia met in a quick, hard embrace.

"Zenobia, listen carefully. There's something urgent I have to tell you. Two hours from now—"

"Later, Jason. There's no time now. Come on, we've got to go."

"But Zenobia—"

"Jason, *we've located the Teloi!*" Zenobia's dark eyes, bionic or no, were alight, for now the hunt was on in earnest. "You and Alexandre get your weapons. Chantal, you probably ought to stay here."

"Like hell!" snapped Chantal, out of character.

"Well . . . maybe it would be best if we all keep together. Now, everyone get moving!" And Zenobia was out the door, the Maroons in tow. Jason and the others could only follow.

She led them north, into the most noisome parts of the dockside area. *And even deeper into the area that's going to fall into the sea,* Jason thought. He resisted the temptation to consult his clock display. Instead, he hastened his steps, catching up to Zenobia.

"What happened?" he demanded. "How did you find him?"

"You know that ship that's been lying out in the harbor to the east, flying no flag?"

"Yes. With all the paranoia around here, people thought it was a pirate or a French scout. But the last I heard, it had turned out to be a Bristol merchantman that had somehow managed to work its way in using whatever occasional breeze came along, and was waiting for this morning to offload its cargo and passengers."

"Right. Well, it turns out that on the way here it stopped in Hispaniola for food and water. While it was there, the *houngan* Donnez used loot his followers had stolen from the French plantations to buy passage here. But they've been becalmed, so they didn't get here on schedule."

"That must have been fun for the Teloi," remarked Mondrago, who had also caught up despite his relatively short legs, with Chantal somehow keeping abreast. "Didn't you say something about a large crate . . . ?"

"Yes." Zenobia's expression was notably devoid of sympathy. "The ship's captain off-loaded at dawn today, which was why we missed it last night. My informants among the dockworkers tell me that the box was brought ashore then, by boat, and that it was hastily taken to a location somewhere around here. We need to split up and cover as much territory as possible."

"Right. But let's stay in groups of three. I'll be able to track you, as long as we don't get too far separated, because I can detect your bionics." *Unfortunately, she'll have no way of knowing where I am,* Jason reflected. *And God knows when I'm going to get another chance to talk to her. And . . . the clock is still ticking.* "Alexandre, Chantal, let's go!"

They headed right, in the maze of alleys, while Zenobia led the two Maroons to the left. Jason's map display was of some use, for the general layout of Port Royal was known to twenty-fourth-century scholars; otherwise it would have been easy to get lost in the chaotic, tightly packed warren of taverns, whorehouses, and assorted mercantile houses of varying degrees of disreputability. Jason fought down his anxiety and forced himself to methodically seek information. As he did so, he saw the little blue dot that denoted Zenobia's position flicker and go out as her own search had led her outside the implant sensor's very limited range.

A series of inquiries at various establishments finally yielded a tavern keeper's nodding recollection of having seen "some niggers with a prodigious great wooden chest" headed up a certain alley not long before. Jason led the way, noting with relief that the blue dot had reappeared. She had evidently looped back around, having found nothing in her area. *If only I had a means of communicating with her . . .*

"Chantal, get behind us," he said as they reached the corner of the alley. "And no argument!" He and Mondrago hefted their muskets to the position of high port, and they rounded the corner.

There were only a few passersby in the narrow, noisome street. About halfway along it, a black man in sailor's garb, armed with a musket, stood watchfully outside a shack that leaned against the side of a somewhat more substantial structure. He spotted them at once, and something about their approach warned him. He brought up his musket and aimed it. At once, Jason and Mondrago did the same.

The bystanders immediately scattered, always a good policy at moments like this in Port Royal. For a moment the tableau held. Then a scream from behind them split the air. Jason whirled, to see a black man with his left arm around Chantal's throat. His right hand held a dagger in an underhand grip, its point just over her heart. When he spoke, his voice held the accent of a native speaker of the French-based slave *patois* of Saint Domingue.

"Since this bitch is white, maybe you care whether or not she's killed. So lower your muskets."

# CHAPTER TWENTY-FOUR

For a time that seemed longer than it was, the standoff remained frozen in place.

Mondrago and the guard by the door continued to cover each other with their muskets across a distance of a few yards, although the former's eyes occasionally flicked over his shoulder in the direction of Chantal and her captor. Jason remained facing in that direction, musket leveled but unwilling to risk attempting a head shot with such a crude and misfire-prone firearm, even at this range.

The man holding Chantal shattered the moment with a harsh rasp. "I said drop your weapons, you damned slavers!" he pressed the knife-point against Chantal's blouse, eliciting a choked yelp.

"That would be real smart on our part, wouldn't it?" Jason forced himself to speak levelly. "I've got a better idea: you release her, alive and unharmed. Your other choice is to die . . . and my friend here knows how to make it last."

The man's eyes ignited with the most intense hate Jason had ever seen on a human face. "Oh, yes," he said, almost crooning, "I know all about how you slavers know how to make it last! Like the way you nail a rebellious slave flat on the ground with crooked sticks and burn him alive little by little, first the hands and then the legs and then the head!"

"We're not slavers—" Jason began. But the man was now in full rant, his voice rising gradually to a full-throated shriek.

"Liar! All you *blancs* are slavers! And you can feel like good Christians at the same time, because black people don't matter, do they? God made black people out of His own shit, didn't He? *Didn't He?*"

"It's too bad you feel that way about yourself," said Jason quietly. "But don't put it on me."

At once, he decided he'd gone too far. The dark face was transported with a rage that left no room for anything else, not even self-preservation, not even sanity. The man's body quivered with the force of his need to plunge the dagger through Chantal's white skin and into her heart.

Jason's trigger finger tensed as he prepared for a desperate shot.

From behind him a familiar voice shouted, "Donnez!"

Jason, who hadn't exactly been paying attention to the little blue dot of his sensor, risked a quick glance over his shoulder. Beyond Mondrago and the guard he was facing, Zenobia stood at the far end of the alley, cutlass in her right hand and flintlock pistol in her left.

"You!" hissed the *houngan*, his captive momentarily forgotten. "Don't try your tricks on me, witch! I know about them, so you have no power over me." This, Jason knew, was true. Zenobia's vocal enhancement implant could not overcome conscious resistance to its siren song by a target who was aware of it.

She advanced a couple of steps into the alley, leveling her pistol. "I can still put a lead ball through your putrid guts." Behind her, the two Maroons appeared, muskets at the ready.

The guard at the door, now caught between Mondrago (who had kept his musket motionlessly leveled through all of this) and the new arrivals, was beginning to look jittery. He blurted something in the slave *patois*. The door opened cautiously and two other musket-armed black men emerged from the shack, pointing their weapons at Zenobia and her men with cautious slowness.

Jason forced himself to keep his attention focused on the sights of his musket, keeping Donnez covered, not daring to move even though he knew he was in Zenobia's line of fire. *This standoff is getting both complicated and crowded,* he thought.

What finally broke it was almost farcical.

Three piratical-looking seamen, who had obviously gotten started early on the day's drinking, came lurching around the corner into the far end of the alley, behind Zenobia and her Maroons. Their purpose in entering the alley was clear, for one of them was awkwardly lowering his pants. The other two immediately came to a goggle-eyed halt, as the realization of what was transpiring in the alley penetrated the alcohol mist. But the one seeking to urinate, absorbed in the task of untying his rope belt, staggered into the Taino, sending him off balance.

At once, the tableau dissolved with an ear-shattering blast of musketry, and the alley filled with the rotten-eggs smell of burning black powder.

One of the newly-emerged cultists fired first, sending a musket ball into the Taino's midriff. His companion also got off a shot, but missed the other Maroon and hit one of the drunks. Some small fraction of a second later, Zenobia brought him down with a pistol shot. At the same instant, Mondrago fired, and the first guard slammed back against the door of the shed before sliding to the ground, painting a trail of blood down the door from the brain matter adhering to it.

Just as Jason was turning, Chantal gave a heave that must have taken every erg of strength in her slight body, jabbed an elbow backwards into the *houngan*'s stomach, and broke free, dropping so the knife only raked her shoulder. She fell to the ground with a sobbing gasp of pain.

*Ha!* thought Jason exultantly as he brought his musket to bear on the now exposed Donnez.

As he began to squeeze the trigger, there was a crash behind him. He involuntarily looked over his shoulder, just in time to see the shed's door flung open with a force that sent the one surviving guard sprawling forward onto the point of Zenobia's cutlass. With a powerful thrust, she drove the weapon through him, its bloody blade emerging through his back.

But no one paid attention, for what now emerged from the open door in a crouch and rose to its full height had no business in this world.

It all came back to Jason in a rush. The nearly eight-foot stature. The almost dead-white skin. The fine hair like an alloy of silver and gold. The features, more disturbing in their elvish near-humanity than something honestly weird would have been, with up-tilted brow ridges and cheekbones, almost nonexistently thin lips, and long narrow nose with flaring nostrils. And, worst of all, the eyes: huge, tilted, opaque, with no clear demarcation between the pale-blue "whites" and the azure irises.

He wore what Jason remembered as the jumpsuit uniform of the *Tuova'Zhonglu*, in surprisingly good shape after all these years—doubtless some self-repairing nano-fabric. But his hair had grown to wild length, and across the gulf of species and worlds anyone could see the flicker of insanity behind those eyes. Even by the standards of his own race, this Teloi was mad.

The strange eyes darted around, and fixed on Zenobia. The alien throat, in the deep, strangely timbred voice Jason remembered, shouted a series of sounds that Jason's imperfect command of Teloi could not precisely interpret. He knew only that the Teloi was vomiting hate.

The obviously supernatural apparition was enough for the two surviving drunks, who screamed and fled. *They're not supposed to have seen a Teloi in Port Royal,* flashed through Jason's mind. But he had no time to worry about it, because the alien was lunging at Zenobia, who was still trying to wrench her cutlass free of the body it transfixed.

Jason stood paralyzed by indecision, for he couldn't risk a shot at the charging Teloi's back for fear of hitting Zenobia, beyond him.

The black Maroon stepped in front of Zenobia and leveled his musket. With a sweep of his arm, the Teloi knocked the musket aside just as it fired and sent the Maroon staggering. But it had given Zenobia time to release the cutlass hilt, step back, and scoop up the dead Taino's still-unfired musket.

The Teloi's insanity was evidently less than total—or at least he was having a lucid interval—for he halted his rush, turned and ran up the alley in Jason's direction. The abrupt reversal of direction threw Zenobia's aim off, and her shot went wide. Mondrago, who had dropped his musket and was drawing his cutlass, was buffeted aside by the alien's rush. Before Jason could get off a shot at an unmissable range of a few feet, he was bowled over, falling across the prone Chantal into the mud and filth of the alley. Then the Teloi was past, fleeing with Donnez into the street beyond.

Immediately, screams erupted at the alien apparition that had burst onto the crowded street.

*This isn't right*, thought Jason again as he examined Chantal. He had barely had time to see that her wound, though bleeding freely, was shallow, when Zenobia and the maroon came running past, cutlasses in hand.

"Come on!" she cried. "They're getting away!" With a curse, Jason sprang to his feet, drew his cutlass and ran after her into the street, leaving Mondrago to haul Chantal to her feet and follow.

They emerged into a scene of confusion. Terrified sailors, whores and other pedestrians scattered, howling their panic, as the Teloi ran past. *This* definitely *isn't right!* Jason couldn't let himself dwell on it as they pursued the alien "god" and his priest. He summoned up his map. They were going more or less in the direction of Morgan's fort, but working their way toward the waterfront. To the right, soaring above the irregular rooftops, the steeple of St. Paul's cathedral, the pride of this notoriously godless town's respectable element, was visible. Up ahead, Jason glimpsed the two very different figures darting northward into a side-street.

"That way!" he called out. But Zenobia, just ahead, had already seen. They all turned right, with Mondrago bringing up the rear, grasping Chantal's hand and urging her on as fast as she was able.

Then Zenobia stopped short and glared, perplexed, into the empty side-street. "Where—?"

It at once became obvious that the Teloi's lapse into rationality had passed, or perhaps had merely been overborne by his fanatical hatred of the killer of his colleague and lover. With a nonverbal sound that was flesh-crawlingly different from a human scream, he dove from the second-story balcony onto which he had climbed and landed atop Zenobia, smashing her to the ground beneath his not inconsiderable weight, sending her cutlass spinning away. His hands groped for her throat. Writhing like a wildcat, she grappled with him, matching his size with her gene-engineered strength.

The Maroon, after a fractional second of stunned immobility, surged forward with a roar, cutlass raised. But Donnez stepped from the recessed doorway in whose shadows he had been lurking, stepped behind the Maroon, and drove his dagger into the broad, lash-scarred back.

Jason sprang forward and brought his cutlass down in a whistling arc. But Donnez, with almost superhuman quickness, withdrew his dagger from the dying Maroon, spun around, and caught the descending cutlass on its blade. For an instant the two men strained together, close enough to smell each other's breath. Then Jason brought a knee up into the *houngan*'s crotch. As Donnez doubled over with a grunt, Jason gave a twist of his right wrist that forced him to drop the dagger, then brought the cutlass's handguard up like a knuckle-duster into the contorted black face. Donnez went sprawling, and Jason raised his cutlass again . . .

Before he could bring it down, the ground under his feet began to tremble and roll. There was a sound like a booming of thunder, except that it came from beneath the ground.

With a cold shock, Jason realized how long it had been since he had consulted his clock display. He gave a mental command.

It was 11:43.

*Well*, he thought, oddly calm, *I can stop worrying about the fact that nobody in this time and place is supposed to have seen a Teloi in the streets.*

*All the people who've seen him are going to die.*

# CHAPTER TWENTY-FIVE

Donnez didn't look horrified. He didn't know what was coming, and people in Port Royal were so long accustomed to minor earth tremors that they hardly noticed them anymore. This was unusually severe, and more of an oceanlike rolling than the typical shocks, but no real cause for alarm.

But, looking up from his supine position, the *houngan* could see the expression on Jason's face, and the lapse of attention that went with it. His cut, bleeding lips formed a hyena-like grin of triumph, and with a convulsive motion he sprang to his feet and rushed Jason, getting in under the cutlass and grasping Jason's wrists. The two of them toppled and rolled over and over into the main street.

Jason, locked in combat with Donnez, fleetingly noticed Mondrago standing over the two writhing, struggling figures, trying for a cutlass stroke that would spit Donnez alone. He could not see Zenobia and the Teloi.

It was at that moment that the ground swelled and then dipped, like the deck of a ship in heavy seas, and the subterranean thunder rose to a rumbling that could be heard—or, more accurately, *felt*—by the entire body, not just the eardrums. And then even that was drowned out by the repeated thudding roar as multistory brick buildings, built to the architectural precepts of earthquake-free England, began to implode. And then, above everything, rose a crash from the north as St. Paul's collapsed. Jason happened to be facing in the right direction to see the towering steeple topple over, just before his ears were assaulted by a plangent metallic clang as the great tower bell hit the pavement,

Now panic awoke on Donnez' face. In fact, he and all the running, screaming people in the street were even more panicked than they would have been had they known the true facts of what was happening. But of course they had no knowledge that this was an active tectonic region where the Caribbean Plate atop which they lived had been moving slowly east for ages, while the North American Plate just to the north of Jamaica had been pushing west, resulting in a fault: a "slip-strike" zone where the two plates ground against each other.

Roderick Grenfell had told them all of this. He had also told them about the Modified Mercalli Intensity Scale of "shaking severity" that seismologists had used since the twentieth century. Earthquakes of Mercalli Value I through VII wreaked steadily rising levels of destruction. Values VIII through X were devastating. Value XI was apocalyptic. What was now beginning under this cloudless blue sky would, in places, reach Value XII.

But none of that would have meant anything to these people. They *knew* that this was the Day of Judgment, and that the seven seals were about to be broken.

Donnez, eyes bugging out with terror, released Jason and bounded to his feet. Mondrago, already off balance, was thrust aside by the suddenness of the move. The *houngan* fled, rushing out into the street . . . but not far.

For the earthen street was liquefying, and chasms were opening.

Grenfell had explained it to them. With the earth's oceanlike heaves, the rising water instantly saturated many areas of the sandy soil. The seismic waves changed the soil structure, sending sand molecules downward to meet water rushing up to fill empty space. Under these conditions, sand simply ceased to act as a solid.

As Jason watched, Donnez, along with various other fleeing people, was pulled down into the viscous sand. And then cemented there, for with the next upward heave of the earth the briny water that had surged up into the sand was sucked out just as quickly, leaving the fugitives trapped in the ground. Some only had a leg caught; others were in up to the waist; still others were trapped entirely, with only their heads showing above ground. One such was Donnez, from whose screams all vestiges of sanity had now fled.

From Grenfell's account, Jason knew there was no point in finishing the *houngan* off. Nor could he be saved, even had Jason felt so inclined. If he was lucky, the hardening ground would squeeze the life out of him, suffocating him before the wild dogs came to eat his head.

As Jason watched, a third and still greater tremor came with a deafening roar, sending him and Mondrago sprawling. Chantal, eyes wide with horror and pain, clung to the windowsill of a building. Zenobia and the Teloi were thrown apart and the latter staggered away, struggling to keep upright. Zenobia got unsteadily to her feet and started to pursue him.

"No!" Jason, with an unsteady lunge, grabbed her arm. "Let him go! We've got to get to higher ground, south of here, or we'll die." *Or, more accurately,* you'll *die,* he gibed at himself.

She stared at him. "Jason . . . what . . .?"

"It's what I tried to tell you. The northern two-thirds of Port Royal is going to be obliterated. Now let's go!" He pulled her along. Mondrago went to Chantal's side and, as gently as possible, disengaged her arm from the window frame to which she was clinging with desperate strength.

"Come on!" shouted the Corsican over the din. "You've got to get away from this building." Chantal seemed to understand, and let him half-guide and half-carry her. They were barely clear when the building collapsed in an avalanche of debris. She turned to Jason and yelled to make herself heard.

"For God's sake, Jason, get us out of here! Activate our TRDs!"

For a moment, Jason's impulse was to do just that. He started to form the mental command . . . but then he met Zenobia's eyes.

"Not yet!" he barked. "Follow me!"

Before anyone could protest, he took Zenobia's hand and led the way southward, in the general direction of Morgan's Fort. In the other direction, as he knew from Grenfell's account, the wharves had sunk almost at once, buildings were flowing into the sea as the loose sand of the waterfront area liquefied, and ships were capsizing. A backward glance assured him that Mondrago and Chantal were following, hand in hand, through the landscape of Hell.

They pressed on, managing to keep their footing despite the nauseating rise and fall of the earth, with Jason's map display guiding them toward the relatively safe areas. They carefully avoided the gleaming, rippling areas where earth had turned to water and people were being swept along, bobbing like corks, frantically clutching at passing wreckage. They dodged showers of falling brick and timbers. They grimly tried to ignore the sights they saw, of people who were less lucky. Some, running from toppling buildings, fell into chasms, tumbling into a hellish sunken world, a whirling maelstrom of water, sand, and flotsam. But others were shot into the air as much as a hundred feet by high-pressure waterspouts before falling to the ground and into it, vanishing again. *Grenfell mentioned these "sand volcanoes,"* thought Jason, hard though it was to hear oneself think above the ear-bruising roar.

Then they turned a corner . . . and saw the Teloi, covered in filth but still unmistakable.

Zenobia and the alien locked eyes for an instant. Then they sprung for each other, Zenobia breaking out of Jason's grip.

But then one of the sinkholes opened under the Teloi. With an unhuman bellow, he dropped away and vanished into the ooze.

"He's gone," shouted Jason, grabbing her around the waist. "Now come on! I can see what looks like a safe area ahead."

They went on, with more and more of the scene of devastation visible above lower roofs. They entered a relatively stable area which must, Jason thought, have a stable base of gravel or limestone. They passed a man in clerical garb, standing resolutely and praying with a circle of wailing people, two or three of whom looked suspiciously like they belonged to Port Royal's small Sephardic Jewish community.

"And so, brethren" the pastor shouted over the din to his flock, "let us kneel down and await the breaking of the Seventh Seal, as foretold in the Revelation of St. John the Divine." The devout looked about them as though expecting to see the Four Horsemen of the Apocalypse come riding. But Jason's eyes were turned toward the harbor.

"Look," he said as quietly as possible. His companions turned, and saw the water had receded, leaving a stretch of wet sand littered with wreckage and capsized ships. But only momentarily, for beyond that a wall of water was rushing shoreward at sixty miles per hour.

"Tsunami!" gasped Chantal.

"*Maremoto*, as the Spanish call it," said Jason, who had once, in 1628 B.C., ridden one from exploded Santorini to the coast of Crete. This three-story wave was, he knew, not nearly as high as that one. In fact, it might not have been a classic tidal wave caused by tectonic buckling at all, but merely the ocean rushing in to fill the vacuum left by the plunging sand. But this time he was ashore on the receiving end of it, not atop its deceptively gentle deep-water swell.

As Jason watched, the foamy top of that surge of water crested over the battlements of Morgan's Fort.

Mesmerized as he was by that oncoming monster of destruction, he was taken completely by surprise when a "sand volcano" erupted in front of them and the Teloi appeared, emerging from the saturated earth, drenched and gasping.

Chantal screamed at the apparition. But Jason recalled something else from Grenfell's lectures. Some of those sucked into chasms in the liquefying soil encountered horizontal subterranean rivers of high-speed water which carried them underground for as much as a half mile until they hit one of the geysers and were expelled back to the surface. He wondered if the Teloi could hold their breath longer than humans.

But Zenobia lacked any such intellectual curiosity. With a shout, she whipped out a knife and lunged for her enemy before Jason could even attempt to restrain her.

The alien and the renegade Transhumanist grappled, but only briefly. Zenobia brought her knife up into the pit of the Teloi's stomach and pulled it upward with savage strength.

Teloi guts were different from human ones.

At that moment, the waters of the tsunami, tunneled by a side street, surged over both of them, stopping just short of Jason and his two companions. At the same moment, Jason watched a ship carried over the lower rooftops on the crest. But then, abruptly, the waters flowed backwards, bearing a tide of flotsam that included Zenobia and her dying victim.

"*NO!*" bellowed Jason, as he sprang forward, splashing into the torrent that irresistibly sucked Zenobia toward the harbor, reaching desperately for her.

He fell prone in the liquid sand as Mondrago tackled his legs from behind. The outrush almost drew both of them with it, but Chantal, on firmer ground, grasped Mondrago. Her inconsiderable added weight was just barely enough.

"You can't save her, sir," said Mondrago.

"And getting killed yourself won't help her," Chantal added.

And Jason knew it was true, as he watched Zenobia vanish under the foam, to be seen no more. He ceased his struggles, and Mondrago released him. He stood up slowly. The tremors and the last echoes of the great booms had faded away. Mechanically, he consulted his clock display. 11:49. *Yes, Grenfell said the destruction of Port Royal took six minutes.* He looked out across a vista of desolation, in which the roofs of half-sunken houses stood amid a sparse forest of masts, where ships had been swept into the city. The ship they had seen crest the high-water mark was still floating outward.

"Sir, we've got to get out of here," said Mondrago urgently. "Remember what Dr. Grenfell told us about the aftermath."

Jason nodded dully. Down below, the looting had already begun. Two thousand of Port Royal's sixty-five hundred inhabitants had been killed outright in six minutes of hell. But the real hell was just beginning, in the absence of food, drinking water, and even the rudimentary law and order Port Royal had previously enjoyed. Three thousand more would die in the next few days from starvation, disease and human-on-human violence.

But for a space he could do nothing but stare at the spot where he had last seen Zenobia's dark head bobbing above the foam.

He became aware of Chantal's hand resting on his arm. She was leaning against Mondrago, who was supporting her with an arm around her shoulders, carefully avoiding her wound. When she spoke, all trace of the acerbity her voice had held earlier was gone. "There was nothing you could have done, Jason."

"Oh, I'd say I've done quite a lot," said Jason without looking at her. "And all of my actions conspired to put her in precisely the position to get killed. Otherwise, she might not have been."

"In which case, your actions and their consequences have *always* been part of the past, if you know what I mean," said Chantal, attempting to console him.

"Maybe that's why Gracchus' letter-writer said you had to be here," speculated Mondrago. "And we still haven't learned who that letter-writer was."

Jason drew a deep breath. "Well, at least I've learned one thing: the Observer Effect cannot be fought." He gave a laugh that held absolutely no humor. "No. On second thought I haven't even learned that. I knew it already. I just chose to forget it."

He looked around. No one was watching. He composed his mind to give a neural command. "Prepare for retrieval. Let's get the hell out of here."

# CHAPTER TWENTY-SIX

"Yes," Kyle Rutherford assured the two men seated across his desk, "Dr. Frey is going to be all right. As you surmised, her wound was superficial."

"Good," said Jason and Mondrago in unison, the latter in what seemed an especially heartfelt tone.

Jason's eyes and Rutherford's met. No words were necessary for Jason to know it was *his* wound—the one inside—that worried the older man.

He had submitted a pitilessly honest report of the expedition. Rutherford hadn't reprimanded him for recklessly delaying their retrieval. (Maybe the priceless imagery of the death of Port Royal downloaded from his recorder implant had helped.) But his silence at Jason's attempt to prevent Zenobia's death had been harder to take than the outburst Jason had feared. Now the director looked at Jason in that same kind of silence.

"I'm fine, Kyle," he gruffly answered the unspoken question. "I just need to keep busy. Specifically, I need to start preparing for our mission to Richmond in April, 1865." His face formed the first smile it had worn since his retrieval from wrecked Port Royal. "After what he went through last time, I was surprised Carlos Dabney volunteered to go again."

He had asked for the historian despite his dislike of having to worry about keeping civilians alive on Special Operations missions, for Dabney's in-depth knowledge of Confederate Richmond might prove invaluable. And Rutherford made no attempt to conceal his tight-lipped disapproval of sending Dabney to a milieu where he would be temporally coexisting with the slightly younger version of himself that had gone on Pauline Da Cunha's expedition. But Jason had reminded him that he had been prepared to do just that, before they had been imprisoned in Stoneman's reverse-stasis field. And besides . . .

"Yes," Rutherford nodded. "I had my misgivings. But I must approve anything that may enhance your chances of success. It is imperative that we deal with the remaining cache—the one of which Inspector Da Cunha became aware—after the Observer Effect ceases to preclude our doing so."

"Assuming that it's the *only* remaining one," Jason cautioned. "As I told Angus Aiken when I last saw him, we have no real justification for such an assumption. Stoneman and his crew might have already emplaced another . . . or they may have sent yet another expedition back, as a result of a message drop from Stoneman alerting them to the destruction of their fallback cache by Angus and Gracchus."

"Ah, yes." Rutherford sounded gloomy. "From what this, ah, Stoneman told you, there is no denying that the Transhumanist underground has made more imaginative use of the message drop system than we ourselves have."

Mondrago spoke up thoughtfully. "I guess that's only to be expected. They get more chances to practice with it. Our research expeditions, by their very nature, have always gone to milieus where something historically important or interesting was happening, so they've been sort of in the thick of things. This has always made it difficult for us to find locations that are both accessible and so out-of-the-way that messages can lie undisturbed for centuries. But the Transhumanists are deliberately dealing in the 'blank spaces' of history, so they normally operate away from the hustle and bustle."

"The point is well taken, Superintendent," said Rutherford ponderously. "But the fact remains that they have an advantage in tactical flexibility, and they may have used it. So a great deal depends on Constable Aiken."

"Right." Jason did a quick mental calculation. Their preparations for the Caribbean expedition, and the expedition itself, had taken seventeen days, while the "linear present" had marched on. "Where Angus is, it's now February 18, 1865. I wonder what he's doing?"

Dark as it was in the concealed space behind the wall panel, Angus Aiken was sure he could see Dolly Richards' grin. He could certainly smell Hern, wedged in as the three of them were. And he himself was definitely grinning as he listened to the choleric curses of the Yankees ransacking "Green Garden," the Richards family home.

Sheridan's latest Ranger-hunting expedition from the Valley had shown that he was finally learning Mosby's methods. He had sent Major Thomas Gibson, 14th Pennsylvania Cavalry, through Ashby's Gap into Fauquier County with 237 men, guided by two deserters and moving under cover of darkness without clanking sabers or wheeled transport. At Paris, Gibson's command had split into two columns, with Captain Henry Snow, 21st New York Cavalry, leading the second one and heading due east to Upperville. Searching every "safe house" in their path, Snow's men had netted three Rangers. But by the time they had surrounded "Green Garden," Richards had been warned and concealed along with his two companions.

"Captain Snow, sir," came an out-of-breath voice from beyond the paneling. "The men back in town have gotten into two barrels of whiskey. About a third of them are drunk."

"God damn it!" exploded the young New York officer. "I'll have their hides! Let's get back immediately, Sergeant. We're going to take our prisoners back to our camp in the Valley."

"But, sir, aren't we under orders to rendezvous with Major Gibson at Upperville?"

"No time! With my command in this condition, I don't want Mosby's men to have a chance to rally and cut us off. We're going back without him."

"There are half a dozen men I don't think will be able to sit their horses," said the sergeant dubiously.

"Then we'll leave the damned drunks behind! Come on!" There was a clumping of boots and a jingling of spurs, then silence. After a moment, Richards' father removed the trapdoor. They emerged gratefully, for the air behind the paneling had been getting stuffy.

"Are you all right, Angus?" inquired Richards. "Hern, I know you're used to this kind of thing."

"I'm fine, sir." After Commander Thanou's premature retrieval, Gracchus had slipped away to rejoin his comrades of the Order of the Three-Legged Horse. Aiken had managed to locate Richards, who had accepted his story that he had gotten separated in the night fighting on New Year's eve. For the next couple of weeks there had been practically no Yankee activity. On February 8 the Rangers, claiming a need for recreation, had actually organized a foxhunt. It had been a new experience for Aiken. But, seeing these men riding through foot-deep snow, yelling in response to the baying of the hounds, he could sense that to them this was a way of reliving, if only for a fleeting moment, the life they had known before the war in a world that was so rapidly slipping away beyond their grasp.

But now the wintry idyll was over.

"All right," said Richards, and his blood was up just as it had been for the foxhunt. "Let's go, and get the word out to as many of our men as we can. Snow will be long gone before we can rendezvous, but I'll bet we can catch Gibson when he's going back through Ashby's Gap. I'll want those men who are in a good position to do so to gather at Paris and see if they can delay Gibson there. The rest of us will join them."

"Gibson's sure to have us outnumbered," Hern observed.

"When did that ever stop the Colonel? And remember, he's coming back in a couple of days to resume command. Do you want to be the one to tell him we were chicken? Now, let's ride!"

It was 10:00 the following morning, February 19, when Richards and his following arrived at Paris, to loud huzzas from the Rangers crouched behind a stone fence on high ground. The smoke of their rifle fire was still in the air, and the last of Gibson's column was vanishing in the distance into Ashby's Gap.

In the course of their all-night gallop, Richards had gleaned intelligence through the usual sources. The Union orders had been confused, and Gibson had expected Snow to rejoin him at Piedmont, not Upperville. By the time he realized Snow had not received the changed orders and gone to Upperville, Snow had been two hours gone. All the random motion had delayed Gibson and enabled the Rebels to gather at Paris, but Gibson, deeming the terrain disadvantageous, had ignored their fire and proceeded on with his hundred and twenty-five Pennsylvania troopers and sixteen prisoners.

"My Jeremiah is one of 'em," declared a disheveled young woman. "Jeremiah Wilson, my fiancé. We're supposed to get married tomorrow, right here in Paris. I begged that Yankee major to let him go, but he wouldn't even speak to me."

Richards gave her a courtly bow from his saddle. "Rest assured, miss, I have every intention of returning him to you in plenty of time for your wedding. Hern, how many men do we have?"

"Counting the ones that just rode in with us, I count forty-three," said Hern in his customary tone of dour skepticism.

"That will be enough." Richards pointed in the direction the Union column had taken into Ashby's Gap. "Knowing where Gibson's base camp is, it's my guess that after passing through the gap he'll turn right onto Shepherd's Ford Road at Mount Carmel Church. That road is so narrow, with the mountains on the right and a tangle of rocks and underbrush on the left, that the Yankees won't be able to form a defensive line, much less turn around and counterattack. Now load both your Colts. We're getting those prisoners back!"

The usual noise-suppression techniques of the Partisan Rangers brought them close up behind the Union column undetected. As they turned onto Shepherd's Ford Road, Aiken remembered this landscape, for they passed the trail he and Gracchus had followed up the mountain to the Transhumanist cache beyond the ridge. But then the rear of the blue-clad column was visible ahead, and Richards gave the command to charge. With ear-shattering Rebel yells, the Rangers thundered into the surprised Union rear guard, which panicked and stampeded into the main body, spreading their panic. The Rangers were in among them, blazing away at close range, the crackling roar of the Colts mingling with the screams of wounded horses. The Union cavalry, unable to maneuver, tried to fire back, but they were armed with Sharps carbines, ideal for dismounted action but unwieldy to use from horseback. Under these conditions, Federal numbers only meant more targets. Within less than a minute, some of them were beginning to surrender, including those guarding the prisoners, while those at the head of the column were breaking off and fleeing down the road.

Aiken, caught up in the swirling mêlée, found himself face to face with a Union trooper, awkwardly trying to control his half-panicked mount and aim his carbine at the same time. He managed to get off a shot, but Aiken ducked, leaning down on his horse's other side and firing from under its belly. Blood spurted from the base of the man's throat, under his beard and just above his yellow kerchief, and he toppled from his saddle. Aiken heaved himself back up into a sitting position and rode on. Then another Yankee was ahead, turning his horse's head to join the men up front who were escaping. As he did so, he momentarily turned. His eyes and Aiken's met.

For a split second, Aiken failed to recognize Stoneman in a blue uniform.

That hesitation allowed the Transhumanist to finish his maneuver and gallop off down the road with the other fleeing Federals. Aiken started to spur his horse in pursuit, but at that moment Richards shouted the recall. Reluctantly, Aiken turned and rode back through the dissipating smoke.

Often, when the Rangers had emptied their revolvers in battle, they grasped them by the barrels and used them as clubs. This hadn't lasted long enough for that. In mere minutes, twenty-five Federals had been killed or wounded and sixty-four captured, including Major Gibson himself.

"And we only suffered two casualties," Richards exulted. "John Iden was killed and Richard Sowers was wounded. But we got all the prisoners back." He turned to the latter. "Jeremiah, let's get back to Paris. I believe your fiancée is waiting!"

A scene of cheering jubilation greeted them when they rode back into the hamlet with their prisoners (who outnumbered them by a factor of almost one and a half) and the sixteen liberated men. The cheers rose an octave when Jeremiah Wilson embraced his intended. But Aiken slipped away, unnoticed in the revelry, and walked up Paris' one "street" to a side alley between two houses. After assuring himself that no one was watching, he passed between the houses and crossed a short stretch of ground to a row of shanties, with one of which he had become familiar. He gave the rickety door a certain combination of knocks. It creaked open and a middle-aged black woman gazed out.

"I need to have a message delivered to Gracchus without delay. It's about Stoneman. He'll know what you mean."

Two days later John Singleton Mosby, now completely recovered though seemingly even thinner than ever, and sporting a full but neatly trimmed light-brown beard, arrived to resume command. Aiken was in the vociferously cheering throng as he greeted Richards.

"By God, Dolly, you'll put me to shame!" exclaimed the colonel. "That action of yours at Mount Carmel Church day before yesterday was as brilliant as anything the Rangers have ever done. You and your battalion don't even need me."

Aiken knew it wasn't false modesty. One of the most striking things about the 43rd Virginia Cavalry, formerly 43rd Battalion Partisan Rangers, was its depth of leadership, almost reminiscent of Nelson's "Band of Brothers." Daring young officers like Richards and William Chapman and others had so completely assimilated Mosby's techniques and style that their victims often mistook them for Mosby himself, even in official reports. And Mosby had always taken full advantage of this, effectively cloning himself and sending small raiding parties to widely separated targets simultaneously, so that it seemed he could be in two places at once. It enhanced the Union troops' almost superstitious fear of the "Gray Ghost."

"We know better than that, Colonel," Richards demurred with a grin. "And so do the governor and the House of Delegates, judging from the honors they paid you earlier this month in Richmond."

"Yes. It was most gratifying. But," Mosby added, his expression darkening, "they made me pose for an official photograph holding binoculars, as though I was still a regular cavalry scout, and carrying a *saber!*"

Richards smothered a laugh. "I can imagine the scene that ensued."

"I argued myself hoarse with them about that saber. I told them it was a useless piece of tin that I never carry. But they were adamant, insisting that people expect it." Mosby gave his head a shake of resigned exasperation. "Ah, well, on to more important matters. I believe our chief focus for now must be the gathering of forage in Loudoun County—Fauquier is pretty much stripped bare for now. For this purpose, we need to divide our companies into ten- and twelve-man detachments."

"Yes, sir. I'll begin organizing that at once. But let me raise one matter first. You recall Captain Landrieu of the Jeff Davis Legion?"

"I do indeed! Just after the incident of my wounding at the Lake house, he departed on his original mission for General Lee. Is he here now?"

"Unfortunately, he and his men vanished into the Valley. Since that was almost two months ago, they are presumed dead or captured."

Mosby's face fell. "That is unwelcome news. I owe Captain Landrieu a great debt."

"Yes, sir. But one of his men, Private Angus Aiken, became separated from his detachment and later linked up with us. Under the circumstances, Bill Chapman and I allowed him to attach himself to the Rangers." Richards motioned Aiken forward. "He's done good service, and now he has a request to make of you."

"Certainly." With the characteristic informality of the Partisan Rangers, Mosby drew Aiken aside. "What can I do for you, Angus?"

"Well, sir, it concerns Captain Landrieu's mission, to which Major Richards just alluded, and concerning which I'm still not permitted to speak. You see, through certain sources of information—of which I'm also not permitted to speak—I have reason to believe Captain Landrieu is still alive." Mosby's eyes became blue lasers of intensity, and his thin, sharp face took on the hawklike look that could be chilling, but he said nothing. "And it is imperative that I be in Richmond the first few days of April, in order to meet him."

"I see. Well, Captain Landrieu saved my life. The least I can do is see to it that you arrive in Richmond by that date. I wish you and the captain good fortune in the mission you pursue, whatever that mission is . . . and whatever good it may do now."

With the last words, Mosby's expression changed to one that Aiken was sure his Rangers were never permitted to see. It was the face of a man too intelligent to conceal the truth from himself. He stood undefeated, and was constitutionally incapable of giving in, but he knew nothing he and his men could do could stave off the doom that stalked across the ashen landscape of the South's blighted dream. Putting a hundred Union troops out of action, such as Dolly Richards had just done, counted for nothing along the titanic clash of scores of thousands at Petersburg and in the Carolinas. The Partisan Rangers could not prevail; they could only endure, and leave a legend.

The moment passed. They walked back to where Richards awaited. Mosby turned briskly to organizing the struggle he could not abandon any more than he could pretend he could win it. Aiken went off to see if there was any word from Gracchus.

# CHAPTER TWENTY-SEVEN

"All right, let's review the sequence of events that brought us here," said Jason, running his eyes over the three members of his team. Besides Mondrago and Carlos Dabney, he had been allowed one additional Special Operations officer. He had asked for Constable Tom Corbett, who had been with him on his first incursion to April, 1865 and had sustained a non-serious wound, arguing that if three men were to be contemporaneous with their earlier selves on this expedition a fourth could hardly make much difference. And, this being the case, it made sense to take advantage of Corbett's previous exposure to the target milieu, thus maximizing the team's chances of success. But Rutherford had made this his sticking point; three were more than enough already, thank you very much. So Jason had settled for Constable Basil Novak. This briefing was largely for his benefit.

"As we all know," Jason continued, "I and Alexandre led a Special Ops mission to Richmond in April, 1865, in response to a message drop from Pauline Da Cunha, whose research expedition—including you, Carlos—had turned up evidence of Transhumanist activity. By the time I arrived—or, for convenience, let's say *Jason Mk I* arrived—on April 1, she had investigated further and determined the exact nature of the threat by means of the detection feature of her brain implant. This expedited my investigation, and we destroyed the nanobot cache in the course of the following night, and departed on

April 3. Afterwards, with the threat seemingly removed, Pauline saw no need to monitor that function of her implant for the remainder of her stay.

"After her retrieval—I was off-world at the time, en route to and from Hesperia, before our expedition to the seventeenth century Caribbean—Pauline was of course debriefed, and her implant's records downloaded. But, again, there was no sense of urgency about reviewing them. And there had been some sort of malfunction after April 3 that resulted in their being fuzzy. So they just sat until after I had returned from the Caribbean expedition on which Pauline was killed." Jason said this last expressionlessly, not meeting Mondrago's eyes, for Dabney and Novak were still not privy to the details. "But there were some bothersome anomalies amid the fuzziness, which finally led to an in-depth examination while I was again off-world. It turned out that on April 4 the detector had revealed the existence of a cache of nanobots which had been emplaced earlier than the one we destroyed . . . and which hadn't been there before."

There was dead silence, and not just from Novak, to whom this was new. None of them had to have the implications spelled out. It was the sort of contingency everyone knew was possible but preferred not to think about.

"Evidently," Jason resumed, "after April 3, surviving Transhumanists informed their uptime superiors, either by message drop or on their retrieval or both. And a second expedition was sent back—or *will be*, since for all we know it will come from our future. Our own expedition under 'Jason Mk II' to counter it was intended to remain until April 5, since we know the second cache in Richmond existed on April 4 and therefore the Observer Effect precludes our destroying it before that date. Basil, as you've undoubtedly learned from Rumor Central by now, all of us except Angus Aiken were captured and held prisoner under circumstances resulting in our unprecedented premature retrieval. So there was no 'Jason Mk II' in Richmond in early April after all. Angus, however, is still in 1865." (Everyone understood that his use of the present tense referred to the "linear present." It was one of the accommodations the language had to make to time travel.) "And he will remain until the scheduled retrieval date, slightly before which he is to meet us in Richmond. Thanks to him, an additional nanobot cache was destroyed in the Blue Ridge Mountains."

Novak gestured for attention. "Commander, something else Rumor Central is handing out is that Aiken did it with the help of some kind of secret organization drawn from the enslaved segment of that era's North American population—and that this organization somehow knows about, and is opposed to, the Transhumanist underground. How can this be?"

"The organization to which you're referring is called the Order of the Three-Legged Horse, after a legend from Jamaica, where it originated. The answer to your question is that it was founded in the seventeenth century by a Transhumanist renegade—I won't say 'defector,' because she had no great opinion of our side either—whose acquaintance we had made. The real mystery was that the Order's leader Gracchus was expecting us, thanks to a letter some unknown party had written in the late seventeenth century, predicting our advent in detail. The letter also stated that it was important that I, personally, go back to the letter-writer's era." Jason smiled at Novak's expression. "Yes, this is the part that's been kept seriously under wraps. Shortly after our return, Alexandre and I, accompanied by Dr. Chantal Frey, went to 1692 Jamaica as instructed. The results were inconclusive." Jason left it at that. "So for now, at least, we have to file away Gracchus's letter under the heading of 'unexplained' and concentrate on our immediate objective, which is the destruction of the Transhumanists' second nanobot cache in Richmond.

"We'll be operating under Special Ops protocols, including the use of 'controllable' TRDs. We will arrive on the morning of April 2, 1865. Basil, you know from the basic historical orientation you've already received that this was the date on which the Confederates evacuated and burned the city. I can tell you from personal experience as 'Jason Mk I' that it was a harrowing night, which I don't relish experiencing again. But the confusion should enable us to go about unnoticed locating the cache, especially inasmuch as we know it's not far from the original one, on the island known as Belle Isle."

Jason activated the briefing room's display screen, which showed a map of a short segment of the James River, at the fall line at the western edge of nineteenth-century Richmond. An oblong island lay near the south shore. "Carlos, would you take over the briefing at this point?"

Dabney cleared his throat. "Belle Isle is a fifty-four acre island with a rocky spine. Before the war, it was home to the Old Dominion Iron and Nail Works, and was used as a recreation area for Richmonders. You will note," he added, using a cursor to point to a railroad bridge connecting the island to the southern shore, at a sharp west-to-east angle, "the connection with the Richmond and Danville Railroad. This bridge became known among Union prisoners of war as the 'bridge of sighs.' For after the First Battle of Bull Run, when the Confederacy was swamped with more than anticipated numbers of prisoners, the Confederate government purchased the island and established a camp for enlisted prisoners on the north side of the island, in an area formerly used as a racecourse."

"'Enlisted' prisoners?" Novak queried.

"The officers were housed in Libby Prison, in the city of Richmond, north of the river. Conditions there were notoriously bad, but were nothing compared to Belle Isle, where there was a rudimentary hospital for the prisoners, but no barracks—only a tent city. The prisoners baked in the summer and froze in the winter, and suffered disease epidemics and inadequate rations, although the number who actually died is disputed. And the encampment grew seriously overcrowded after the Union army's frequent defeats. At one point, it held more than twice its theoretical three-thousand-man capacity.

"The island was used for this purpose because of its security advantages—the whitewater rapids on the north side, where the camp was located, discouraged attempts to escape by swimming, although some prisoners became desperate enough to try it—and also for the ready railway access, as it was always intended primarily as a holding facility for prisoners to be transferred further south. By October, 1864 they had all been shipped out and the prison was abandoned."

Novak looked puzzled. "I don't quite understand, then. Why don't we materialize right there on the island after April 5, 1865, find the cache, and destroy it at our leisure?"

Jason answered the question. "Two reasons, in ascending order of importance. First, the Transhumanists will be expecting us to do precisely that, and may plan to have a presence on the island then to prevent us. So we'd better show up earlier than they expect, and deal with them first. Secondly, Angus Aiken is under instructions to be in Richmond around the first of April, and I promised I'd meet him shortly thereafter. I also have reason to believe that Gracchus is going to be there, and we've learned how helpful he and his organization can be." *Although,* the bothersome thought surfaced, only to be dismissed as not immediately relevant, *I don't know* why *he told me he was so determined to be in Richmond then.*

"Also," Dabney put in, "even though the nail factory wasn't reopened until after the war, we can't be certain that the island was completely deserted on April 5."

"But, Commander," Novak persisted, "if we arrive on April 2, won't we overlap in time with Jason Mk I?"

"Also Alexandre Mk I," Jason admitted. "And even more of an overlap with Carlos Mk I. Believe me, I'm all too well aware of that." He had to smile, recalling the effort he'd had to expend to soothe Rutherford's jitters. "But it can't be helped. And remember, none of us in our 'Mk I' manifestations reported any weird encounters with ourselves, so we have the Observer Effect on our side. Something will prevent any such encounters.

"Angus should be in Richmond by April 2, and I should be able to locate him. My computer implant will be set to pick up the tracking device in his TRD as well as the ones in you three's. Also, in the course of Jason Mk II's expedition, we located a potential safe house in the city—the Van Lew mansion. We probably won't be using it, because it will be best if we can get back across the river before dawn on April 3, when the last bridge is destroyed. But if necessary, we will proceed to the mansion after our arrival, and Angus will probably do the same."

"Assuming," Mondrago cautioned with unwelcome realism, "that he'll still be alive."

"There's always that," Jason admitted reluctantly. "All sorts of things could happen to someone riding with Mosby's Rangers."

Angus Aiken held his horse's head, silently waiting with the other hundred and twenty-seven men in the wooded hollow a mile east of the village of Harmony, which in turn was two miles east of Purcellville, awaiting Mosby's command.

It was now March 22, and the harsh winter was past. Sheridan had departed the valley on February 27, handing command over to General Winfield Scott Hancock, a hero of Gettysburg but a man who did not understand counterinsurgency. He had gone into a static defensive posture, complete with frontier-like stockades, to protect the B&O Railroad, and only sent large, cumbersome patrols into Mosby's

Confederacy. Finally he had organized a massive circular hunt by eighteen hundred infantry, cavalry and artillery to trap Mosby's two hundred men. While infantry detachments sealed Ashby's Gap and Snicker's Ferry against westward escape, and an additional force from Fairfax Court House performed the same function to the east, Custer's protégé Marcus Reno had moved south from Harper's Ferry with the main force of a thousand two days before. His ponderous advance had given Mosby plenty of warning. Now he was proceeding from Purcellville toward Leesburg in standard formation, with the infantry marching along the road and the cavalry paralleling its flanks. And Mosby was ready.

As the flanking column of bluecoated cavalry appeared on the edge of Harmony in the distance, Mosby gave a hand signal. Lieutenant Jim Wiltshire acknowledged with equal silence, and led two dozen men of Company A, including Aiken, out of concealment and onto the road. They proceeded west, toward the advancing Federals—the 12th Pennsylvania Cavalry, Mosby's sources had indicated.

Presently, shouts could be heard from up ahead, followed by a thunder of hooves. The Yankees had taken the bait.

"Back, boys!" yelled Wiltshire, wheeling his horse around.

They fled back down the road, with the Northerners charging in pursuit.

When they drew level with the strip of woods behind which the other hundred-odd Rangers waited under the command of Mosby and Lieutenant Alfred Glascock, they wheeled again, into the faces of their startled pursuers, and began to pour revolver fire into the head of the onrushing Union column, bringing down men and horses in a welter of confusion that caused the column to crumple up into a congested mass on the roadbed . At the same instant, Rebel yells erupted to the left as the Rangers waiting in ambush erupted from the trees, crashing into the flank of the jammed mass of Union cavalry, blazing away with their Colts at point-blank range.

The Pennsylvanians held only momentarily before breaking, their only thought to disentangle themselves from the jam and get back to Harmony and take shelter behind an osage orange hedge where the infantry was deploying. As the pursuing Rangers reached the outskirts of town, fire from behind the hedgerow began to rake them, killing two and breaking the momentum of their charge. But that momentum carried some of them into the town even as Mosby was ordering a retirement.

Aiken was one of them. He saw a Ranger shoot a Union trooper down on the front porch of a house. Some of the men seemed disposed to stop and loot. But then he heard Mosby's shouted command.

"Come on, men! Let's skedaddle while we have the chance," he yelled. The men came around, although he saw one pause to cut a ring-finger off a fallen man's hand first. Most of them extricated themselves from Harmony and rejoined the withdrawing main body, which Mosby was leading south. The Federals showed no inclination to follow them.

Aiken spurred his horse and drew abreast of Mosby as the latter was receiving a report from Lieutenant Glascock. "I make it nine Yankees killed, twelve wounded and thirteen prisoners. We also got fifteen horses."

"Good," Mosby nodded. "We only lost two dead—the ones caught in that infantry volley—and five wounded. Another four were captured—they didn't get out of the town in time." He noticed Aiken. "There would have been more of those if it hadn't been for you, Angus. Good work. And now," he added, looking at the sky to the west, "Those clouds rolling in from over the mountains portend a rainstorm tonight. We'll bivouac in southern Loudoun County. But after this, Reno is sure to be reinforced—probably tomorrow or the next day. So we'll disperse further south, into Fauquier County. And," he continued, turning to Aiken again, "it's only a week before you need to be in Richmond. We'll see about getting you there. But I may not see you again. If not, good luck."

"Thank you, sir." Aiken met those extraordinary blue eyes, and felt a sense of impending loss. He also felt an almost uncontrollable urge to tell Mosby he was going to survive the war, and eventually be memorialized in countless ways. But of course he couldn't.

The rain was falling, and they had donned their rubber ponchos, when a rider trotted out of the stormy darkness, off to the side in thin woods. By now, Aiken could recognize Gracchus even in these conditions. He inconspicuously detached himself from the column—easy to do, given the Rangers' informal marching order, especially at night—and approached the black man.

"I haven't seen you in a while," he said, as softly as he could and still make himself heard over the rain.

"I've been busy, trying to learn if there are any more caches."

"Are there?"

"Not that I've been able to find out about. But . . . I know where the one in Richmond is."

Aiken was instantly alert. "You can't come to Richmond with me. We'll have to meet there. How will I find you?"

"Don't worry. I'll find you. And," Gracchus added in a tone Aiken could not interpret, "I'll *definitely* find Commander Thanou."

# CHAPTER TWENTY-EIGHT

"Now I see why they put the POW camp on the north side," said Mondrago as he stepped gingerly from one wet boulder to another. "Too easy to get off the island here."

They had materialized—at dawn of April 2, as per standard procedures—in an out-of-the-way location south of the James River, as close to the Richmond & Danville railroad bridge as they had dared. But walking across the bridge to Belle Isle would have been too conspicuous even this early in the day. Fortunately, as Dabney had explained, getting across the relatively narrow strip of water separating the island from the south shore was a matter of fairly easy boulder-hopping as long as the water level wasn't exceptionally high. Today it wasn't. So they were working their way under the bridge, unnoticed, proceeding carefully in the early morning light and a dissipating fog.

Only part of Jason's mind was on the effort of keeping his footing. The rest contemplated the fact that he was about to witness the fall of Richmond a second time.

Once had been more than enough.

At least the weather was more comfortable than the winter conditions from which he had departed on his last excursion into 1865 Virginia. The fog burned off to reveal a somewhat hazy and humid day, but there was a slight breeze. That breeze muffled the sound of distant shelling to the south, the direction of Petersburg. Richmonders had long become accustomed to such sounds from that direction. But this had been going on since just after midnight.

Dabney had explained what that sound meant today. Yesterday, the Union armies had finally crumpled Lee's right flank in the Battle of Five Forks, to the west. Grant, sensing his opportunity, had finally ordered a frontal assault on the Petersburg lines. Hundreds of guns had shelled the Rebel trenches unmercifully for hours. Then, at 4:45, with the fog still thick, the Union infantry had advanced in the predawn darkness and eighteen hours of continuous fighting had commenced.

But as yet Richmond knew nothing of its onrushing doom, as it prepared for communion services on this Sunday morning. Not until 10:45 would the War Office receive Lee's message that this time the Yankee juggernaut could not be stopped, that he was retreating westward in an effort to join Joe Johnston's army in North Carolina, and that the Confederate government should evacuate its capital.

Yes, Jason had seen all this before.

*Or, rather, I* am seeing *it all before,* he thought with the sense of dizzying unreality that often accompanied time travel. For even as he splashed ashore on the southern side of Belle Isle, Jason Mk I was north of the James, in the city, where he had made contact with Pauline Da Cunha yesterday. And later today, amid the chaos of the Confederacy's Gotterdammerung, that same Jason Mk I would come to this island after crossing the Mayo Bridge, making his way through Manchester, and crossing the Richmond & Danville railroad bridge that no one was bothering to watch. But he would never encounter himself, so Jason (Jason Mk III, as he decided he must think of himself, even though as Jason Mk II he had never made it to this point in spacetime) would surely be gone from Belle Isle by then.

Jason sternly dismissed such thoughts from his mind, for his immediate concern was the whereabouts of Angus Aiken. The red dot denoting the young Service man's TRD was worryingly absent from his neurally projected map of Bell Isle's immediate environs. So he expanded the map's scope.

There! North of Richmond, moving slowly south. At least Aiken was alive.

Angus Aiken waved goodbye to the two Rangers who had been

accompanying him, and turned his horse's head southward, riding parallel to the railroad tracks toward Richmond.

Various delays had prevented him from reaching Richmond by the first of the month. But finally Mosby had lent him an escort and sent him south. He was sorry to say farewell to those men, beside whom he had fought so often. He lacked Carlos Dabney's in-depth knowledge of history, and he had no real appreciation of the rights and wrongs of this more-than-five-centuries-old conflict. But he knew good men when he saw them.

And at any rate the war was just about over. He lacked Dr. Dabney's erudition or Commander Thanou's experience, but he had received a basic historical orientation. So he knew that the Confederate capital he could now see before him in the dissipating James River morning fog was innocently experiencing its final moments. Later today it would be evacuated by the Confederate government and army, and tonight it would be burned.

He badly needed to make contact with Commander Thanou before any of that happened. For that, he would just have to rely on the commander's cyberneticized ability to locate him. And, perhaps, on whatever ill-defined help could be provided by Gracchus, who had seemed very emphatic about his desire to be in Richmond around this date.

He wished Gracchus was with him now, for without Commander Thanou's neutrally displayed map he would have to ask directions to find his way around in the city. With a sigh, he urged his horse onward.

"Well, here it is," said Jason, standing beside an overhanging crag and staring down at the rather artfully concealed hole where a plug of rock had been removed and then replaced over the nanobot cache below.

From memory, he'd had no trouble locating the cache that Jason Mk I would destroy tonight by the light of burning Richmond from across the river. Naturally, they had left it scrupulously alone, but it had served the purpose of confirming that his implant's detection feature for such things was functioning properly. Unfortunately, that feature was extremely short-ranged. So it had taken them longer than he would have wished to find this second one, even though it wasn't far from the first. Both were on the southern side of Belle Isle's rocky, wooded spine. The opposite side would one day be quarried for rock, leaving a cavity which would fill with water and become a lake that would further enhance the scenic quality of the island's northern side. But this slope would be practically unfrequented even in the twenty-fourth century, when Belle Isle had once again become a recreation area alongside the falls of the James.

It was, Jason thought, a bit of foxiness of the part of the Transhumanists to emplace this second string to their bow so close to the first—the last place one would normally think to look for it. Also, this was probably the only place where it could lie undisturbed for centuries of change and upheaval in the greater Richmond area. And this area, with its hub location in the eastern North American conurbation of the twenty-fourth century, was a natural target for the initial civilization-destroying effects when the nanobots woke to malevolent life on *The Day.*

"Well," said Mondrago, interrupting his thoughts, "now that we know where it is, we'd better backtrack and get across the river to the city."

"Right," Jason nodded. "We need to link up with Angus and find a place—maybe Elizabeth Van Lew's house, which according to Carlos is outside the area that gets burned—where we can lie low for three days." But even as he spoke, his somber gaze remained on that inconspicuous circular crack in the flat rock. His left hand, moving by an unconscious impulse, went to the Confederate cavalry canteen that held a small but very powerful explosive device. And he brooded on a subject never far from his mind since his return from Port Royal: the Observer Effect.

*Pauline Da Cunha's implant is going to pick this up two days from now, when she comes here to confirm that Jason MK I succeeded in taking care of the first cache. That's why we're here now. And that's why we have to wait three days before blasting it. But . . . what if I were to simply blast it now? What's to prevent me—?*

At that moment, he noticed a tiny, flashing blue dot at the lower left corner of his field of vision. With a spasmodic motion, he whirled around.

That motion saved his life, for at the same instant a *crack!* was heard and a bullet missed him so closely he could feel the wind of its passage. It smashed into the rock wall behind the spot where his head had been, sending slivers of stone flying into his face.

They all dove for cover behind boulders, as more shots rang out in fairly rapid succession. One of them grazed Dabney's left upper arm. *He must be using a Henry repeater*, thought Jason, recognizing the sounds as those of a rifle rather than a revolver. They drew their Colts—already loaded, just in case—and returned fire, sending the shooter ducking behind the rock outcropping that had concealed him, on the crest just above them. There was a brief lull in the shooting, and Jason, ignoring the stinging cuts on his face, looked around him. To the left was a declivity that seemed to offer a way to flank the rifleman's position.

His Colt had only two rounds left, but this was no time to reload. "Alexandre," he hissed. "Cover me and keep him down." The Corsican nodded, and fired off a fresh fusillade. While the Transhumanist was sheltering behind his rock, Jason slithered off into the declivity and began scrambling up a steep slope, circling around as fresh rifle shots rang out.

The shooting had paused again when he emerged from behind the boulders and, sheltering behind a tree growing through a crevice in the rock, saw the Confederate-uniformed Transhumanist lying prone, reloading his Henry and talking.

Implant communicators did not require audible speech; subvocalization sufficed, which was very handy for covert operations. But the Transhumanist, unconcerned with concealing his presence under the circumstances, wasn't bothering with that. He was speaking in a low voice. Jason activated his implant's recorder function, complete with the same sound amplification feature he had used while sitting in Jefferson Davis's waiting room.

". . . and so I have them pinned down," the goon-caste Transhumanist was saying. "But there are four of them, and . . . Yes, sir. Understood. I'm to slip away, get back across the river, and rejoin you in the city. But what if they . . . ? Oh, I see. Of course. They *can't* destroy it now . . . No, sir! I never intended to question your orders. I abase myself! . . . Understood, sir. Signing off." The Transhumanist peered over his rock barrier, fired three shots in rapid succession, then slid backwards down the slope, got to his feet and turned around . . . to find himself squarely facing Jason, who stood with leveled Colt, its hammer drawn back.

With the unnatural quickness of his caste, the goon brought his rifle around. Before he could complete the movement, Jason squeezed his trigger and sent a bullet crashing through the butternut-clad chest and the heart behind it. The Transhumanist swayed and fell face-down, dead before he hit the ground.

"Come on up here!" Jason called out. The others joined him, and Novak, who was particularly skilled in low-tech first aid, tied a bandage of torn cloth around Dabney's arm. Meanwhile, Jason and Mondrago examined the dead Transhumanist. As expected, he was carrying nothing of any use to them.

"But," Jason explained, "I overheard him reporting to his boss—Stoneman, I imagine—who is over in Richmond now."

"If it is Stoneman, I wonder if he's been here all along, since we last saw him in January," Mondrago wondered, "or if this is a different 'mark number.'"

"There's no way to know. And it's not something we need to know just now. The point is, he's expecting this goon to report to him. So that's one more reason for us to get over to the city before he expects us." Jason turned to Dabney. "Carlos, are you up to it?"

"I'll be all right, Commander. It's just a shallow wound." Gamely: "In a way, it's a good thing. There are so many wounded men in Confederate uniforms around here just now that we ought to have at least one."

"Then let's go. We have to get back across the shallows to the south bank, then north across the Mayo Bridge."

Dabney got unsteadily to his feet. "Of course you realize what we're going to be walking into, don't you? By the time we enter downtown Richmond, the news of Lee's message to the War Department will be starting to spread, and—"

"Believe me, Carlos, I know. In fact, I remember." Jason smiled briefly, as he recalled seventeenth century Port Royal. "I seem to be making a habit of being on hand for the deaths of cities." Then other recollections of the seventeenth century banished his smile. "And of course we're going to have to think about the need to avoid any contact with our own previous 'mark numbers' . . . and with Pauline Da Cunha . . ." He gave his head a shake. "Let's go," he repeated.

Dabney touched his arm. "Commander, let me ask you something. You've never told me how Inspector Da Cunha died on your last expedition to the Caribbean. In fact, you've been quite reticent about it. May I know the circumstances of her death?"

Jason's first impulse was a surly refusal. Then he decided that this man had been through enough with him to deserve an answer. He spoke very levelly.

"We were shipwrecked on the southern coast of Hispaniola. Before rejoining Henry Morgan's men, we were captured by the Transhumanists who had been planting the seeds of one of their hidden cults—in this case a perversion of Voodoo that included, as did the historically attested *Secte Rouge* of later times, ritual cannibalism. They used Pauline as a victim. I watched, bound and unable to do anything about it, as she was butchered alive, cooked, and eaten. Afterwards, when I spoke to the Transhumanist leader, her grease was still on his lips . . . and I could smell his breath . . ." Jason could hear his voice start to waver. He clamped control on himself. "The Transhumaist leader paid. I was able to do that, at least. But now perhaps you understand why I don't relish the thought of seeing her, still alive, knowing what I know."

He turned and started toward the island's south shore, leaving the shock-stunned Dabney to follow him.

# CHAPTER TWENTY-NINE

It was late morning and the Virginia April sun was blazing when Angus Aiken rode south along Ninth Street, past stately homes and upscale hotels and stores, listening to the sound of Richmond's various church bells. After crossing the rails of the Richmond, Fredricksburg & Potomac Railroad that ran east to west along the center of Broad Street, he proceeded another block south and found himself with the landscaped slope of Capitol Square rising gently to his left up to Jefferson's Classical capitol building. Across the street on his right was St. Paul's Episcopal Church. From within, he could hear a hymn coming to an end—something about "Jesus, lover of my soul."

The street was largely empty, at this hour on Communion Sunday, and thus it was that Aiken could clearly see a figure in Confederate uniform emerge from a building one block ahead, on the right, and run in his direction. As the man approached, Aiken could see he was clutching what appeared to be one of this era's telegrams. He dashed past and, to Aiken's surprise, flung open the door of the church and entered. Aiken caught the sound of a sonorous German-accented voice reading the Communion service. He turned his horse's head again and prepared to continue southward.

Then he saw four uniformed figures ahead, turning right off Main Street and advancing toward him on foot. The officer leading them was waving to him.

Recognition dawned, and he spurred his horse half a block before flinging himself from the saddle and clasping arms with a broadly smiling Jason Thanou.

"Commander! I don't mind telling you it's a relief to see you. I was delayed, and I'm only just getting into Richmond."

"I know, Angus. I've been homing in on your TRD. Now, listen: we've pinpointed the secondary nanobot cache that we're going to have to destroy subsequent to the day after tomorrow. In the process, we had a run-in with a Transhumanist who'd been left on watch. His boss is somewhere here in the city. We're provisionally assuming he's Stoneman—"

"I caught sight of him in the course of a skirmish in late February," Aiken interjected. "Up around Ashby's Gap, when we whipped the tar out of the Yankees at Mount Carmel Church."

"All right." Jason showed no sign of reaction to Aiken's turn of phrase. "We'll continue to assume it's him, and that he's not alone. And my ability to detect their bionics is, as you know, very short-range. For the next couple of days, we're going to have to be on the alert every second . . ." Jason's voice trailed off, and he stared past Aiken, who noticed that Carlos Dabney was staring in the same direction. Following their gaze, he turned and looked back at the church.

A small group of very grim men, some in uniform but most not, were emerging from the open door, through which Aiken thought he could hear the minister's German accent growing thicker and his voice shakier. The group was led by a tall, gaunt, well-dressed man. They walked quickly south on the cobblestones of Ninth Street.

"Ten-*hut!*" said Jason as they passed. The time travelers came to attention, and Jason saluted, as Jefferson Davis passed without acknowledgment, staring fixedly ahead, his pale eyes seemingly focused on something that was slipping rapidly away and would soon be lost to sight forever.

"You know who he is, don't you, Commander?" said Dabney.

Jason nodded. "I once glimpsed him through his office door, in the Confederate White House. He's not headed in that direction now."

"No. He'll be going to his working office in the Treasury building just south of Capitol Square, where he'll convene his cabinet and staff. A courier from the War Department just brought him Lee's telegram telling him Richmond must be evacuated. He's never really believed it, you see, so he's made no real plans for this contingency. The Confederate government will have to pack up and leave in a matter of twelve hours." Dabney gestured toward St. Paul's. "Dr. Minnegerode will manage to finish his sermon, but as the churches empty out, the word will rapidly spread and panic will start to set in."

"Yes, I remember," said Jason, gazing around with a haunted look. "Although Jason Mk I missed out on these early scenes. Even though he's already here," he added wryly.

"But you know what comes later."

"Yeah," remarked Mondrago grimly. His Mk I version had also been—and, in fact, currently was—here.

"Right," Jason agreed. "So we've got to find a place to go to earth. Someplace where our earlier selves aren't."

"How about that train station where we hung out for a while after leaving Elizabeth Van Lew's?" suggested Mondrago. "It will be a madhouse, with people trying to get out of town, so we can lose ourselves in the crowd. And the Transhumanists won't try any funny business there."

"The Virginia Central Railroad depot," Jason nodded. "Good idea. Let's go."

He led the way toward Sixteenth and Broad, turning left and skirting the southern edge of Capitol Square. Across the street were government office buildings. Stacks of documents were being piled up on the sidewalks, and set afire. On the lawn of Capitol Square itself, the same was being done to wheelbarrows full of Confederate paper currency. The smell of smoke began to fill the air.

"Now it begins," murmured Dabney.

By the time they reached the depot, there was another aroma in the air, one which only the most insensitive could fail to smell: that of incipient panic.

Jason knew it well, from various times and places. It grew as rumor spread, and wagons arrived under heavy guard, loaded with gold and silver to be loaded aboard railroad cars. To the south, a low rumble of sound could be heard as government officials frantically tried to secure passage on James River Canal packet boats. As the afternoon wore on, lines of frightened depositors at the banks grew longer and less orderly, and the streets grew more and more full of people and animals and every kind of wagon, and the noise from the direction of the river rose as a steadily growing stream of refugees poured along the canal's towpath in the direction of Lynchburg. But so far there was nothing shrill about any of it. Most people stumbled about in a state of unreality, determined to continue to make the motions of normalcy.

Then, just after 4:00, criers rode through the streets with the City Council's official evacuation announcement. Like a cloudburst suddenly dissipating a stifling miasma, full-blooded panic erupted.

"The council and Mayor Mayo—that really is his name—authorized a citizens' committee to meet with the Union commanders and arrange the city's surrender," Dabney explained to Jason, raising his voice to be heard over the uproar from the increasingly choked streets: rumbling wagon wheels, shouting people and the pathetic shrieks of whipped animals. "They also passed a number of resolutions intended to maintain order. One was to destroy all liquor supplies, smashing the barrels and pouring the whiskey into the gutters. Another was to set fire to the tobacco warehouses. Both of those are going to turn out to be terrible mistakes."

Jason glanced at Aiken. The young Service man's face wore an unmistakable look of sadness as he watched the Confederacy's death throes. Jason placed a hand on his shoulder. "Remember, Angus, we can't take sides."

Aiken smiled. "Is it that obvious, sir?" Then he spoke forthrightly, almost defiantly. "I can't help feeling that something of value is being lost. I lived and fought with Mosby's men for months. They had a certain naïve dash, an innocent gallantry. The world won't see their like again."

"No, it won't," Jason admitted. Then he noticed a man who had "slave dealer" written all over him enter the depot, leading a coffle of chained blacks. He argued furiously with a guard who barred the way to one of the trains reserved for government use. The guard shook his head and hefted his bayonetted rifle meaningfully. The slave dealer threw up his hands in disgust and, with a resigned expression, unlocked his human property and walked away.

"No, it won't," Jason repeated. Then he indicated the newly released slaves, standing bewildered. "But it also won't see *their* like again."

"I know," said Aiken in a voice almost too small to be heard, lowering his head. After a moment he looked up, and his young eyes sought Jason's. "Sir, aren't things ever unambiguous?"

"No. You'll learn that." *But you'll never learn to like it*, Jason decided not to add.

"One exception to that," Mondrago demurred. "The Transhumanists are unambiguously evil."

"Amen," intoned a deep voice behind them.

They all whirled to face Gracchus. The black man was dressed in his usual rough, nondescript laborer's clothes, and stood inconspicuously in the depot's turmoil. "Remember I told you I intended to be here around on this day, Commander."

"So you did. I didn't understand why at the time. Still don't, in fact."

"Simple. I knew this city is going to fall tonight. And I know Mr. Lincoln is coming day after tomorrow. I want to be here for that."

"You know—?" Jason swung around and stared at Aiken.

"Yes, Commander, I told him," said Aiken miserably.

"You *what?!*"

Aiken wilted under Jason's glare. "I thought I owed it to him, sir. And I didn't reveal anything else."

Jason opened his mouth to say more. But then he closed it again and shook his head. "Well, what's done is done. We won't bother Rutherford with things he doesn't need to know. And," he added, turning to Gracchus, "I'm glad you're here. For one thing, I can tell you that I kept my promise." He looked around anxiously, but under the circumstances no one seemed to be taking any notice of their conversation, which was practically inaudible above the uproar anyway. "I went back to Jamaica on the date your letter required."

"Ah." Gracchus's face was unreadable.

"And I saw your founder Zenobia die." Jason said it bluntly, and watched Gracchus's face carefully. But those dark features now went entirely—and strangely—expressionless.

"Yes. I knew she was going to die around that time," the black man said in a carefully neutral voice.

"And so," Jason continued, "I still don't know why your letter-writer wanted me there at that time, since I accomplished nothing." *Except the death of a Teloi, which is somewhat more than "nothing,"* Jason mentally amended. But he held his peace, for Gracchus wouldn't have understood, and it had no apparent relevance to the enigmatic letter.

"However, that's water over the dam. Here I am now, and here's where we stand." He described their finding of the second nanobot cache and their encounter with the Transhumanist on Belle Isle. "So," he concluded, "we worked our way across the river to the city to rendezvous with Angus—and, we hoped, you as well. But now we need to get back across to the south shore of the river before dawn tomorrow."

"Why?"

"I may as well tell you that that's when the retreating Confederates are going to burn the Mayo Bridge—the last one left—as soon as the last of their troops are across it. We've got to be with them."

"Again, why?"

"Because, for reasons you don't need to understand, we can't destroy the cache before the fifth. With all the bridges gone, we wouldn't be able to get to Belle Isle from this side of the river without a boat—and we can't count on being able to get one, with the city under military occupation."

"Why not go across the river now?"

"I know for a certainty that there are Transhumanists here in Richmond now, most likely including Stoneman. If it can possibly be done, I want to find them and deal with them before they can try and interfere with us on the fifth."

"I understand," said Gracchus. "And I think I might just have an idea of where they are. But let's wait here a little longer, until things get to the point where nobody will notice us on the streets."

"That won't be much longer," said Dabney.

It was a little past five when Jefferson Davis arrived with his staff. The chaos was such that he was barely noticed. Dabney explained that his wife and children had already left on a train for Charlotte, North Carolina. The plan was for him and his cabinet to depart for Danville, Virginia at 8:30, one railroad car per department, but in fact he didn't get away with his peripatetic government until eleven, beginning a forlorn flight south.

Midnight came, and Gracchus led them out of the depot, unnoticed, amid the mounting exodus. Jason became aware that they were headed southeast, toward the lower-class housing areas near the river and Shockoe Creek.

Dabney realized it too. "Wait! We don't want to go in this direction."

"That's right." Jason, who had never exactly been noted as a mindless rules-robot, nevertheless swallowed hard before he could speak. "Later tonight, large areas between the river and Capitol Square are going to burn to the ground."

Gracchus's eyes grew wide. "Then we've got to go there and get my people out! Come on." He pressed ahead, and the others followed after only the slightest hesitation.

As they entered the Exchange Alley area south of Main Street, they were startled by a sound of shattering glass. Moments later, a trio of raggedly dressed men emerged from a broken store window, loaded with merchandise, and hurried shiftily on.

"The looting has started," Dabney told Jason. "The inmates have broken out of the unguarded jails, and the lowlifes are starting to come up from the riverside tenements. And there's nothing to keep order except a token force of Confederate troops left behind to burn the Mayo Bridge as soon as the last of Lee's rear guard is across it. The respectable people who haven't fled are barricaded inside their houses. From now on, the mob rules the night."

They continued south, and the signs of pillaging grew worse and worse. Ahead, they heard a roar of shouting voices. Then they emerged into the intersection of Fourteenth and Cary Streets, where the commissary depot was located, and entered a scene from hell.

A hungry mob had descended on the commissariat, and was looting those stores of food which had not been transported. Nearby, the militia had followed the City Council's well-intentioned order and smashed the heads of three hundred barrels of whiskey, pouring thousands of gallons into the streets. Now the looters, on all fours like animals, were scooping and lapping it up from the gutters, heedless of how much foul, muddy water went with it. And the more they swilled, the more the frenzy grew. The looters were no longer furtive. They smashed their way into any abandoned building, fighting with each other over their plunder.

The smell of whiskey might have been overpowering, but it was already overlaid by another aroma: that of smoke. And to the south the glow of flames was lighting the sky.

"They've carried out the council's other order and fired the tobacco warehouses along the riverfront. And the fire is already spreading."

"Yes. I remember." Even as Jason said it, he felt a stiff southerly wind begin to blow.

As they watched, the flames leapt from building to building, igniting the old colonial-vintage timber of many. As the roaring, crackling, hissing inferno rolled up from the waterfront, consuming the commissariat, the heat and smoke grew stifling and even the rioters fled. Old buildings came crashing down in showers of sparks and flying bricks and plaster as their beams split.

They stumbled on, until Gracchus recognized a black man—particularly black, with soot—up ahead. They spoke briefly, and Gracchus turned grimly to Jason.

"The rest of my people have already headed northwest, toward Capitol Square. Lots of people are sheltering there—at least it's away from the burning buildings."

"And maybe the Transhumanists are up there," Novak speculated, coughing on the smoke that made it increasingly difficult to speak.

"Maybe," said Jason. He summoned up his implant's digital clock display, and frowned. His eyes met Mondrago's in an instant of shared understanding. "We're going to have to be very cautious in that area. You see . . ." He decided not to explain why; there was no time, and Gracchus wouldn't have understood anyway. "All right, Gracchus, lead the way."

# CHAPTER THIRTY

They headed west along Cary Street, until the canal basin was on their left, its water reflecting the flicker of flames to the southeast. To the right, up Eleventh Street three blocks, they could glimpse the darkened expanse of Capitol Square, on Council Chamber Hill. They started to turn in that direction.

It was at that moment that a tiny cluster of blue dots flickered at the edge of Jason's field of vision . . . to the west, further along Cary Street.

"Gracchus, the Transhumanists are this way."

Gracchus didn't bother asking how Jason knew. He pointed north. "I've got to go find my people."

"All right. We'll find you later."

"Or I'll find you." And Gracchus was gone, up the hill.

"Let's go!" Even as Jason said it, the dots flickered again, and were gone. Cursing the short range of the bionics-detector function, he led the way by the light of the flames to the south, past the packet office from which the last canal packet boat had long since departed and on across the railroad tracks that ran along the center of Eighth Street. There, the blue dots blinked tantalizingly, only to vanish as the Transhumanists again opened up the distance between them. He urged greater speed on the others. Ahead, the fire was spreading and they went cautiously between burning buildings, wary of collapsing walls. Just ahead and only a block to the right, at Fifth and Main, the flames had engulfed the United Presbyterian Church, and its tall steeple was swaying drunkenly.

"Commander!" gasped Dabney, struggling to keep pace. "Surely you realize we're headed in the direction of—"

"I know," said Jason impatiently. "Remember, I was here before." *And, in fact, Jason Mk I is here right now*, he reminded himself. He consulted his clock display. It was almost three A.M. "But we've got a little time. In fact—"

All at once, an idea occurred to him.

*The Transhumanists, aside from a few not-very-well-regarded specialists, have no interest in history—in fact, such an interest is slightly suspect among them. Stoneman will, of course, have been briefed by those specialists. But he may be hazy on the exact sequence and location of events tonight.*

*Maybe . . . just maybe. . . .*

"Come on!" he snapped, and continued along Cary Street.

Dabney was openly jittery now. Even Mondrago looked a little nervous. "Uh . . . sir, are you keeping an eye on your clock? We're headed toward—"

At that moment, just a block to the right, the burning, tottering United Presbyterian spire finally toppled over and, with a rending crash and a shower of fiery debris, crashed to the street amid the screams of the watching crowd.

It was so startling and so distracting that Jason didn't notice the reappearance of the little blue dots until it was too late.

"Halt! Don't move!" came a horribly familiar voice, this time with the undertones of a vocal enhancement implant. Caught unaware, they were susceptible to that subsonic suggestion for the second or two before they could nullify it by conscious resistance. They froze as commanded. By the time their mental defenses had taken hold, four goons had stepped out from an alley, aiming Colt revolvers. They stayed frozen under those guns, in hands whose trigger fingers were actuated by genetically upgraded reflexes. Jason had a feeling the goons were under instructions to watch his face for indicia of the mental concentration required to activate his party's "controllable" TRDs, and that their retrieval would return four bullet-riddled corpses to the Authority's displacer stage, leaving one red-haired one lying in Cary Street until April 5.

Behind the goons came Stoneman, smiling.

The fleeing, panic-stricken people in the street paid no attention. On this night of horror and lawlessness, one group of Confederate soldiers pointing guns at another was hardly to be noticed, and certainly not to get involved in. No one interfered as one of the goons relieved them of their own revolvers under the watchful eyes and steadily aimed Colts of the other three. Stoneman sauntered up before Jason, wearing his infuriating smile. His revolver was, Jason noted, held nonchalantly.

"So you're still here," Jason observed in a tone he hoped was as irritating as Stoneman's smirk.

"Quite. I remained in northern Virginia for some time after your escape, during which time I informed my superiors of what had occurred via message drop." (*Meaning,* Jason mentally interjected, *that you weren't using a "controllable" TRD. Of course, that doesn't necessarily mean the Transhumanist underground doesn't have them.*) "So these reinforcements were dispatched." Stoneman indicated the goons. "They brought the cache you have located on Belle Isle, and which I gather you haven't already destroyed, doubtless for some reason connected with the Observer Effect. Now, of course, you'll never destroy it."

"Speaking of which," asked Jason levelly, "why are we still alive?"

"You won't be for long. But to answer your question, there are two reasons." For an instant, Stoneman's mask of insouciance slipped to reveal sheer, gloating malice. "The first is that before you die I want you to know what a chance you missed when you blew up my cabin. All the delicate advanced equipment was destroyed, true. But *this* survived the blast, as I discovered when I sifted through the rubble afterwards." With a theatrical gesture, he reached inside his tunic pocket and produced a tiny lozenge-shaped plastic case. Jason recognized it, for it was standard: what appeared to be simple plastic was in fact a superhard composite laminate substance, for this was a damage-resistant casing for a data chip.

"The chip," Stoneman explained, "was one which we required for various functions. It also bears certain data which needs to be returned uptime. Otherwise I would have destroyed it after finding it, to eliminate any possibility of you subsequently obtaining it. For, you see, it contains a great deal of incidental data about our technology—including our time travel technology—which you would have liked very much to possess. Oh, yes: very, very much!"

Jason commanded his face to expressionlessness, not wishing to give Stoneman the satisfaction of revealing that which the Transhumanist so avidly wanted to see there. But inwardly, his thoughts were raging. *My God! A clue to the hole in Weintraub's math that causes our temporal displacement hardware to be almost prohibitively massive and inefficient and energy-intensive, while theirs is compact enough to be concealable and even semi-portable. There's nothing we wouldn't give for it!*

"You indicated that there's a second reason," was all he said.

"Yes." Stoneman seemed slightly miffed by Jason's seeming impassivity. "I want to know if you have any more men at large in or around this city, and if so where they are. I advise you to tell me. Remember, you can go quickly and cleanly, or else . . . otherwise."

Once again, Jason kept his features immobile with an effort, for now his earlier half-formed idea came roaring back. He summoned up his clock display. Yes. Almost 3:00 A.M.

*It might actually work.*

*I've got to play it very carefully, though. I can't fall down at Stoneman's feet, slobbering and begging for mercy. He's too smart—he'd know it was fake.*

"What makes you think I'd tell you?" Jason infused the question with the truculent defiance Stoneman would expect, but he insinuated the barest quaver, the subtlest hint of underlying apprehension.

"This." Stoneman seemed to seize on the slight suggestion of weakness. He held up his seemingly standard Colt Model 1860 .44 caliber Army. "It incorporates an undetectably miniaturized but quite effective nerve-lash."

It took very little acting skill for Jason to break out in a sweat. In his time, the nerve-lash was seriously illegal to possess, much less use. But in the nightmare years of the Transhuman Dispensation, a century and a half before that, it had been a common instrument for control of "lower life-forms." Thankfully, it was only usable by direct contact. By direct neural induction, it stimulated the human nervous system to the ultimate capacity of its pain receptors short of driving the mind in question, shrieking, into the refuge of insanity.

But even now, he knew Stoneman wouldn't buy a too-facile

surrender. And thus he knew, with gut-churning certainty, what had to be done next.

"You're lying," he made himself say.

At once, a goon grasped his arms from behind and pulled them up into an immobilizing position. With a smile, Stoneman touched an invisible control on the side of his revolver and, very gently and briefly, brushed the muzzle against the side of Jason's neck.

At that fleeting contact, his entire body, mind and soul contained nothing but excruciating agony. Heedless of the relatively trivial pain in his arms, he arched convulsively in the goon's grip, then went limp, shuddering, as the nerve-lash was instantly withdrawn. The goon released him, to fall in a shivering, nauseated heap.

"All right," he gasped, "I'll tell you." He wished, in defiance of the negative results of centuries of research, that there had been something to telepathy, so he could mentally command his followers not to queer the pitch. Because this was crucial.

He needn't have worried. Dabney understood, because he knew what was about to happen, and the Service men grasped it at once. In fact, Mondrago comprehended it so well that he broke in with his own contribution. "Don't tell him, Commander! God damn it, don't betray the others!"

Stoneman gestured impatiently to one of the goons, and a pistol barrel was backhanded across the side of Mondrago's head, not hard enough for him to lose consciousness but sufficient to send him to his knees, dizzy and bleeding. Stoneman turned back to Jason. "Well, Commander?"

Jason got unsteadily to one knee (but *not* to his feet, for he knew what was coming) and consulted his clock display again. *Yes, it must be just about time.* He gestured southward. "A couple of my men are waiting at Seventh and Arch Street. They're still there, even though the fire is spreading into that area."

For an instant, the look on Stoneman's face made him fear he had blown it after all. But then he realized it was a look of mildly surprised disappointment, not one of suspicion. The Transhumanist gave rapid orders to two of the goons, who departed in the indicated direction. The other two, with two revolvers each, kept the prisoners covered.

"I must admit to a degree of disillusionment, Commander

Thanou," said Stoneman. "Even under nerve-lash, I expected better from you, Pug though you are. But one never knows, does one?" He shook his head, then turned brisk, playfully tossing the little case up and catching it. "Now, as to the manner of your death: I know what I said before, but assurances to Pugs of course mean nothing, so—"

A flash to the south suddenly flooded the scene with light. At the same instant the night was shattered by a deafening roar and a concussion that sent everyone staggering, as the fires reached the National Arsenal and thousands of artillery shells exploded in a blast that shook Richmond's seven hills, shattering windows and sending chimneys toppling over blocks away as a great pulse of heated air and smoke spread outward, bearing a shower of fragments . . . including the fragments of two goon-caste Transhumanists. *The best use to which the Confederate States of America's munitions were ever put,* flashed through Jason's stunned mind.

It was, he knew, only the beginning of Richmond's climactic agony. One after another, a hundred thousand shells, including those on the Confederate Navy ironclads that had been run aground on the riverbank, would explode all through the remainder of the night and into the morning, without letup: four nerve-wracking hours of continuous, ear-bruising blasts, worse by far than a Union bombardment would have been.

Jason, who was expecting it and was kneeling, remained steady. The Transhumanists were sent stumbling forward by the shock wave from behind them. Stoneman practically fell onto Jason, who grasped the wrist of his gun-hand. At the same time, he dropped the tiny case, which went skittering and bouncing playfully off along the cobblestones. He and Jason grappled, the latter handicapped by apprehension that the nerve-lash feature of the Colt his opponent was still grimly clutching might still be activated.

A succession of shots distracted his attention, and he saw out of the corner of his eye that one of the goons was getting off a succession of rounds from his two revolvers—probably fewer rounds than he would have with one, and the other hand free to "fan" the hammer. But he was doing so while off-balance, and his shots went wild. Novak went under those shots and sent him sprawling with a *savate* kick, then rushed him and grappled for the pistols. The other goon, whom the concussion had sent to his knees, was unable to get off a shot before

Aiken brought a knee up into his face and sent him sprawling over backwards, dropping one of his revolvers. With the resilience of his gengineered breed, he sprang back to his feet—only to be shot through the midriff by Mondrago, who, though still exhibiting the after-effects of dizziness, had scooped up the dropped pistol.

All of which distracted Jason just enough for Stoneman, with a surge of genetically upgraded muscles, to bring his Colt's muzzle into contact with Jason's cheek. For the second time, he convulsed with sickening agony, and Stoneman broke free. He started to bring the Colt—no doubt also useable as an ordinary pistol—to bear on the uncontrollably shuddering Jason.

Then, as though in slow motion—or so it seemed to Jason, in what he was coldly certain was the last second of his life—Mondrago swung around to bring his revolver into line on Stoneman. At the same instant, Novak smashed his opponent's left hand against the cobblestones, forcing him to drop the pistol it was holding. In appreciably the same motion, he brought his right elbow down on the goon's throat, crushing the larynx, then swept up the dropped pistol and brought it around.

In that fractional second, Stoneman must have instantly analyzed the situation and decided he had more important business than a gunfight he probably wouldn't win.

Without even pausing to shoot Jason, he dived to the street, sliding along on his stomach as Mondrago's and Novak's bullets whizzed over him, grabbed the little laminate case, then sprang to his feet and sprinted east down Cary Street. The Service men fired after him, but the Colts were inaccurate beyond short ranges, especially in the flickering light of burning Richmond. He was soon gone.

Dabney, whose non-combat-trained reactions hadn't kicked in before the brief fight was over, helped Jason to his feet with his good arm. "Are you all right, Commander?"

"Yes, I'm fine," Jason lied as he forced down his residual trembling and shook his head to clear it of nausea. "Alexandre?"

"I'll do," said the Corsican, wiping away the blood that was trickling down his cheek.

"Then let's go!" The blue dot denoting Stoneman's bionics had already wavered out of Jason's field of vision, but he had a pretty good idea of where the Transhumanist was headed. "We *have* to get that data chip! It would be the intelligence coup we've been hoping and praying for. That's become our top immediate priority."

"Killing Stoneman would be all right, too," Mondrago commented as they started out at a run.

# CHAPTER THIRTY-ONE

It soon became evident, as the little blue dot flickered on and off, that Jason had been right about Stoneman's destination.

They turned left on Ninth Street, and soon the bell tower at the southwest corner of Capitol Square rose before them. Beyond it, the intricately landscaped grounds sloping up to Mr. Jefferson's capitol building were carpeted with sheer human misery. Here, away from the fires, now-homeless Richmonders huddled with whatever possessions they had been able to salvage. Old people sat staring into nothing. Parents tried to calm their wailing children as the nerve-shattering blasts of exploding artillery shells went mercilessly on and on and on.

Dabney had explained that the public buildings here would survive—although it would take heroic efforts by bucket brigades to save the governor's mansion. And in this throng of refugees, Stoneman would undoubtedly seek to lose himself.

"Let's spread out," Mondrago suggested.

"Right. But don't get too far from me; if my implant picks up on his bionics, I want you all to be able to converge quickly. The one thing in our favor is that he can't simply throw that case away; he indicated that his superiors want it back."

"The bad news," said Novak, "is that a fire-fight would cause even these shell-shocked people to panic, and he might get away in the confusion."

"And anyway," added Aiken, looking around at the civilian bystanders of all ages and both genders, "we *can't* start a fire-fight here."

"Then we'll have to subdue him with as little violence as possible," said Jason. "Although he won't have any such compunctions. Let's go!"

In the ghastly light of the flickering fires and occasional flashes of explosions, they threaded their way through the crowd, tightly packed and somehow listless, as though these people were drained and deadened by hours of outrageous assaults on their senses as well as on their very world. The adults seemed to have become desensitized even to the repeated crashes of the exploding shells, although the children continued to scream and beg their parents to make it stop. No one paid any attention to armed and uniformed men moving among them.

Apparently no one paid attention to the presence of a black man either, here amid the rubble of a collapsed society, for Jason spotted Gracchus up ahead.

Gracchus saw him too. "Commander! What happened? Did you find Stoneman?"

"Or he found us." Jason briefly described what had happened. "And so here we are, trying to find him in this crowd."

Gracchus looked puzzled. "Why? Oh, I know: killing the son of a bitch would be a pure pleasure. But you said you have to get back across the river while you can, so you can get to Belle Isle on the fifth and blow up the cache there. I don't know how much time you've got. The railroad bridges have already been burned; Mayo's Bridge is the only one left, and they've got tar and pine knots and kerosene all along it so they can burn it in a flash as soon as the last Rebel troops get across it. Then it'll be too late. Let's get across now."

"Gracchus, Stoneman is carrying something—don't ask me to try to explain what it is—that we've *got* to try to get from him. It's a case, no bigger than a matchbox, made of . . . a material you've never seen."

The black man's expression changed to one of skepticism. "Is something that little really worth the risk?"

"Trust me. This is more than the opportunity of a lifetime. If we can take this thing back to our own era, it could mean the beginning of the end for the Transhumanists. It would be like . . . well, like Gettysburg was in *this* war: the turning point. If there's any chance at all, it's our duty to take it."

"Let me round up my men," was all that Gracchus said.

*Actually,* thought Jason as he did the same, *I haven't even told him all the risks involved—because I know who is going to be in this part of Richmond, headed toward the Mayo Bridge, in a very short time. But he wouldn't understand. And I can't let myself think about it. I already have more than enough on my mind.*

The two groups worked their way around, to the east of the governor's mansion, where they saw fire brigades quelling an incipient blaze in the kitchen outbuilding. Here, another black man joined them and had a hasty colloquy with Gracchus, who turned to Jason. "This man thinks he spotted Stoneman a little to the north, around Broad Street. But now he's turned around and is working his way around, back toward the Mayo Bridge, in an indirect sort of way."

"So," said Dabney, "he also wants to get out of Richmond while he can. But he knows we're looking for him and is trying to elude us."

"He probably can, in the winding streets to the east of here," was Mondrago's pessimistic assessment.

"Then we won't try to track him down," Jason decided. "We'll go straight to the bridge and wait there, where he'll have to get past us."

Unnoticed by the firefighters, they scrambled down the slope and continued a block to Fourteenth Street, littered with the detritus of evacuation: broken furniture, dead animals, fire-blackened silverware, shattered crockery, pathetic lost toys. There, all of Gracchus's men except one named Rufus fanned out to the east, in an effort to form a net behind the Transhumanist. The rest of them fell in with straggling Confederate troops trudging south between the burning buildings toward the Mayo Bridge. Jason grew more nervous, checking his clock display repeatedly and trying to remember the exact time at which he and the others, including Pauline Da Cunha, had crossed over in the company of these retreating troops, whose departure would mean the end of the last vestige of law and order in Richmond until the Union army arrived.

They crossed Exchange Alley, passed the burned-out ruin of the commissariat, beyond which Fourteenth became Pearl, and approached the bridge. It was still not quite dawn, but the fires gave enough light to see it extending ahead over the river and Mayo's Island. A few engineers were crossing over to the south, having put the finishing touches on the combustibles along the bridge's length. A single engineer remained, near the closest abutments, as did a mounted man, who, like Jason, wore the three bars of a Confederate captain on his collar.

"Captain Jason Landrieu, of the Jeff Davis Legion, sir," Jason introduced himself. "Whom do I have the honor of addressing?"

"Captain Clement Sullivane, sir," the horseman replied in an accent that Jason by now was sufficiently experienced in this milieu to be fairly confident in identifying as South Carolinian. "I've orders to hold this bridge until the last of our troops have crossed it. But I'm still awaiting some ambulances, with cavalry escort, of General Gary's command. So I've had to stay here and watch . . . this." He gave a gesture that encompassed the landscape of Hell that was Richmond. A moment passed before he could speak again. "You may as well get your party across. As soon as the last of Gary's men are gone, I'm to fire the bridge."

"Thank you, Captain, but we're waiting for someone. We'll stay over here for a while."

"As you will—but at your own risk. I can't delay blowing the bridge for anyone." The engineer shouted some question, and Sullivane sketched a salute. "Excuse me, Captain. And good luck!" And he trotted his horse away.

"Let's get back here," said Jason, pointing to a narrow side street, little more than an alley, extending toward Shockoe Slip, surrounded by burned-out hulks of buildings. They slipped into its shadows to lie in wait.

They were just doing so when Gracchus turned, as though noticing something in the shadows of a partially collapsed wall. "What—?"

A shot rang out and Gracchus spun around ninety degrees with a gasp of stunning pain. Before the rest of the could draw their revolvers, Stoneman sprang out from behind the wall, grasped the disabled Gracchus by his left wrist and, eliciting a fresh cry of agony, swung him around to serve as a shield, with a Colt pressed to his right temple. "One move and he dies!"

Jason seemed to exist in a state of protracted time as various sense-impressions and the conclusions drawn from them flashed through his brain.

First, Gracchus's wound. The bullet had entered a few inches down from and to the left of his right shoulder. But there had been no cinematic spurt of blood – no major artery had been hit. He was losing blood now, though, and artfully immobilized by Stoneman. And no help could be expected from Sullivane; the captain was otherwise occupied and far enough away that he hadn't even heard the shot over the distant cacophony of exploding shells. And if Jason shouted for him, Gracchus would die. For Stoneman's thought processes were no trouble figuring out. The Transhumanist, seeing he couldn't shoot all of them, had decided to settle for a hostage. His next words confirmed it.

"Now, then. I'm going to go across the bridge with him. If anyone asks, he's a Union spy I've caught and am taking him for questioning. I'm not sure anyone will even notice, though." He glanced out onto the main street, where the last Confederate elements were coming through. "You will remain here. If I see you following me, he will die."

"He'll die anyway," said Jason, "after you have no further use for him." He was playing for time, for those retreating Confederates had reminded him of something. He consulted his clock display. *Yes. Any moment now.*

"Perhaps, and I know you won't believe any pledge of mine. But there's a chance I'll release him once I've crossed the river and they've burned the bridge behind me; after all, he's in no shape to do me any harm. And if I know Pugs, as long as that that chance exists, you'll have to take it." Stoneman started backing toward the street, keeping Gracchus interposed between himself and the five revolvers pointed at him. "We're going now."

"First," said Jason, "I think you'd better look behind you."

Stoneman seemed about to spit contempt for such a childish trick. But then all of them were staring past him at the street. Rufus stood paralyzed, and Dabney gasped. The Transhumanist risked a glance over his shoulder . . . and saw the small party among the knots of straggling Confederate troops. There was a dark-haired woman in a bedraggled crimson dress in what seemed the fashion of the Gulf Coast, and a few soldiers led by a certain captain . . .

*Now I think I remember,* thought Jason in the midst of unreality. *Just before we crossed the bridge, I thought I noticed, out of the corner of my eye, some kind of confrontation going on in an alley. But of course I couldn't stop to look into it.* He continued to stare at what he couldn't help thinking of as the ghost of Pauline Da Cunha . . . and also the ghost of his own slightly younger self, as were Mondrago and Dabney. Aiken and Novak simply stared.

But he at least had been prepared for it. Stoneman hadn't. The Transhumanist's jaw fell at the utterly unnatural sight of the seeming doubles, and his grip on Gracchus went limp and his revolver wavered slightly out of line.

With the strength of desperation overcoming the weakness of blood-loss and pain, Gracchus broke free of Stoneman's grip on his left wrist and brought his left elbow back into the Transhumanist's midriff, while dropping down.

Stoneman's trigger finger convulsively tightened, and the revolver barked. But the shot merely grazed the top of Gracchus's head and the black man collapsed, leaving Stoneman's chest shieldless.

Jason had known—or, rather, remembered—what to expect. So he was able to wrench himself into action at that crucial instant. His Colt crashed in the alley, and Stoneman stood, swaying, for a fractional second before collapsing to the filthy cobblestones.

"Basil, take care of Gracchus," Jason ordered as he hurried to Stoneman's body and knelt beside it. He tore open the bloodsoaked tunic front, reached inside and fumbled in the inside pocket. There! He withdrew a tiny laminate case, held in a hand that trembled slightly.

"So that's it?" Gracchus asked. The black man blinked away a trickle of blood from his scalp wound. "Are you sure it's really so important as to be worth all this?"

"Gracchus," sighed Jason as he put the case in a pocket and buttoned it, "have you ever heard of the legend of the Holy Grail?" Without waiting for a reply, he stood up and looked at the street. Jason Mk I and Mondrago Mk I and the other ghosts—including Pauline Da Cunha, whom Jason thankfully would now never need to fear confronting—had moved on, and would now be crossing Mayo's Bridge. The street was filled with a procession of ambulances, being driven at reckless speed.

"That will be the next-to-last element of General Gary's force to cross," said Dabney. "Afterwards will come their cavalry escort, after which the bridge will be gone."

"Right. We've got to move. Basil, Aiken: help Gracchus along. Let's go."

It was just after six and dawn had broken when they reached the bridge, just as General Gary's cavalry was dashing across it. "You're just in time," said Captain Sullivane. "There'll be enough of a delay in the fuses for you to get across." He paused and looked around—a young man prematurely aged by war and the death of dreams. The rising sun was a sooty red ball in the smoke still-burning fires, and it revealed only scenes of desolation. In that gloomy light, Jason couldn't be sure if he saw the glint of tears in Sullivane's eyes as he took his last look at the corpse of the Confederate capital. Then the last of the horsemen were across, and Sullivane took one last look, touched his hat and said, to no one in particular, "All over. Goodbye." Then he turned to the engineer. "Blow her to hell." And he turned his horse's head and started across.

Jason and his party followed him on foot as the engineer lit the fuses. Slowed as they were by the need to support Gracchus, the engineer passed them in his haste to reach the south shore. They were still on the bridge when the tar barrels began to erupt in a chain reaction of fire behind them.

The had just reached the south shore when Aiken glanced back, stiffened, and shouted, "Look!"

There was a figure running—or, rather, hobbling rapidly—after them, frantically keeping ahead of the advancing flames.

"Stoneman!" gasped Jason.

He had been certain the Transhumanist had been dead. In fact, he probably *had* been very nearly dead. But his bionics must have included the kind of automatic-release packet that, by electrical stimuli and multiple chemical injections, could jack a body that was by most legal definitions dead into a ghoulish simulation of life. Such was the thing that now staggered along the bridge, silhouetted by the flames approaching from behind.

He evidently saw them, for he began to raise his revolver.

At that moment, another tar barrel caught fire directly behind him, and the gout of flame enveloped him, turning him into a writhing human torch. There was nothing human in his scream.

"Welcome to Hell, Stoneman," Jason heard Mondrago say.

Moved by an impulse he could not define, Jason aimed his Colt.

Before he could fire, the portion of the bridge under Stoneman's feet collapsed. Like a flaming comet, the Transhumanist fell into the river along with all the other burning debris, adding to the hissing steam rising from the waters.

For a moment, they all gazed at the river. Then, without a word, they turned and trudged south.

# CHAPTER THIRTY-TWO

Rufus led them to a tarpaper shack not far from the railway, on the bluffs overlooking the riverbank. There they could wait until April 5, without any chance of encountering Pauline Da Cunha. (Jason Mk I and his party had, by this time, already departed.) As they rebandaged Gracchus's wounds and Dabney's less severe one, they could look out across the river from Mayo's Island to the city, as the sun rose higher in the smoke-fouled sky to reveal a scene of hideous desolation.

Between the north shore and Council Chamber Hill, over twenty blocks lay in smoldering ruin—"the burnt district," Dabney said it would always be called afterwards, even when all trace of the conflagration had vanished from everything except the collective memory. Some fires were still burning, and there was still the occasional roar of exploding shells, when the first Union troops appeared at about 7:00 AM, less than an hour after they had crossed the bridge. Blue-clad cavalry and artillery began moving along the debris-littered streets, through a scene of pandemonium as the drunken, looting mobs, swelled by the newly homeless, ran riot, their howling faintly audible even across the river. Also audible were the tunes played by military bands—Dabney identified them as "Yankee Doodle" and "The Star-Spangled Banner"—as the endless blue columns of infantry snaked through the streets toward Capitol Square.

At 8:00 they could discern activity at the capitol building. The Confederate flag came fluttering down, and the Stars and Stripes went up. And above all the distant sounds rose what were clearly roars of jubilation.

"The Union forces include the all-black Twenty-Fifth Corps," Dabney explained. "Most white Richmonders who still have homes are staying inside them with doors locked and shutters drawn. But the blacks are pouring into the streets, mobbing the Federal troops, plying them with flowers and fruit and jugs of whiskey—although the officers will smash those with their swords. And later this morning, when the black troops march through, they'll be almost unable to believe their eyes." The historian chuckled. "The Union officers were as unable to understand the euphoria as the white Southerners were."

"They would be," said Gracchus from where he lay on a filthy blanket. He let out a long sigh. "I wish I was over there to see it. But tomorrow, I *will* be there, one way or another."

"Don't rush it," advised Novak.

"I'll be there," said Gracchus, his voice beginning to slur. "I'll be there. . . ." He slipped off into unconsciousness.

In the afternoon, with nothing to do but wait and with a very strenuous and entirely sleepless night catching up with them, they all drifted off. Jason was the last, for Gracchus's words troubled him. *Yes, he reflected before finally letting sleep take him, he's determined to endanger himself by going there, come hell or high water, because I broke the rules with an audible snap and told him who is going to be in Richmond on April 4.*

*I'm never going to tell Rutherford. He'd be even more insufferable than usual.*

The next morning, Rufus found a small rowboat, which had doubtless washed ashore after coming adrift from one of the abandoned Confederate Navy ships. Now it was early afternoon, and they stood looking east toward the ruined naval base at Rocketts, where a side-wheel steamer had pulled up to the dock and a commotion was visible. Of course, it was too far to discern a tall stovepipe hat above the throng. But Dabney had assured them that Abraham Lincoln and his son, guarded by ten sailors, were about to commence the two-mile walk to Capitol Square.

"Are you sure you're up to this?" Jason asked, indicating Gracchus's immobilized right arm.

"Sure. Rufus will do the rowing. And in all the excitement, nobody will notice us tying up at Shockoe Slip." The black man started to turn away. Then he stopped and, with an obvious effort, turned. "Commander, you saved my life night before last. There's nothing I can do for you that will repay that. But at least I owe it to you to start being honest."

"What do you mean?" asked Jason, puzzled.

"I've lied to you," said Gracchus bluntly. "That letter—the one that said you had to go to Port Royal . . ."

"Yes," Jason prompted. "Nobody knows who he was who wrote it."

"Except that he's not really unknown. Or, rather, *she* isn't unknown."

For a very long moment, there was silence. Or at least it seemed a long moment to Jason, who wondered if, on some level, he hadn't known all along what he now knew, on some other level, what Gracchus was about to tell him.

"You mean..?"

"Yes. Zenobia wrote that letter."

"But she couldn't have!" blurted Jason, angrily unwilling to believe. "She died in the Port Royal earthquake of 1692. I saw her die. Damn it, I saw the tsunami carry her out to sea!"

"You saw that. But you didn't actually see her die. She survived. There was a ship, the frigate HMS *Swan*, that the tsunami carried inland, over the tops of houses—"

"Yes, I think I remember seeing that."

"—but which then stayed upright and served as a kind of life raft for many, as the wave crested as high as some of Port Royal's tallest structures and then swept wreckage and people back out toward the harbor. Zenobia was one. She was badly battered, but she held on. And despite her internal injuries she lived on—for nine more months." Gracchus smiled briefly. "And she knew what she had to do. She wrote the letter I showed you—the letter you had told her you had read, and which had meant nothing to her at the time you told her about it. And she also wrote a *second* letter, to be handed down to her descendants, telling them that when one of them would encounter you in 1864 he was show you the first letter and tell you the lie I told you. And that you couldn't be allowed to know the truth until you came back to 1865 a second time—as you have now."

For a moment, Jason simply existed, stunned, in a maelstrom of whirling thought. But then a single word separated itself from the chaos and registered on his consciousness in all its manifest impossibility.

"Wait a minute . . . did you say 'descendants'? Zenobia had no children!"

"She had none when you last saw her." Again, Gracchus smiled. "Remember I said she lived nine more months?"

For several seconds, Jason simply stared, in a silence that the other members of his party were disinclined to break. They all wore looks of incomprehension . . . all except Mondrago, who understood.

"I don't know whether or not she already knew she was carrying your child," Gracchus resumed. "Probably not—it was too soon. But she soon realized it. And given her injuries, the childbirth was very difficult. She died. But the child lived." The black man took a deep breath. "There's something else I haven't been honest about with you. I've spoken of her 'successors.' I didn't mention that the succession is through her bloodline."

As though from a great distance, Jason heard himself speak. "You mean . . . ?"

"Yes, Commander. I'm your descendant. Your great, great, great grandson, to be exact. And it has been an honor and a great gift to meet you."

This time the silence lasted very long indeed before Jason could speak again, because for the second time in as many days he felt the immanence of ghosts. "No . . . it is I who have been given a gift." He extended his left hand. Gracchus took it.

"And now," Gracchus finally said, "I have to go." He stepped aboard the boat with the help of Rufus, who poled it out onto the river and then began to row.

"Gracchus," Jason called out, moved by a sudden impulse, "tell me one more thing. Do you have children?"

"Yes. A young son, back in Jamaica. So you see, Commander, the bloodline goes on."

Jason said nothing, for he lacked the words. He stood watching the boat recede into the distance. Presently Dabney joined him.

"While passing the docks between Rocketts and downtown Richmond, Lincoln is going to be mobbed by the newly freed blacks. They'll swarm around him, trying to touch him, practically worshipping him as a messiah. One of them will go to his knees before him. Lincoln will remind him that he is now free, and say, 'Don't kneel to me. That is not right. You must kneel to God only.'" The historian smiled. "I wonder if Gracchus will see that?"

"Maybe that will *be* Gracchus," said Jason . . . but absently, for most of his mind was on one thought.

*You were honest with me, Gracchus. But I wasn't entirely honest with you. I couldn't be. I withheld one piece of information, for your own protection. I didn't tell you that the man you're crossing this river to see is going to be killed in ten days.*

*I couldn't tell you that, because if I had you might have gone to Washington and tried to prevent it. And I couldn't let you try to defy the Observer Effect, which you can't possibly understand. Reality protects itself. It might have killed you to do it.*

*Please don't think less of me, a week and a half from now.*

He blinked the beginnings of a tear from his eyes. When he could see again, the little rowboat had rounded the eastern tip of Mayo's Island and was lost to sight.

The next morning, the morning of April 5, came. The nanobot cache on Belle Isle could now be destroyed.

Temporal retrievals were always timed for the small hours of the morning, when the locals were most likely to be asleep. So it was still dark the following morning when Angus Aiken's TRD was timed to activate. Jason couldn't give him a second-by-second countdown, but they knew approximately when he would vanish. Hands were shaken all around, and then they waited.

"Just before dawn, we'll do the deed and then I'll activate our TRDs," Jason told him. "So tell Rutherford that we'll be along shortly."

"Understood, sir."

"Angus, it was never in the plan for you to have to survive for months in this milieu on your own. You've performed outstandingly, and I'm going to tell Rutherford as much."

"Thank you, Commander," the young Scot stammered.

"In fact, I think you deserve something." Jason reached inside his tunic and withdrew the tiny laminate case. He placed it in Aiken's hand. "I want you to have the honor of being the one to take this back with you and give it to Rutherford—and tell him what it contains, and what it means."

Aiken turned as red as his hair. "But . . . but, sir, I couldn't possibly—"

And he was no longer there. Jason felt a faint breeze on his face as the air filled the man-sized vacuum that had momentarily been created by his vanishment.

Mondrago cocked an eyebrow at Jason. "I can't believe you're passing up the opportunity to see the look on Rutherford's face."

"You know," said Jason with a smile, "I have a feeling that it's still going to be there when we arrive."

They turned, and started toward Belle Isle.

# AUTHOR'S NOTE

The present writer was born in Virginia in 1946 and therefore grew up visualizing God as a slightly imperfect version of Robert E. Lee. One always tries to recognize, and compensate for, the biases inherent in one's upbringing. But no revisionist historian has ever shown me any compelling reason to disagree with Carlos Dabney's assessment of Lee at the end of Chapter Nine. His opinions on slavery and secession were as I have represented them, based on his own writings and recorded utterances; his advocacy of freeing and arming the slaves is a matter of historical record. If any are still in doubt as to his statesmanship—along with that of Generals Grant, Johnston and Sherman—in averting the postwar devolution of America into Bosnia writ large, I refer them to that brilliant work *April 1865* by Jay Winik.

The White House of the Confederacy (which in fact is, appropriately enough, gray) has been beautifully restored. It, and the adjacent Museum of the Confederacy, are very much worth a visit—if, that is, you can find them, tucked away as they are among the large modern buildings of the Medical College of Virginia.

Elizabeth Van Lew's story is an epic of espionage. Everything herein about her, including her appearance and opinions, is accurate. So, to the extent possible, is everything about that altogether more shadowy figure, Mary Bowser—or Mary Richards, or Ellen Bond—except, of course, for her obviously fictional connections with the entirely imaginary Gracchus. The same, incidentally, goes for the slave boy Daniel Strother. If fact, except for Gracchus and his associates in the Order of the Three-Legged Horse, every nineteenth-century individual I have named actually lived.

The skirmish in Chapter Ten is fictional, and in fact the period in question was one of relative inactivity for Mosby's Rangers; but it is an accurate representation of the tactics used by them and the psychological effect those tactics had on the Union forces. Everything else herein about John Singleton Mosby, a.k.a. the Gray Ghost, and his Partisan Rangers is true to history and biography, again with the obvious time-travel-related exceptions. These exceptions include those connected with the unexplained fusillade of shots outside the Lake house on the night of December 21, 1864 when Mosby received one of his numerous wounds. They also include the involvement of Angus Aiken and Gracchus in Adolphus ("Dolly") Richards' raids in the Shenandoah Valley in January, 1865, which otherwise occurred exactly as I have depicted them, even to such details as Richards' attested exchange with Hern in Chapter Eighteen. The same goes for Aiken's role in the Mount Carmel action in Chapter Twenty-Six, which is otherwise factual even to the recapture of Jeremiah Wilson in time for his wedding; no one seems to know which two Rangers hid with Richards behind a wall panel, so I have felt no compunctions about making them Hern and Aiken. In these matters, I have relied on *Mosby's Rangers* by Jeffrey D. Wert, *Gray Ghost* by James A. Ramage, and of course Mosby's own memoirs. And I make a particular point of acknowledging my indebtedness to Curt Phillips, who has generously given me the benefit of his expertise in Civil War history. Any inaccuracies or infelicities are entirely the fault of the author.

It is a safe bet that Mosby never read Sun Tzu, even in his later years in China, but if he had he would have discovered a kindred mind. In his still-mentally-acute eighties, commenting on the stupid slaughter then occurring on the Western Front of World War I, he practically paraphrased Sun Tzu: "The object of war is not to kill. It is to disable the military power." Judging from photographs and paintings (and one bust) dating to various periods during and after the Civil War, the man simply could not make up his mind whether to be clean-shaven or full-bearded; I have therefore felt at liberty to represent him one way or the other at any given time.

The plot to assassinate Lincoln by bombing the White House is factual. The attempt was made only a few weeks before the end of the war, and was foiled as a result of a chance encounter with a Union patrol. The idea that this was a *second* attempt (the first having been aborted by the loss of one infernal machine in January, 1865) is a product of the author's imagination, but the dates work.

The Transhumanist perversion of Voodoo in *Pirates of the Timestream* and the present novel is of course fictitious. But it is synthesized from actual elements of the Afro-Caribbean syncretic religions, on which subject (and also that of Jamaican folkways) I am deeply indebted to Zora Neale Hurston's *Tell My Horse*.

Contemporary eyewitness accounts of the Port Royal earthquake of 1692 read like something out of the imagination of Hieronymus Bosch, but modern seismology verifies them. My depiction follows them without exaggeration, and does not even cover the *real* horrors that followed in the lawless and starving aftermath.

I have likewise not exaggerated the fall of Richmond, which is so well documented that I have been able to attempt accuracy even about such details as the stage Dr. Minnegerode's Communion service at St. Paul's had reached when the courier rushed in and gave Jefferson Davis the fatal news, even to the hymn that was being sung. Equally factual is the incident of the release of the slaves in the railroad depot, as are all incidents connected with the fire, although it is not always possible to ascertain the order in which they occurred. Captain Sullivane's final seven words before burning Mayo's Bridge are a verbatim quote. Unlike Port Royal, Richmond was subsequently photographed; the photographs of the burned-out districts resemble Hiroshima after the bomb.

I have used the nineteenth-century names of all the Virginia hamlets that figured in Mosby's operations, even though some of them have subsequently changed. Salem, for example, is now called Marshall; Harmony is now called Hamilton. Incidentally, Mosby's ambush of Reno's men at the latter place as described in Chapter 27 was the Partisan Rangers' last significant action. They never surrendered. A few days after the surrender at Appomattox, Mosby slipped a man into Richmond to ask Lee if they should take to the hills and carry on guerrilla warfare as many, up to and including Jefferson Davis, had proposed. Lee replied as he always did to everyone who would listen—which meant everyone, because he was Lee: "Go home, all you boys who fought with me. Help to rebuild the shattered fortunes of our old state." Mosby obeyed. On April 21, 1865, he called the Rangers together at Salem and simply disbanded them. They left the field with honor.